DEEP SOUTH

DEEP SOUTH

A Traveler's Guide to Alabama, Mississippi and Louisiana

by

Dana Facaros and Michael Pauls

HIPPOCRENE BOOKS
New York

 For information, address:
Hippocrene Books, Inc., 171 Madison Avenue,
New York, N.Y. 10016.

Published in the United States by Hippocrene Books, Inc.
in 1986.
ISBN 0-87052-237-X

Cover photo courtesy of Louisiana Office of Tourism

Printed in the United States of America.

Contents

Foreword: The South

> "Ah'm from the South, boy! In mah class ah graduated magnolia cum laude, and ah was voted the most likely to secede . . . When ah pass Grant's tomb ah shut both eyes. Ah never got to the Yankee Stadium! Ah won't even go to the Polo Grounds unless a southpaw's pitchin'!"
>
> —Senator Beauregard Claghorn, the Dixie Foghorn

The honey warm names of the Southern states read like a list of belles at a ball at Mockingbird Plantation under a June moon—Virginia, Georgia, Florida, North and South Carolina, Louisiana. They encompass regions as diverse as the Okeefenokee Swamp, the Everglades, Louisiana's gator-filled bayous, sugar white beaches, cities like New Orleans and St. Augustine, which belong more to the Old World than the New, and others like Atlanta and Fort Lauderdale, toadstools of our own soggy age.

No region in the United States has attracted—or believed so fervently in—more of its own myths, nor has any region changed so drastically in the last thirty years. Yankees who formerly dismissed the South as the "Problem Child of the Nation," the home of poor sharecroppers, blustering pot-bellied sheriffs, fragrant demagogues, magnolia-scented women and country fried colonels, a land that its inhabitants willed them to forget, received a shock when Jimmy Carter, the technocratic symbol of the New South, was elected president. Overnight, on the cover of *Time Magazine*, the South had shed its hackneyed Dixie image to emerge as the "Sunbelt," and Northerners who had chortled at the jokes of Senator Claghorn, on Fred Allen's old radio show, found their employers moving the company plant to the South, where taxes and energy bills are lower and unionism stillborn.

It has been over a hundred years since the War and Reconstruction and now the South is getting its revenge. Not only are Southern industries, corporations and ports booming, often at the expense of their Northern counterparts, but regional exports like Bible beating T.V. evangelism, stock car racing and country music have infiltrated Yankeeland at an alarming rate, while 20th century Southern literati gleefully expose many of the Yankee's gods for the shams they really are.

The cultural exchange, however, has gone both ways, for better but usually for worse. Visiting the region isn't quite the journey to a foreign country that it used to be—desegregation is now a way of life, as are some of the North's biggest mistakes like suburban sprawl, shopping malls and urban renewal, all new and raw and perverting the landscape even more glaringly than in New Jersey. But it symbolizes one of the South's principal distinctions as a region, that it is unfinished, still waiting to fulfil its destiny.

Introduction

Getting Around

The South is not particularly blessed with public transportation; if you're not driving, a Greyhound or Trailways bus pass is the best bet for traveling around, particularly if you plan on visiting rural areas. If you are flying or taking a train, be sure to inquire about car rental packages (fly-drive) that are sometimes very economical.

By Air. The major international airports in the South are in Atlanta, Tampa, Miami, New Orleans, Washington D.C., Nashville, and Memphis. There are smaller airports in all the state capitals and resort centers, particularly in Florida. Don't neglect to check the ads in the travel section of your newspaper for discounts, charters, etc. Southern routes are very competitive; anyone who pays full fare hasn't done their homework.

By Train. Amtrak, the government subsidized passenger railway, has several daily trains to the South. From New York or Washington D.C. there is a coastal route that splits between Petersburg and Savannah, one line passing through Raleigh and Columbia, the other through Charleston and Fayetteville. From Savannah the route returns to the coast until Jacksonville, where it again splits, one fork running to Miami, and the other to Tampa. Another train from Washington goes to New Orleans, via High Point, Charlotte, Greenville, Atlanta, Birmingham, and Hattiesburg. You can also get to New Orleans from Houston, or from Chicago, via Memphis and Jackson. A line from Chicago to Texas crosses Arkansas. For detailed information on routes and stations, see the individual states. Families traveling Amtrak are eligible for discounts; see your travel agent, who can also make reservations—which are usually required.

By Bus. Greyhound and Trailways are the two major interstate carriers: each offers unlimited travel passes for a week, two weeks, or a month. Discounts are available to travelers over 65, between 6 and 11, while children under five ride free. On city buses and subways we have left out the fares, as these are always subject to increases. Note, however, that you'll always need exact change when boarding a city bus.

By Car. To rent a car in the USA you must have a major credit card for the deposit and be 21 years old. Foreign visitors, however, may pay the deposit in cash, and can rent a car if they're 18 as long as they have an International Driving Permit, and a return ticket home. Many companies let you rent the car in one place and return it to another. Most also offer unlimited mileage, and have lower prices the longer you rent the car. If there are more than two of you traveling, renting a car and splitting the cost may be less expensive than public transportation.

If you are cutting costs, consider the new breed of auto renting agencies that specialize in second hand cars. Two of these agencies have gone national and have toll free numbers to call for information: Rent-A-Wreck (800-228-5958) and Ugly Duckling (800-854-3380). In most cities there are independent companies that rent mechanically sound older cars—even Cadillacs, campers, and mini buses—for a small percentage of the fees charged by Hertz or Avis. Check the yellow pages in the telephone book when you arrive. Another good bet, if you plan to travel fairly long distances, are the Drive Aways, where you make arrangements through a company to drive someone's car in a certain amount of time from point A to point B. There are many of these to Florida in particular. Look in the yellow pages of the phone book under "Automobile Transporters and Drive Away Companies" and often times in the personal ads of newspapers for drive away opportunities.

Another possible option is to buy a used car and sell it when you're ready to fly home. The best place to look for one is the classified section of a small town newspaper. A decent used car may cost between $300 and $500; later models will be more, but probably not worth it. Shiny bargains often turn out to be lemons. After purchasing a car, you'll have to get a license for it (temporary ones are available) and in many states buy insurance. When it's time to leave, sell it through the newspaper or a used car dealer.

If you do drive, the first thing to do is buy a good road map, or pick up one at the state's tourist office. The Rand-McNally Road Atlas, covering the fifty states, is good and sufficiently detailed. It is also a good idea to join an auto club, like the American Automobile Association (AAA) which has offices in practically every town in the country. They offer not only advice, maps, and travel booklets, but also a discount on traveler's cheques, lists of campgrounds, a degree of insurance, bail bond, and cover the cost of a tow in an emergency. They can also help you get a license if you buy a car, and if you're from abroad, write to them for a copy of their *USA Travel Information* (AAA National Headquarters, 8111 Gatehouse Road, Falls Church, VA 22042), a free guide to all aspects of driving in the United States. If you want to join, a year's membership costs $28.

Driving regulations are standardized throughout the country: 55 mph speed limit on highways, and right turns on red are legal after giving pedestrians the right of way. In the South, small towns sometimes earn their main revenues by creating speed traps, so beware, and obey all posted signs. Gasoline is priced by the American gallon (a fifth less than an Imperial gallon, about 4½ litres) and is generally cheaper at self-service stations. Try to avoid buying gas along turnpikes or in the center of cities, where it's bound to be much more expensive.

Hitchhiking. The South is probably the worst region in the country to thumb a ride; the police are generally less tolerant, and motorists more suspicious and less likely to pick you up. Although it is technically not illegal in any state, each town may have its own ordinance on the subject. Stay off the Interstates (stand on the ramp in front of the "No Hitchhiking" sign) or the roadway, which in Arkansas is defined as the side of the highway as well as the paved section. Some general suggestions: always go to the edge of a town before you start, travel lightly (if you're from another country, sew your flag in a prominent place on your rucksack—Americans love foreigners), hold a sign stating your destination, avoid hitching at night, and smile. A good way to find rides is to ask around at gas stations, truck stops, or diners on the way.

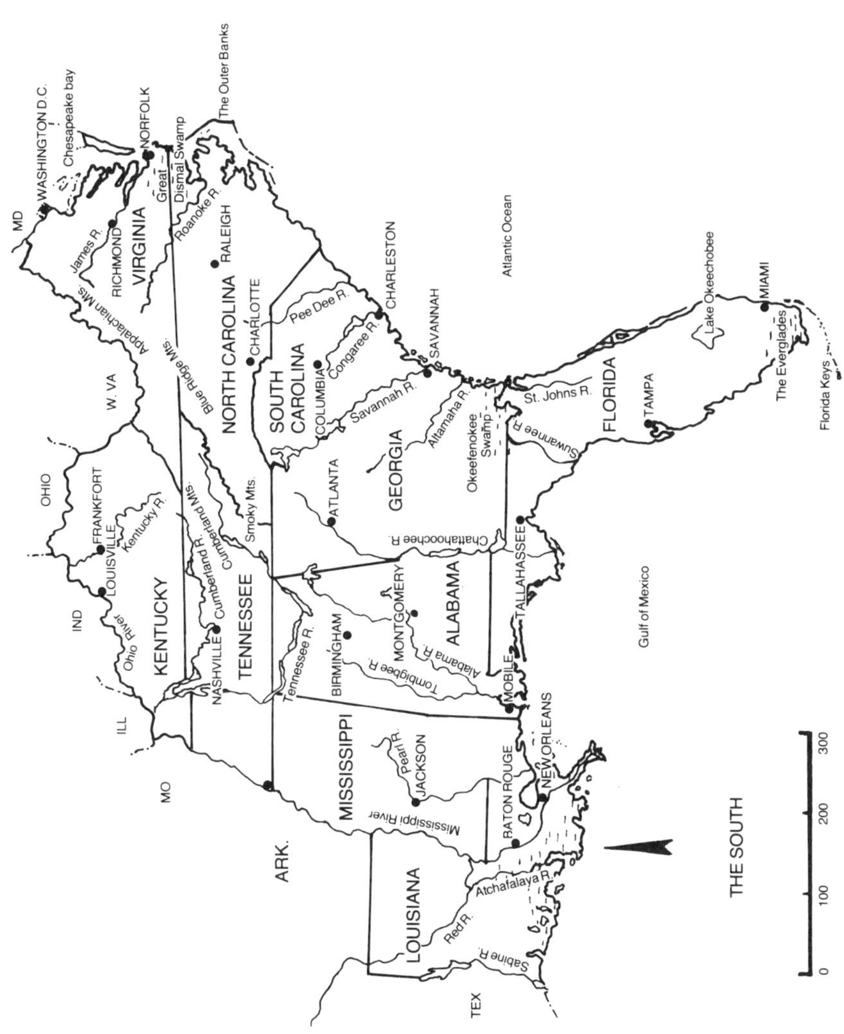
THE SOUTH
0
100
200
300
WASHINGTON D.C.
MD
Chesapeake bay
NORFOLK
Great Dismal Swamp
The Outer Banks
Roanoke R.
RICHMOND
James R.
VIRGINIA
RALEIGH
Appalachian Mts.
Blue Ridge Mts.
W. VA
NORTH CAROLINA
CHARLOTTE
CHARLESTON
Atlantic Ocean
Pee Dee R.
SOUTH CAROLINA
COLUMBIA
Congaree R.
SAVANNAH
Savannah R.
Altamaha R.
GEORGIA
ATLANTA
Okeefenokee Swamp
St. Johns R.
Suwannee R.
FLORIDA
TAMPA
Lake Okeechobee
MIAMI
The Everglades
Florida Keys
OHIO
FRANKFORT
LOUISVILLE
Kentucky R.
KENTUCKY
IND
Ohio River
ILL
Cumberland R.
Cumberland Mts.
Smoky Mts.
NASHVILLE
TENNESSEE
Tennessee R.
BIRMINGHAM
MONTGOMERY
ALABAMA
Chattahoochee R.
TALLAHASSEE
Gulf of Mexico
Alabama R.
Tombigbee R.
MOBILE
MO
MISSISSIPPI
Pearl R.
JACKSON
NEW ORLEANS
BATON ROUGE
Mississippi River
ARK.
LOUISIANA
Atchafalaya R.
Red R.
Sabine R.
TEX

A woman thumbing alone is courting disaster, sad to say. On the positive side, there are many people who hitchhike even when they own cars, just for the interesting class of people who offer rides.

By Foot. The major trail of the east coast, the Appalachian Trail, passes through Virginia, Tennessee, North Carolina, and Georgia. For information and a list of hiking clubs in the region, write to the Appalachian Trail Conference, Box 236, Harpers Ferry, W.V. 25425.

Accommodation

Hotels and Motels. Outside the downtown areas of large cities and resort areas like Miami Beach, hotels are scarce; motels are common, but not always less expensive. We have listed after each state a small selection of the available commercial lodgings that do not belong to chains. We are not being elitist, merely saving space. If you prefer the security and reservation networks of a Hilton, a Holiday Inn, or an inexpensive Motel 6, look for their toll-free 800 numbers in the yellow pages of any city, and their operators will be happy to tell you where to find one of their establishments and make reservations for you. The South is well endowed with brand new chain lodgings; some good budget chains are Days Inn, L-K Penny Pincher Inns (tel. 800-848-5767), Scottish Inns (800-251-1962), Econo-Hotels (800-446-6900), Family Inns (800-447-4470), Motel 6, Knights Inn and Red Carpet Inns (800-582-6103). Inquire at the motel desks for free catalogs listing all the motels.

Prices vary widely. What is moderate in Miami in the winter season would be outrageously expensive in Mississippi. The easiest room to find is the double with a double bed; a single will be only a few dollars less, and an extra bed or cot a few dollars more in most cases. Almost all hotels and motels have at least a private shower and toilet, and it really is difficult to find one without a television. If you do not make reservations, the best place to look for reasonably priced accommodation is on the periphery of town, and along highways and access routes. This is unfortunate for the traveler relying on public transportation. We have tried to list all inexpensive and moderately priced downtown lodgings, but often the only choice is the local YMCA.

A place in this book listed as inexpensive will be up to $25 a night for a double room. Moderate ranges from $25 to $40, expensive from $40. Rates fluctuate, depending on the season and major events, like Mardi Gras, when a modest motel in New Orleans may charge over $100 a night. While prices in most of the South go up in the summer, they hit rock bottom in southern Florida. "American Plan" means three meals a day are included in the price; "Modified American Plan" means two meals. Hotels with arrangements like these are generally expensive resorts. Leave a tip if you spend more than one night in a place (at least a dollar per night).

Inns and Guesthouses. An "inn" usually means old and expensive, and there are several guidebooks that tell you where to find them in the South. In some places in the South, you can spend the night in ante-bellum plantation houses for $50 or $60 a night. Guesthouses (similar to Bed and

Breakfasts in Great Britain) are rooms in private homes, and are fairly inexpensive. For a list, write to the Tourist House Associates, Inc., P.O. Box 355a, Greentown, PA 18426 for their *Guide to Guest Houses and Tourist Homes USA* ($4).

Youth Hostels. The name is deceptive; these are for everyone, regardless of age. Although designed for travelers who arrive on foot or bicycle, there are now several hostels in cities as well. Almost all require a youth hostel card, issued either abroad, or, if you're an American, from the American Youth Hostel Federation (National Headquarters, Delaplane, Virginia 22025). A year's membership costs $14, or $7 if you're under 14 or over 59 years of age. When you join, you receive the *AYH Guide and Handbook;* the far more detailed *Hosteling USA,* which describes activities near each hostel, is also available from AYH headquarters for $5.95. Staying in an American Youth Hostel is not the rigid experience it often is in Europe, although there are certain rules, like no drinking or drugs, and you are sometimes expected to help out with the general chores. Check-out time each morning is 9.30. Reservations are recommended, and required at some of the more popular hostels. Prices average $5 a night and sometimes include meals. In summer, colleges and universities often have dormitory rooms for rent at modest prices.

Farm Vacations. These have a strong appeal to city families in particular, and range from old-fashioned farmhouse accommodation on working farms, to resort-style farms with many recreational opportunities. The best guide for these is *Country Vacations USA,* available from Adventure Guides, 36 East 57th Street, New York, N.Y. 10022.

Camping. Camping means different things to different people. There are commercial campgrounds throughout the South for the trailer and camper sets and state park campgrounds on a first come, first served basis. Backpackers and canoeists will find camping spots along major trails in the wilderness; a good book to read on the subject is *Wild Places of the South* by Steve Price, published at $7.95 by The East Woods Press, Fast & McMillan, 820 East Boulevard, Charlotte, NC 28203. Each state can provide information on campsites within its borders; another good source is Rand McNally's widely available *Southeastern Campground and Trailer Parks Guide.*

Handicapped Travelers. As time passes, airlines, airports, hotels, restaurants, museums, etc., are taking care to make themselves more accessible to the handicapped. For sound, specific information on facilities, *The Wheelchair Traveller* by Douglas R. Annand (write to Ball Hill Road, Milford, NH 03055) and *Where Turning Wheels Stop* (put out by the Paralyzed Veterans of America, 3636 16th St. N.W., Washington D.C. 20010) are good sources.

Senior Citizens. There are many discounts available to travelers over 65 years old. A good way to get in on them is to join the American Association of Retired Persons/National Retired Teachers Association, 1909 K Street NW., Washington, D.C. 20006.

Children. An alarming trend among newer establishments, particularly those with pretensions, is the banning of children. On the other hand, many chain motels take children for free or offer discounts. If you have very small children, bring a sleeping bag. Cribs are available in many places. Motels often provide lists of babysitters and many resorts have their own babysitters and special programs to accommodate the children of guests.

If you need help finding a place, or have any other questions, call or visit *Travellers Aid,* which has offices in most cities and is listed in the phone book. Foreign visitors can also call a toll-free number, 1-800-255-3050, for information; this is USADesk, and operators who speak a variety of languages are on duty from 9 am-10 pm Monday-Friday, and noon to 6 pm on Saturdays and Sundays.

Dining

Restaurants in this book (again we spurn the chains; they're harder to avoid than find, especially in the South) are rated by asterisks that reflect only the price, not the quality. One asterisk is inexpensive, around $5-$8 for dinner; two asterisks run from $8-$15, three will cost on the average $15 or more per person, for the average entree. In the world's largest democracy, people who work in restaurants receive sub-minimum wages, and are expected to make it up in tips; 15% of the final tab before tax is a rule of thumb. (Occasionally in Florida, however, you'll find the service included in the tab.) Only in fast-food restaurants and cafeterias are you not expected to tip.

Foreign visitors are often impressed by the large portions most American restaurants dish out, usually more than the average person can eat, a child certainly. Many offer children's portions at a low price, or have "kiddies' menus" with hamburgers, hot dogs, spaghetti and other foods the native children are addicted to. A popular restaurant feature these days is the salad bar, where you serve yourself as often and as much as you wish. Be wary of theme restaurants, another new trend, where you may dine in a castle or a cave, where the waiters on rollerskates dress up in gorilla costumes and bring you an indecipherable cutesy menu and bizarre food.

The coastal regions of the South and New Orleans are a gourmet's paradise, but the hinterland is another story altogether. Traditional, ballyhooed Southern cooking may be an acquired taste, particuarly when you're confronted with the likes of collard and turnip greens, grits (white corn mush), chitterlings (pork intestines) and red eye gravy. Southerners eat more corn than anyone in more forms. Almost all main dishes are fried and accompanied by hush puppies—corn meal balls of deep fried batter that supposedly got their name in plantation kitchens, where the massa's hounds would pester mammy until she hushed them with these delicacies, hot from the pan. Judging by the number of restaurants that proudly advertize them, homemade baking powder biscuits are a Southern obsession for breakfast, so much so that you can even buy them at McDonald's. For lunch or dinner, try the fried catfish, fried chicken, Southern ham, or bar-b-qued meats, with a side order of black-eyed peas, sweet potatoes, or greens. Many restaurants feature gumbo, a Creole specialty that usually includes seafood or chicken, okra, corn, tomatoes, etc. "Tea" in the South means heavily sugared iced tea. Specify if you want it hot. Besides Southern-style restaurants, many towns in the South have Mexican, Louisiana-style, pizza, and Chinese restaurants, the latter, on the average, better than the Chinese restaurants in the north.

If you're on a budget, be sure to check out the menu by the cash register before you sit down. Prices are often lower at lunch time, so you may want to eat your main meal then. Buy your liquor in a state or retail package store, instead of ordering it in a restaurant where you'll pay twice as much. Even the lowliest motels have free ice.

American bars and taverns can be dark, gloomy places where no one talks to anyone, the television providing the only entertainment, or they can be lively and fun places to meet the natives. Ask around before you go. The drinking age varies throughout the country, from 18 to 21, and if you look a little young, you may be asked to show identification. Most bars close at one or two in the morning and on Sundays. Be sure to try the South's famous Mint Juleps, at least once. There are several good regional varieties of Tennessee whiskey and bourbon unknown in the rest of the country; ask the bartender.

Alabama

> Alabama felt a magic descending, spreading, long ago. Since then it has been a land with a spell on it . . . an emanation of malevolence that threatens to destroy men through dark ways of its own . . .

Carl Carmer, a professor and writer from up North who spent six years in the state that calls itself the "Heart of Dixie," wrote these words at the beginning of an extravagant, wild-eyed rouser of a memoir called *Stars Fell on Alabama,* a 1934 best seller that probably made an incalculable contribution to the uneasiness that state has always summoned up in the national consciousness. In the popular mythology, Alabama is the center of a vast terra incognita of Southern cotton farms, courthouse politics, sharecroppers, and feverish murky passions, a steamy plain punctuated by lynchings, cross-burnings, and occasional fits of gratuitous violence. It is the state of Wallace and the Lost Cause, where one sees the U.S. flag everywhere and the Confederate stars-and-bars usually right next to it.

The chronicles of Alabama do admit the event Carmer credited with forever changing the destiny of the land, an event that has lived in the state's folklore for a century and a half. The stars fell on November 13 1833, a tremendous meteor shower from the direction of the constellation Taurus, and whatever vortex they drew Alabama into, it is true that any state—indeed, any beleaguered country of Eastern Europe—would be hard pressed to match Alabama's history for hard fate and unrelieved gloom.

Mention any of this to an Alabamian and he is less likely to be insulted than just contemptuously bored with it. Quite understandably, the state has had enough of histrionics, of being a stage for its own and everyone else's Dixie fantasies. Alabama rejoined the United States long ago, and it does its best these days to be quiet, pragmatic, cautiously open, and as much like the other forty-nine as it feels comfortable with. In an age where the increasing sophistication and homogenization of Southern states is something apparent to even the casual traveler, the old stereotypes no longer serve. Whatever strange magic there was is fading, and whatever destiny was created when the stars fell is something Alabama is no longer willing to accept. Consider, so many years after the assault from the heavens, that Alabama is now shooting back. The nation's first satellite, the rocket that carried it, and dozens more since were built by NASA in the brand-new Alabama city of Huntsville.

One great disservice the old image of Alabama always carried with it was to obscure the distinctiveness of the state's regions. In many ways Alabama is one of the most diverse states in the South. Outlining them from the bottom up, we start with Mobile on the Gulf Coast, whose French influence and historical head start set it apart from the rest of the state, and also, along with the seacoast itself, make it the most interesting corner of Alabama for tourists. Montgomery and the "Black Belt" are undiluted Deep South, and not without their charms and surprises. And once you penetrate a bit further north, into the southernmost reaches of the Appalachians, you'll find a very different Alabama indeed, a mix of the state's oldest and newest, tucked between the long folded ridges that stretch down from Tennessee. This is where you'll find Birmingham, the "Pittsburgh of the South," and also the TVA.

Getting to and Around Alabama

By Air. The major airports in Alabama are located in Birmingham, Mobile, Montgomery and in the Huntsville-Decatur area; smaller airports served by scheduled commercial service are at Dothan, Tuscaloosa, and Gadsden.

By Train. The only Amtrak passenger train that passes through Alabama, The Crescent, stops at Anniston, Birmingham and Tuscaloosa on its route between New York-Washington D.C. and New Orleans. For information, call toll free in Alabama 800-874-2800.

By Bus. Besides Greyhound and Trailways, the major interstate carriers, Colonial Trailways, Gulf Transport Co., Capital Motor Lines, Basden Transportation, Ingram Bus Lines and Thrasher Transportation have routes in Alabama.

By Car. A small section of the Natchez Trace, between Nashville, Tennessee and Natchez, Mississippi cuts across the corner of the state. For more information, see "Mississippi."

History

At about the same time that Pizarro and Cortez were doing their dirty work in Peru and Mexico, other Spanish explorers were appearing in Mobile Bay. Alonzo de Piñeda was the first in 1519, followed by Panfilo de Narvaez, whose boat was wrecked in a storm off the Alabama coast in 1528, leaving as its only survivor that famous liar Cabeza de Vaca. He turned up in Mexico eight years later, publishing stories of great cities, gold and jewels in the American southeast. Among those fooled was Hernando De Soto, and he visited Alabama in the course of his epic journey across the South in 1540. At the time the principle tribes of the area were the Creeks, Choctaws (one of whose tribes was called the *Alabama*) and Cherokees, all of whom practiced agriculture and lived in towns. To these fairly civilized folk, the Spanish hoodlums must have seemed utter barbarians, mongols from the steppe with guns and something even more mysterious—horses. De Soto massacred some Indians, enslaved others, commandeered their food supplies since there was no gold, and generally made a nuisance of himself up and down the Alabama River. At the great town of Maubila, a few miles upstream from today's Mobile, he met the powerful chief Tuscaloosa and promptly murdered him after receiving his hospitality, burning the city and slaughtering its inhabitants. Alabama named both the city of Tuscaloosa and the Black Warrior River after the chief, but the only thing in America commemorating the conquistador was the big, aggressive-looking De Soto car, with tailfins and lots of chrome. People stopped buying them in the 1950's.

Spain did make one attempt to settle this land, if only a half-hearted one. In 1559, Tristan de Luna and 1,500 colonists from Mexico founded a town on Mobile Bay, but hurricanes, internal dissension and a lack of easy wealth made them depart after only two years. As the Spanish lost interest, the French explorers replaced them. Sieur de Bienville, who would found New Orleans seven years later, started the first settlement at Mobile, in 1703. The new town grew slowly and, in fact, it almost disappeared in 1720 when the French government decided it was tired of losing money on their Louisiana Territory and stopped sending supply ships; two years later, the capital was moved to New Orleans. After the Seven Years War, all of Alabama passed to the British as part of West Florida and was in turn seized by the United States in the War of 1812.

As a part of the newly created Mississippi Territory, Alabama began to attract settlers, mostly from Tennessee, Georgia and the Carolinas; the northern part, along the Tennessee River, became for a while the most densely populated area in the Territory. The very presence of these new arrivals, however, squatting on Indian lands or manipulating the law to steal them, led to troubles with the Creek almost immediately upon acquisition by the U.S. At the time a kind of civil war was dividing the Creek nation between those who were trying to assimilate themselves into the white man's culture and those who would rather fight, led by a radical brotherhood of warriors called the "Red Sticks," most of whose leaders, ironically, were half-bloods with names like Peter McQueen, High-Hat Jim and William Weatherford. In 1813 a band of Red Sticks was ambushed by their opponents, who took refuge with the U.S. Army at Fort Mims. The enraged Red Sticks then raided the fort, massacring not only Indians but the white settlers who had taken refuge there. Down came Andrew Jackson, bringing his Tennessee militia and recruits from other states, and the most relentless Indian fighter of them all soon revenged Fort Mims and put an end to the Creek Wars with some massacres of his own. Jackson and his friends presided over the removal of most of Alabama's Indians in the aftermath and made their fortunes speculating in their former lands. By 1817, Alabama was a separate territory and in 1819 it became the 22nd state, with 127,000 inhabitants.

For a while, the major question in Alabama politics was where to put the capital, which found itself first at Huntsville, then at the now ruined and abandoned town of Cahaba, later at Tuscaloosa where north Alabama wanted it and finally back down south in Montgomery. New settlers contested with the "Georgia party" of men from that state who controlled Alabama's economy for political dominance, and that struggle evolved into the usual antebellum Southern politics of Jacksonian Democrats versus Whigs. The population doubled by 1830 and again by 1840, canals and railroads were built and King Cotton added south Alabama to his dominions; an age of easy credit was punctuated by occasional crashes and panics, but on the whole Alabama in its formative years shared fully in the Flush Times, as an almost entirely agricultural state, dependent on cotton and ruled by a class of wealthy planters. The state hardly had a chance to settle down and make a name for itself in industry or commerce when the Civil War arrived to bring all advancement and development to a halt.

In response to the attacks of the abolitionists and to the fight over the extension of slavery into new territories, the Southern hysteria in defense of slavery and the "Southern way of life" took strong root in Alabama. After a curious interlude in the 1850's when the "Know-Nothings," a political party and secret society that flourished in the North on anti-foreign and anti-Catholic sentiments, almost won control of Alabama politics, the state's politics fell prey to the oratory of home-grown "fire eaters" like William L. Yancey and W. F. Samford, who led Alabama into secession in the first week of 1861. Northern Alabama, where there were few slaves and much pro-Union feeling, almost seceded itself after this and a convention was held there to try and form a new, loyal state called "Nickajack," without success. Meanwhile, with Virginia still debating the question of secession, the rebel states installed their capital at Montgomery; the Confederate States of America was declared in the Alabama statehouse on February 4, and Jefferson Davis was inaugurated there two weeks later.

By May, Virginia had made its decision and the rebel capital removed to Richmond. Alabama, however, still had an important role to play in the conflict. Even though no big battles were fought there, the state still knew almost continual military action, beginning with the Federal seizure of towns along the Tennessee River in early 1862 and ending with the capture of Mobile and Montgomery just before Appomattox. And even though Sherman never marched through it, Alabama found itself on the ropes at war's end, with a ruined economy, empty towns and a destitute population largely dependent on Federal relief. Reconstruction, though tainted by the usual political corruption so wildly exaggerated by Southern historians, proceeded smoothly, with the restoration of the state economy, new industries and railroads and the founding of the city of Birmingham. In a state where education had always been somewhat neglected, a number of new colleges and technical schools, both for blacks and whites, were begun by the Republican government. This government, however, was ineffectual in coping with the terrorism of the Klan and its imitators, who started their work in Alabama as early as 1867. By 1872, the Wizards, Klaxons and Kleagles had destroyed whatever slim chance for democracy had ever existed in the state and reduced many rural areas to anarchy. Blacks and Northerners, ministers and teachers, were murdered by the score; most of the state's black churches and schools were burned, but hardly ever was a grand jury moved to turn in an indictment when the Klansmen were caught. In 1874 an election distinguished by equally large helpings of planned violence and ballot fraud, with election day riots in Mobile and Selma, returned the Democrats to power. Reconstruction was over.

If Alabama spent most of the next century in darkness, it was not for lack of effort among the state's better elements. The progressive urge surfaced repeatedly, though usually without success. First there was the farmers' movement of the 1880's. Organizations like the Agricultural Wheel, the Farmers' Alliance, and the Colored Farmers' National Alliance for a time threatened to gain control of the state government but their candidates were consistently defeated in rigged elections. Their network of co-operatives was at the time as promising as that of Wisconsin or Minnesota, but it disappeared as their warehouses were burned, their employees murdered, and some counties literally taxed them out of business. The 1880's also saw the beginnings of industrialization as Birmingham, the "Magic City" that enjoyed a tremendous boom in that decade, and other north Alabama towns turned the state's greatest natural resource into an important iron and steel industry. All this did was to give Alabama a new class of absentee tycoons to ally themselves with the Bourbon Democrats and the railroads, notably the Louisville and Nashville, that ran the state; a growing union movement in the mills and mines was crushed in 1894 by police violence and the use of convict labor as scabs.

Alabama was one of the last Southern states to jump on the Jim Crow bandwagon, but when it did, it was more systematic than anywhere else. A constitutional convention called in 1901 "to establish white supremacy" did just that, enacting every trick a Southerner ever invented to disenfranchise blacks, and also enough poor whites to wreck the Populist Party that had grown out of the farmers' movement. Surprisingly the effect of all this tale of woe was to create a progressive wing within the Democratic Party, partly composed of refugees from the destroyed movements of the past. At the beginning of the new century, reform governors William Jelks and Braxton Bragg Comer passed child labor laws, aided education and fought the railroads. Able Alabama representatives were making their state's delegation the strongest in the U.S. Congress; there was Oscar Underwood, a serious contender for the presidency in 1912, two senators named Bankhead, father and son, and a brother who became Speaker of the House. During the 1930's the younger two Bankheads and another Alabama Senator, Lister Hill, would become the leading Southern supporters of the New Deal.

Even with these successes, however, enough of the old madness was still present to keep the state's reputation blackened. After World War I, three Alabamians, one a crank and the other two successful promoters, resurrected the Ku Klux Klan as a money-making scheme; the promoters grew rich as suckers with $10 flocked to their banner, and the Klan held state politics in its grip through the 20's. It made the Alabama scene perfectly bizarre, as one Klan member, a Yale graduate and Cyclops of the Montgomery lodge named Bibb Graves, became an outstanding progressive governor. Another member was a young lawyer named Hugo Black, who was later to become part of the anti-segregationist majority on the U.S. Supreme Court in the fateful years of the 1950's. In the 20's, America knew Alabama best for yet another politician, one of the great Southern demagogues, Tom Heflin; in the 1928 election he stumped Alabama declaring that if Catholic Al Smith won the presidency, the Pope was set to sail into Mobile Bay in a submarine and have the state forcibly converted to Catholicism. In the 30's there was the famous case of the Scottsboro Boys, nine young black men who were found with white women on a train, and following the Southern custom all were convicted of rape. As American Communists made them their cause celebre of the the decade—and the whole world heard about them daily on Moscow radio—the Supreme Court freed them, Alabama reconvicted them, the Court freed them again, and Alabama convicted them again, this time without the state's bothering to produce any evidence. One of the men escaped to Michigan, where the governor refused to extradite him, and the others were paroled fifteen or twenty years later when the case was safely forgotten.

In spite of this, however, Alabama was changing. The beginnings of the

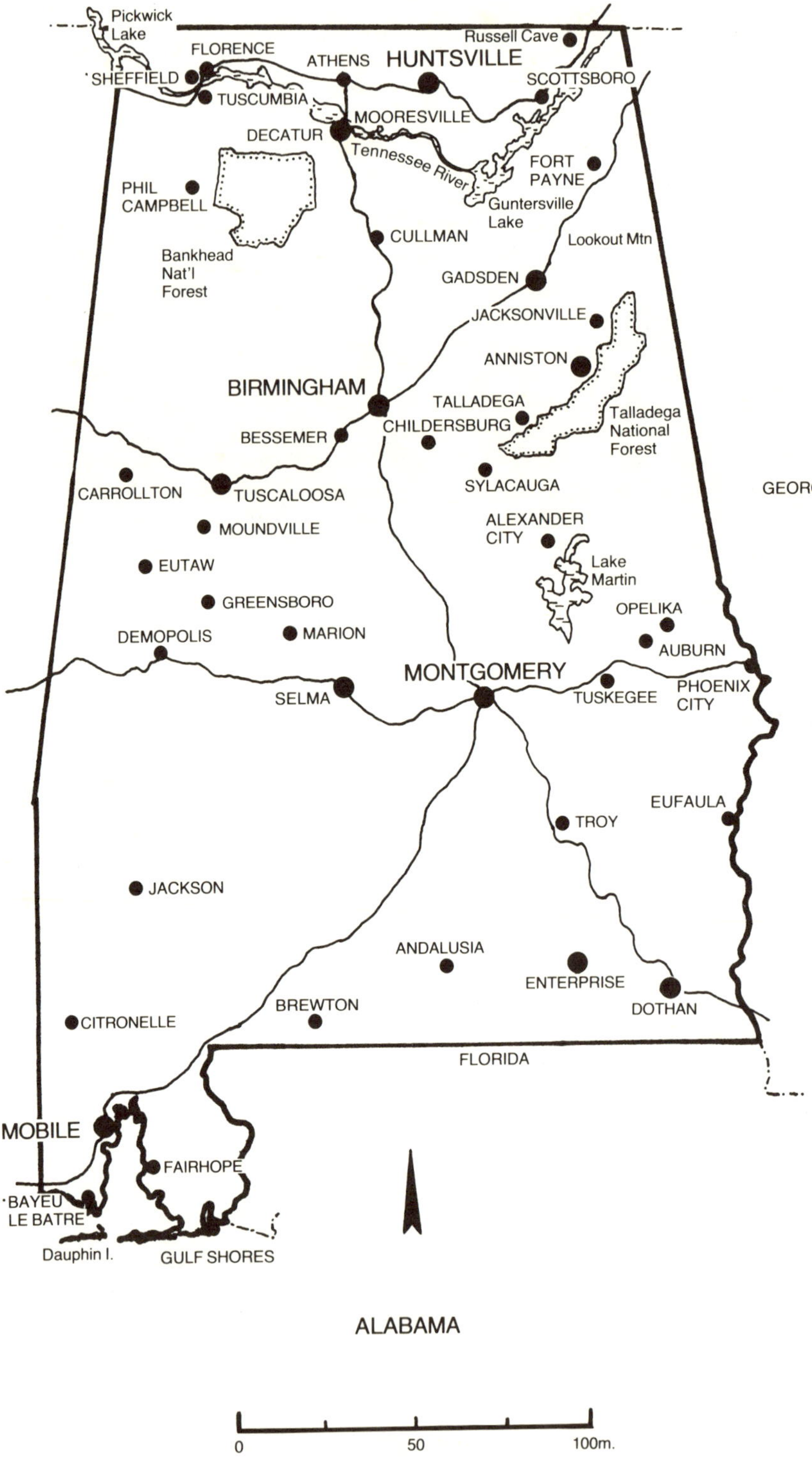

Pickwick Lake
Russell Cave
FLORENCE
ATHENS
HUNTSVILLE
SHEFFIELD
SCOTTSBORO
TUSCUMBIA
MOORESVILLE
DECATUR
Tennessee River
FORT PAYNE
PHIL CAMPBELL
Guntersville Lake
CULLMAN
Lookout Mtn
Bankhead Nat'l Forest
GADSDEN
JACKSONVILLE
ANNISTON
BIRMINGHAM
TALLADEGA
CHILDERSBURG
Talladega National Forest
BESSEMER
SYLACAUGA
CARROLLTON
TUSCALOOSA
GEORGIA
ALEXANDER CITY
MOUNDVILLE
EUTAW
Lake Martin
GREENSBORO
OPELIKA
DEMOPOLIS
MARION
AUBURN
MONTGOMERY
SELMA
TUSKEGEE
PHOENIX CITY
EUFAULA
TROY
JACKSON
ANDALUSIA
ENTERPRISE
DOTHAN
BREWTON
CITRONELLE
FLORIDA
MOBILE
FAIRHOPE
BAYEU LE BATRE
Dauphin I.
GULF SHORES

ALABAMA

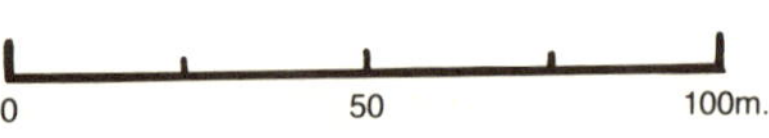

Tennessee Valley Authority were here, not in Tennessee, with the nitrate plant and Wilson Dam which were begun in 1916 by the Federal government at Muscle Shoals as part of the war effort. In the 20's Republican administrations abandoned the half-completed project, which they thought was "socialistic," and tried unsuccessfully to sell it to Henry Ford. When TVA finally came, after the election of Roosevelt, it had a tremendous effect on depressed north Alabama; rapid industrialization continued into World War II, when Alabama liked to call itself the "Nation's Arsenal," and afterwards. Huntsville grew into a major city, and the nation's space program began there in the 50's. Alabama agriculture was changing too, thanks to the boll weevil from Mexico, who ended the self-destructive dependence on cotton.

Just at the moment when Alabama was starting to look respectable again, the Civil Rights revolution arrived to make the state a battleground once more. In 1955, a girl named Autherine Lucy became the first black student at the University of Alabama, but even the federal courts couldn't keep her there longer than a month. That same year saw the beginnings of the assault on Jim Crow laws when Mrs. Rosa Parks got herself arrested for refusing to give up her seat to a white man on a crowded Montgomery bus; the subsequent bus boycott, led by the young Reverend Martin Luther King, attracted nationwide attention, and was eventually successful when the courts outlawed the city's law requiring separate seating. After the first Civil Rights Act in 1960, the fight for voting rights and against discrimination picked up again in the courts and on the streets. The arrival of the "Freedom Riders" in 1961 was met with bloody attacks by local thugs in the bus stations in Birmingham and Montgomery, and U.S. Marshals were sent in to restore order.

In 1963 Alabama got a new governor, a former amateur boxer and country lawyer who started his political career in 1948 defending Harry Truman against the schismatic Dixiecrats. After the events of the 50's, however, George Corley Wallace appeared as a hard core stonewaller, and the words of his inaugural address electrified the South: "I draw the line in the dust and toss the gauntlet before the feet of tyranny, and I say: segregation now, segregation tomorrow, segregation forever!" Such talk couldn't stop the movement, but it did make life in Alabama uncomfortable for everyone. The campaign for civil rights and employment opportunities led by King in Birmingham met success in the face of continuing police riots. Wallace failed to prevent either the integration of the University of Alabama or the famous 1965 march from Selma to Montgomery—this on the second try, after state troopers worked the marchers over the first time—but his actions got him the nationwide attention he needed to make four attempts at the presidency, starting in 1964, as the "white backlash" candidate. In 1968, he drew enough votes from the Democrats as a third party candidate to give us Richard Nixon. Reproach any Alabamian on the subject of George Wallace, and they will remind you that he won primaries in states like Maryland and Michigan while speaking for millions of Northerners who felt themselves dispossessed in the confusions of the 1960's. Most Alabamians would rather forget about the events of the Civil Rights movement in their state—they lost, and it must be said that they have taken it almost graciously—but they remember Wallace as a man who did as much for education and economic development as any governor they've had so far.

During the campaign of 1972 Wallace was shot in a shopping center parking lot in Maryland. Now in a wheelchair, he practices law in Montgomery and awaits a political comeback. When he runs again, speculation has it that it will be with substantial black support. If even George Wallace can change into what diehards used to call "the very worst kind of moderate," who is to say that the "new Alabama" that Dr. King saw at the end of the road from Selma to Montgomery might not be in sight even now?

Mobile and the Coast

Alabama's charm city, Mobile, is the oldest in the state and it wears its age well; its location and the French influence from its early days leave it much more in common with New Orleans and the other towns of the Gulf Coast than with the hinterlands of Alabama. Mardi Gras, azaleas and restoration of their fine old homes are the passions of the Mobilians, but this growing city is not content to live in the past. Besides being one of the nation's leading ports, Mobile has sizable paper and petrochemical industries and builds fishing boats for the entire world.

Bienville founded the city in 1703 as Fort Louis de la Mobile, the capital of French Louisiana. As governor he presided over the difficult early years; his successor, in 1710, was Antoine de la Mothe Cadillac, famous as the founder of Detroit. Even though the government moved to New Orleans in 1720, Mobile continued to prosper; the British snatched it in 1763, only to lose it to Spain during the American revolution and the Spanish in turn saw it seized from them by the U.S. in 1812. The Mississippi and Alabama territories fought over Mobile in the courts and Alabama won, giving the state the peculiarly slanted boundary it has today. In the Civil War, Mobile was the best defended Confederate port, and consequently the last to fall. In August 1864, Admiral Farragut repeated his valorous capture of New Orleans by once more sailing under the guns of rebel fortifications and gaining control of Mobile Bay with the famous line: "Damn the torpedoes, full speed ahead!" The city itself, however, held out until April of 1865, after an eight month siege. The war was not the greatest of Mobile's calamities; in the decades before and after it, several great fires ravaged the city and yellow fever epidemics were common.

Mobile, if the truth be told, taught New Orleans how to do Mardi Gras. The celebration is as old as the city and a carnival society called the Cowbellions provided the model for New Orleans' first "Krewes" in the 1850's. Today such groups as the Infant Mystics and the Krewe of Columbus still entertain the citizens with their parades for a week up to Shrove Tuesday. There's even a ball especially for visitors to the city, held by the Krewe de Bienville.

Downtown Mobile spreads itself around **Bienville Square,** Dauphin and St. Joseph Streets, with an ornate cast-iron fountain commemorating the year the city finally got a good public water system, putting an end to much of its health problems. Two churches in the downtown area are Greek Revival masterpieces: the **Cathedral of the Immaculate**

Conception, on South Claiborne Street, a minor basilica built in 1835, and the **Government Street Presbyterian Church,** at 300 Government (1836), a work of New Orleans' favorite architect James Gallier. Two historic preservation districts grace the downtown area. On the northern edge, between Adams and State Streets, Claiborne and Conception, the **De Tonti Square District** has over forty buildings from the 1850's and 60's; one that would look quite at home in New Orleans' Garden District with its "iron lace" porch, is the **Richards House,** restored and maintained by the D.A.R. as a museum (Tues-Sat 10-4, Sun 1-4, adm.). South of Government Street, two blocks of old Mobile have survived the construction of a freeway interchange looping around them to become a trendy shopping area called Fort Conde Village. **Fort Conde** itself disappeared long ago, but as their bicentennial project the Mobilians reconstructed a part of the bastion from plans in the French government archives and furnished it after the 1730's. There is a museum and Mobilians in French 18th century uniforms who tell you what life was like in this lonely colonial outpost. Lonely, perhaps, but not uncomfortable. It's hard to believe this colorful and decorated place is an accurate job of rebuilding, but it is; the French always built prettier fortresses than their colonial competitors in North America. This one has half-timbered barracks and stores with pitched tile roofs, and one-fifth of the wall is adorned with lovely vedettes (daily 9-5, adm.). Outside the wall, on Theatre Street, the 1822 structure that now pretends to be a gracious home was really the city's first jail; converted to a residence over a century ago, after the demolition of the fort, the **Conde Charlotte House** is full of antiques and run by the Society of Colonial Dames as a museum of period rooms from the city's past—a polite competitor to the Richards House (Tues-Sat 10-4, adm.).

Just across from the fort, near the Bankhead Tunnel that carries traffic under the Mobile River, you'll notice Mobile's **City Hall;** if it looks oddly like a market building, that's because it originally was—produce below and city offices above, built in 1856. It stands at the foot of the city's loveliest thoroughfare, **Government Street,** lined with old oaks, fine homes and gardens full of azaleas in the spring. At no. 335 the 1872 Bernstein-Bush House, once the home of a Mobile mayor, is now the **City Museum.** Mobile has more than enough history to fill this large and elegant townhouse down to the basement, with exhibits from all the periods of the city's past, paintings, ship models, Mardi Gras costumes and some fascinating drawings of old carnival tableaux, and a room full of restored carriages. The Civil War in Mobile is particularly well represented; Mobile claims one of the Confederacy's most dashing heroes as a native son, Admiral Raphael Semmes, who terrorized Yankee shipping with a commerce raider the *C.S.S. Alabama*; he captured over seventy ships. There is a statue to him, by the way, behind City Hall, and his brilliant career earns him a whole room in the museum (Tues-Sat 10-5, Sun 1-5, free). Besides this, the City of Mobile operates two other museums, the **Carlen House,** a restored 1842 Louisiana Cajun-style cottage, at Wilcox and Carlen Streets, and the **Phoenix Fire Museum,** just around the corner from the City Museum at 203 S. Clairborne Street in the 1859 home of the old fire company called "Phoenix," with shiny old pumpers and firefighting memorabilia dating back to 1819 (both museums have the same hours as the City Museum, free).

Nearby on Government Street, the **Spanish Plaza,** flying all the flags that Mobile has lived under since 1711, serves as the front door for the new, round, **Municipal Auditorium.** The neighborhood to the west and north was the preferred residential area of the last century, now revived as the **Church Street East Historical District.** Of the many splendid homes here, one can be visited: **Oakleigh,** a simple but beautiful 1833 structure whose amateur architect, a Mobile merchant, built it for himself. The Mobile Preservation Society has its headquarters here, and they offer guided tours with a wealth of detail about the house, its furnishings of various eras, and its collections of portraits, antiques and memorabilia (on Oakleigh Place, south of Church; Mon-Sat 10-3:30, Sun 2-3:30, adm.).

Another Mobile attraction is the **Fine Arts Museum of the South,** in Langan Park on Forest Hill Drive, with a collection of contemporary painting and decorative arts in an informal setting (Tues-Sat 10-5, Sun 12-5, free). Mobile keeps its ties to the sea not only with an old fashioned riverboat, the *Magnolia Blossom,* offering cruises around Mobile Bay from May to September, but with its very own battleship, the *U.S.S. Alabama.* When the Navy planned to scrap this impressive veteran of World War II, bristling with 16-inch guns, Governor Wallace started a campaign to bring it here, and it currently sits at anchor in the bay east of downtown—the city's most popular tourist attraction—along with a World War II submarine, the *U.S.S. Drum,* and a collection of warplanes (daily 8-sunset, adm. $2.50). And finally, you can go to the dogs, wagering at the **Mobile Greyhound Park;** races 8 pm every night except Sunday.

Mobile's backyard, the narrow strip of Alabama in Mobile and Baldwin Counties that touches the Gulf Coast, serves as the state's oceanside playground, with a number of beaches on the narrow islands that enclose Mobile Bay.

South of the city, the **Bellingrath Home and Gardens** at Theodore were the home of a local industrialist, with 800 acres of flowers and sculpture, and a wildlife refuge (on Rt. 163; gardens open sunrise to sunset, adm. $3; home open the same hours, adm. $3.75). The town of **Bayou Le Batre** calls itself the "Seafood Capital of Alabama," for its fleet of small fishing boats that glean the gulf for shrimp, oysters, crabs and fish. East of town, Rt. 163 follows a causeway over to Dauphin Island, lined with sandy beaches. There is a bird sanctuary here, also some ancient Indian shell mounds, on Iberville Drive, like those in Georgia (some others can be found across Mobile Bay near Point Clear). **Fort Gaines,** one of the redoubts that couldn't stop Admiral Farragut, still guards the entrance to the bay. Built in 1822, the fort houses a small museum (daily 8 am-sunset; adm.).

Across the channel stands **Fort Morgan,** the larger of the two; despite the pounding Farragut gave it, it has been used as a coastal defense point in every war since. The star-shaped fort, built by slave labor in the 1830's, has a lot to see for students of military history and also a museum (daily 8-6, free). The long sand spit behind it, **Pleasure Island,** extends almost thirty miles, all the way to the Florida line, with more beaches, a state-run resort at **Gulf State Park,** and deep-sea fishing charters. Back up the bay, across from Mobile, an unlikely religious experiment survives, the **Malbis**

Plantation near Daphne on US 90. In 1906, a Greek Orthodox monk named Jason Malbis, originally Antonios Markopoulos, came to America commanded by a vision, and after some time in Chicago and Texas he ended up here, and founded a community that attracted over a hundred Greek immigrants and grew prosperous with farms, a canning plant, a bakery in Mobile and other establishments. Most of the Greeks have now assimilated into the Mobile area, but Malbis Plantation is still worth a stop for its impressive blue-domed Malbis Memorial Church, with a lovely interior of white marble and stained-glass windows.

Tourist Information. In **Mobile,** at 108 S. Claiborne St., tel. 433-6951.

Restaurants. *In Mobile*: Malaga Inn***, 359 Church St.; Bernard's***, 407 Conti St.; Constantine's**, 1500 Government St.; Wintzell's Oyster House**, 605 Dauphin; Bayley's Seafood**, Dauphin Island Pkwy.; Filippo's Villa**, 1862 Government St.; Back Porch*, 200 S. Royal St.; Fletchers B-B-Q*, 1503 Government. *In Fairhope*: Grand Hotel Restaurant**. *In Gulf Shores*: Gulf Shores State Park Lodge**.

Montgomery and Central Alabama

Between the Gulf Coast and the red hills of the north lies the region of Alabama called the Black Belt. It's a common misconception that this name refers to black people—who indeed are a majority in several counties; instead, what's black here is the soil, the best in the state and perfect for raising cotton. Consequently, this is the "Old South" corner of Alabama, with all the plantation houses and some pretty towns like Selma and Greensboro.

North of Mobile, sites that played an important role in the state's history have little to show for it today. Where the Tombigbee flows into the Alabama was the Indians' capital Maubila; west of Tensaw is the site of Fort Mims, and along the Tombigbee, the site of St. Stephens, once the colonial capital. In **Citronelle,** the last Confederate forces east of the Mississippi under young General Dick Taylor surrendered on May 4, 1865. Many of the people around Citronelle belong to Alabama's oddest minority group, the "Cajans." They have nothing to do with Louisiana Cajuns, but are descended from Spanish, Indians, French, blacks and —they say—pirates. A very private and little understood people, credited with outlandish ways and superstitions, they were held back for years by a government that accorded them the same official discrimination it did the blacks.

The heart of the Black Belt, however, is to be found much further north in Marengo County, the only county in Alabama named after a horse—Napoleon's horse in fact. A group of ruined French aristocrats who followed the fallen emperor came here in 1817, founding the "Vine and Olive Colony" to see if they could make a new life for themselves from those two Old World products. After building the town of **Demopolis,** they found it really wasn't on their land, and consequently lost it to speculators. A second attempt nearby proved equally unhappy; the climate was too hot for wine grapes, and the soil proved murderous to the olive trees. The colony folded in the 1830's, and most of its members found their way to Mobile or New Orleans. Little remains from this brief experiment, but Demopolis is worth visiting for two fine mansions of the cotton planters who succeeded the French. **Bluff Hall,** on the bluffs over the Tombigbee next to Demopolis' Civic Center, started as a Federal-style townhouse in 1832, but had a columned portico tacked on later for conformity's sake. The Marengo County Historical Society operates it (Tues-Sat 10-5, Sun 2-5, adm.). At 805 Whitfield Street, off US 43, **Gaineswood** is an impressive if somewhat quirky Deep South Monticello, designed and built by the owner, a planter named Nathan Whitfield, and it took him over forty years to complete. Most of the furnishings are original (Mon-Sat 8-4 pm, Sun 1-5, adm.). Demopolis may well see a new golden age someday, for it is the southern terminus of an enormous Army Corps of Engineers project, the controversial **Tennessee-Tombigbee Waterway,** connecting those rivers to create a kind of alternate Mississippi for water-borne freight.

North of Demopolis, the towns of **Greensboro, Marion** and **Eutaw** each have their share of elegant plantations. In Marion, of architectural interest are the 1855 **Perry County Courthouse** and the buildings of **Judson College for Women** (1838) on Bibb Street. On the Black Warrior River, near Moundville, several great temple mounds mark the spot of a prehistoric Alabama metropolis at the **Mound State Monument.** There's a large museum of artifacts from the site, built over an excavated burial ground, also a reconstructed village and life-size displays of everyday life and religious ceremonies—an ambitious and questionable project, considering how little is really known about these mysterious peoples (daily 9-5, adm.). Up in **Carrollton,** you can see one of Alabama's strangest stories recorded in the **Face on the Courthouse Window.** Once, a black prisoner named Henry Wells was being kept in the garret for his own safety while a lynch mob gathered outside. As he watched them through the window, a bolt of lightning hit and permanently etched the prisoner's terrified expression on the glass. Wells died of shock, but the face can be seen today.

Because the streets of **Tuscaloosa** are lined with majestic old live oaks, this university town, the capital of the state until 1846, has acquired for itself the odd nickname of Druid City. Founded by Creek Indians, and named for the great warrior killed by De Soto, the town was destroyed by Jackson's army in the Creek Wars, and rebuilt on a nearby site by white settlers after the removal of the Indians. Growth was steady, and Tuscaloosa snatched off the capitol and the new university largely by its own efforts at self-promotion. Disaster came when the government departed, and again in 1865 when the Yankees burned the university. The old capitol became a Baptist college, but it too burned in 1923, leaving only its stone steps in **Capitol Park,** 6th Street at 28th Avenue, in the oldest part of the city. Nearby, the **Old Tavern,** built in 1827, has become a museum with mementoes of Tuscaloosa's glory days.

On the west side of town, the **Druid City District** contains many fine homes and shady streets, along Queen City Avenue, 17th, and Greensboro Avenue. The **University of Alabama,** with its large campus off University Boulevard, has risen from the ashes to become one of college football's powerhouses. The Crimson Tide's coach, Paul "Bear" Bryant (the winningest coach in football history) is easily the most popular man in Alabama; at every Presidential nominating convention the state's delegates, sober or otherwise, throw his name in for consideration. Since desegregation came in 1963—after Governor Wallace "stood in the schoolhouse door"—Alabama has won or shared five national championships. Attractions on campus include the 1829 **Gorgas House,** once the residence of the father of another famous Alabamian, William C. Gorgas, the man who found the cure for yellow fever at the Panama Canal (Tues-Fri 10-noon, and 1-4, free). Also, there is the **Alabama Museum of Natural History** on 6th Avenue (Mon-Fri 8-4:45, free). West of the city, two historic parks surround the remains of once-flourishing early Alabama ironworks that contributed much to the Confederate war effort: the **Brierfield Ironworks Park,** on Rt. 139 south of Montevallo, and **Tannehill State Park,** off Interstate 59, with a museum, restored houses and iron furnaces, and demonstrations of crafts and production methods.

Selma: This town, also, was a great producer of munitions in the Civil War—though there isn't much industry today. Federal troops changed Selma's destiny in the spring of 1865, when after defeating a ragtag army of defenders under Nathan Forrest they found a warehouse of Confederate whiskey and looted, raped and burned their way though town. Selma had been founded back in 1820 by William Rufus King, later Vice President of the U.S., who gave it a name taken not from the Bible, but from the Ossian poems of Macpherson. Most Americans remember Selma only for its unfortunate lapse of good behavior in 1965, and this must have come as a profound embarrassment to this peaceful, pretty town. Actually, Selma worked hard to avoid trouble when Martin Luther King came to town in one of the first voter registration drives, and only a bloody-minded thug of a county sheriff got Selma splashed across the headlines of the nation's newspapers. Today the city includes in its tourist brochures the **Brown Chapel** at Selma University, for a while the spiritual center of the movement, and also the **Pettus Bridge** across the Alabama River. Here, on March 7 1965, Sheriff Clark's men and state troopers met 600 peaceful, singing blacks and whites on the first march to Montgomery with gas, clubs and whips, while the nation watched aghast on television. For this, and other incidents that attracted so much sympathy and support to the movement, the Southern Christian Leadership Conference jokingly offered the sheriff an honorary membership.

All that is in the past now (veterans of the march held a reunion here last year) and Selma would rather point out to you its historic district, the largest in Alabama. At its center is the lovely restored commercial district along **Water Avenue,** its 19th century buildings with arcades and balconies picturesquely draped over the bluffs above the river. Nearby on Union Street, the **Smitherman Building,** built in 1847, is now the city's museum (Mon-Fri 9-4, Sun 2-4, free) and at 713 Mabry Street, one of Alabama's finest antebellum homes, **Sturdivant Hall** (1853) has been faithfully restored by the city (Tues-Sat, 9-4, Sun 2-4, adm.).

A few miles downriver from Salina, accessible by Rt. 22, are the scanty remains of Alabama's first capital, **Cahaba.** Old maps show the buildings and streets of this once-important city, built on a grid plan around the semicircular park that contained the first modest statehouse. Persistent flooding, once necessitating the removal of the legislature from the second floor of the capitol by rowboat, caused Cahaba's long decline; it survived as a ghost town into this century until vandals burned most of it. The ruins can be visited anytime, sunrise to sunset.

Montgomery: In the middle of this typically southern city there's a small park, and in the middle of that the simple, domed, **Alabama State Capitol.** Here, on the west portico under the Egyptian revival columns, a star in the pavement marks the spot where Jefferson took the oath as the first and only president of the C.S.A. George Wallace, with careful symbolism, gave his famous inaugural speech on the same spot. That capitol still dominates Montgomery from "Goat Hill" at the foot of Dexter Avenue, the city's main street. Additions were built in 1885 and 1905, but little has changed since its construction—on the site of an earlier capitol of the same design that burned—in 1851. The famous clock that marked the first hours of the Confederacy is still in operation and prominent plaques in the Senate and House chambers commemorate Alabama's secession and the adoption of the rebel constitution by the representatives of the Southern states in February 1861. Highlights of the building (which, in this state with its long tradition of parsimonious government, is very poorly maintained) include the scenes of Alabama history in murals around the rotunda, and the cantilevered wooden spiral staircases, climbing three floors without support.

Also interesting, on the ground floor under the rotunda, is a bust of Governor Lurleen Wallace, decorated with plastic roses. In 1966, her husband George discovered an absolutely novel means of evading the Alabama constitutional requirement that forbids governors a second term. He had Lurleen run in his place; she won, and proved an able governor (with some help from George) until her untimely death from cancer in 1968. Her demise in office, like John F. Kennedy's, has resulted in a kind of popular canonization, and you can learn all about her life and brief political career at the **Lurleen Wallace Museum,** in a restored 1850's "Steamboat Gothic" house across Monroe Street from the Capitol (daily 8-5, free). On the other side of the Capitol, among the collection of government buildings that have appeared to house the growing bureaucracy of a growing state, stands the **First White House of the Confederacy,** the home of Jefferson Davis for the five months Mongomery served as the capital. The "Stars and Bars" still fly here, and the home, built in 1825, contains many articles that belonged to the Davis family in rooms furnished after the period (644 Washington Avenue; daily 8-5, free). Next door, aficionados of offbeat museums will love the one in the **Alabama Department of Archives and History,** an enormous attic full of fascinating clutter left behind by the Indians, the Spanish, the French and the Alabamians themselves. There's an entire room devoted to the life of William Rufus King, another to the Vine and Olive colony, hundreds of stuffed birds, a doll collection and a portrait gallery of famous Alabamians where Bob Jones, the bigot Bible-thumper who founded Bob Jones University, hangs next to Booker T. Washington (Mon-Fri 8-5, free).

Down Dexter Avenue from the Capitol, at Decatur Street you'll pass the Judiciary Building, which once was a Masonic temple, and the **Dexter Avenue Baptist Church.** The Rev. Martin Luther King became minister here in 1955, just before the bus boycott; this, it can be said, is the place where the Civil Rights movement started. At Montgomery Street,

Dexter meets a lovely new decoration for downtown, recently redesigned **Court Square,** with the ornate 1885 **Mac Monnies Fountain.** There's a legend of an Indian priestess prophesying that the city will prosper as long as the underground spring that feeds the fountain continues to flow. At Court Square, an area where new skyscrapers are changing the face of downtown, Dexter curves and becomes **Commerce Street;** here, sloping towards the Alabama River, Montgomery has built its new **Civic Center** across from two blocks of 19th century commercial buildings that were once the heart of downtown, the **Commerce Street Historic District.** Here also is another of Montgomery's architectural landmarks, the Union Station, like any proper fancy 19th century depot part royal palace and part Victorian penitentiary. Behind it, **Riverfront Park** displays the world's first electric trolley car, one that ran in Montgomery in 1886. The dock is here for the *General Richard Montgomery,* a riverboat offering tours on the Alabama in the summer.

Also downtown, there are two more antebellum homes to tour: the **Murphy House,** on Bibb Street at Coosa (Mon-Fri 8-5, adm.) and the **Ordeman-Shaw House,** on Hull Street, a part of the **Old North Hull Historic District.** This isn't the usual restored neighborhood, but a collection of homes, both modest and elaborate, and also a church, store and tavern, all built between 1818 and 1895, and moved to this site by the City Landmarks Commission as a kind of open-air museum of early urban life in the South (Mon-sat 9:30-3:30, Sun 1:30-3:30, adm. $2.50). The real restoration district lies south of downtown, with some fine homes along Perry and Court Streets. Nearby at High and Lawrence, the **Montgomery Museum of Fine Arts** has a collection strongest in 19th century American painters and decorative arts (Tues-Sat 10-5, Thurs until 9 pm, Sun 1-6, free). A few blocks away at Perry and Adams Streets, an odd-looking building houses something called the **Tumbling Waters Museum of Flags, Inc.** (Mon-Fri 10-4, free).

Just west of the city a major contributor to the local economy is **Maxwell Air Force Base,** home of the "Air University." This is one of the oldest air bases; none other than the Wright Brothers came down here to establish a flying school in 1910.

Northeast of Montgomery, along the Tallapoosa River, beyond the power company dam that has created big **Lake Martin,** is the **Horseshoe Bend National Military Park,** on Rt. 49, the last stand of the Red Sticks. On March 27, 1814, Andrew Jackson and his Cherokee allies surrounded the heavily outnumbered Creeks in this fortified bend in the river and annihilated them. Operated by the National Park Service, the park has a museum, a battlefield tour and occasional demonstrations of firearms used at the battle (daily 8-4:30, free). Directly east of the capital are two of Alabama's leading educational institutions. **Auburn University,** at Auburn, is also the largest; its teams are the arch rivals of Alabama's Crimson Tide. Some fine buildings grace the campus, including the 1840 **University Chapel** and the very academic-looking 1888 **Samford Hall.**

Tuskegee Institute, in Tuskegee is, of course, the famous school founded in 1881 by Booker T. Washington, with some aid from the state government, for the vocational training and spiritual uplifting of blacks. Despite a polite controversy between Washington and other black leaders, such as W. E. B. DuBois, over the question of whether Tuskegee's practical and realistic approach would only serve to confirm the subordinate status of blacks, the school became nationally famous, attracting the philanthropies of such men as Carnegie and Rockefeller. Hundreds of Tuskegee graduates became teachers, spreading their skills as well as Washington's message of hard work and dignity, and contributing immeasurably to the welfare and capabilities of Southern blacks. Since 1927, Tuskegee has been a degree-granting college, and it thrives today on a lovely tree-shaded campus on Rt. 126 just west of the town. Most people know the Institute best as the home of George Washington Carver, the great scientist who made hundreds of useful things from peanuts and other farm products and changed the face of Southern agriculture. At the **Carver Museum** on campus, much of this scientific wizardry is displayed, but even more interesting is the insight into the man himself and his uniquely spiritual approach to science and the inter-relationships of man and nature. Carver was also an artist of exceptional talent, and some of his works are here. The museum is a part of the **Tuskegee National Historic Site** (Mon-Sat 10-noon, & 1-4, Sun 1-4, free), which also includes an 1850's Greek Revival mansion called **Grey Columns,** now the National Park Service's reception center, and Booker T. Washington's home **The Oaks,** built and furnished, like most of the Institute's original buildings, by the students themselves.

Beyond Tuskegee there's **Opelika,** with an impressive 1896 county courthouse, and **Phenix City** which was for a while in the 1950's the "sin city of the South". Right on the Georgia border, near a major military installation, organized crime got hold of this town and turned it into a violent wonderland of brothels and gambling dens. When Phenix City's citizens rose up to throw out them and the corrupt politicians that permitted them, the crooks responded with murders and firebombings. Hollywood turned the brave struggle of the reformers into a movie, but they were unsuccessful until the Governor declared martial law in 1954 and sent troops to clean up the mess. **Eufaula,** in George Wallace's own Barbour County, is an eastern outpost of the Black Belt, a modern city with a fine collection of pre-Civil War buildings and an annual "pilgrimage" like the one in Natchez. Among them: the **Wellborn House,** 630 Broad Street (Mon-Fri, 8:30-2, donation); **Fendell Hall,** 917 W. Barbour (open by appointment, adm.); also the **Shorter Mansion** on N. Eufaula Avenue, housing the **Eufaula Historical Museum** (Mon-Sat 10-4, Sun 1-4, adm.). In the town of **Troy** on US 231, the **Pike Pioneer Museum** recalls early Alabama with a group of authentically furnished cabins, everything from the general store to an outhouse.

Further south the Black Belt gives way to the southeastern "wiregrass country" a plain dotted with stands of pine; the land is relatively poor here and consequently this is one of the last parts of the state to be settled, a peculiar frontier country in the 1880's. It wasn't good territory for growing cotton but, of course, they did it anyhow until the boll weevil came up to devour two-thirds of the crop in 1915. In the middle of the agricultural town of **Enterprise** stands one of the world's strangest memorials, the **Boll Weevil Monument.** There's a story that it came about by accident: in 1919 the city was erecting a fountain surmounted by a female figure with arms extended. A traveling salesman asked the workmen about it and got the facetious reply that it was in honor of the weevil. He believed it and called all the big city newspapers. The city was cornered and added a plaque and a big fat weevil between the lady's arms. Enterprise, however, claims they meant it, and with good reason. The weevil taught area farmers the virtues of diversified agriculture and Enterprise became the prosperous and pleasant town it is today courtesy of the new monarch, King Peanut. Between Enterprise and **Dothan,** a large industrial town, home of the National Peanut Festival, the big Army installation at **Fort Rucker** invites you to the **U.S. Army Aviation Museum,** with "the largest collection of helicopters in the free world" (Mon-Fri 10-5, Sat & Sun 1-5, free).

Restaurants. *In Selma*: Costa's***, 1629 W. Highland. *In Tuscaloosa*: Moon Gate Inn**, 2431 Universitry Blvd.; Waysider*, 1512 Greensboro Ave.; Ezell's Catfish Cabin*, Jug Factory Rd. *In Montgomery*: Elite Café**, 129 Montgomery St.; SOS Oyster Reef**, 845 W. South Blvd.; Sahara**, 511 E. Edgemont; Beverly Restaurant**, 1250 Air Base Blvd. *In Opelika*: White Columns**, 915 Ave. B. *In Auburn*: Stoker's Seafood House**, 1144 Opelika Hwy. *In Eufaula*: Chewella Restaurant**. *In Dothan*: Garland House**, 200 North Bell.

Birmingham and Northern Alabama

Northern Alabama is different both in its people and its geography. The southernmost heights of the Appalachians fill the top of the state, with a long bend of the Tennessee River wrapped around them, and south of these the Red Hills country extends almost as far as Montgomery. This is industrial Alabama, a land rich in mineral resources. These were barely exploited until after the Civil War, but today the area has not only new and growing industries, but some already past their prime. Northern Alabama is the most densely populated part of the state, the wealthiest and the place with the largest number of union workers in all the South. New cities like Birmingham and Huntsville account for most of this; they are superimposed on an old mountain setting that is closer in spirit to Tennessee than the Black Belt or Mobile.

Birmingham's colossus looks down over the center of the city from Red Mountain, one of the largest statues in the world, built of Red Mountain iron in Birmingham's furnaces. Everyone knows the Iron Man, even if they know nothing else about the industrial center of the South; few cities have chosen a more fitting symbol for themselves. Birmingham's good fortune was an abundance of all three minerals needed to make steel: iron, from Red Mountain and elsewhere, coal, and limestone. The agrarian South ignored them until necessity intervened in the Civil War. Soon after, in 1871, northern interests founded the city and named it for the great British industrial city they hoped it would emulate; Birmingham became a classic example of a deplorable American phenomenon, the city formed entirely by land speculators, with little regard to anything except a quick profit. When two railroad routes crossed near the site, the city's future was assured and the Elyton Land Company raked in the money as industrialists like Henry De Bardeleben and huge corporations like Tennessee Coal & Iron (later merged into U.S. Steel) built their mills. The "Magic City" seemed to appear almost overnight and by 1930 it was almost as big as Atlanta. The Depression, however, hit Birmingham like a hammer and started a long decline in the steel industry that continues today. As in Pittsburgh, only one large mill remains within the city limits, U.S. Steel's Fairfield Works, and Birmingham now imports cheaper ore from South America instead of using its own. Even so, "primary metals" still puts dinner on the table for Birmingham, and the city has successfully diversified into other industries.

Birmingham's large black population had been protesting discrimination since the 1930's, but it was not until the 60's that "Bad Birmingham," the city that Martin Luther King called "the Johannesburg of America," became one of the focal points of the national struggle. Nowhere in the South did Jim Crow have a tighter hold; not only washrooms and buses were segregated, but also taxis, grandstands at the ballparks, elevators and even police paddy wagons. Birmingham was always a rough town, but with the first protests it became a violent, hate-filled city of daily confrontations. Civic leaders tried to pretend nothing was happening, preferring to remind visiting reporters of their large number of churches with "the biggest Sunday school attendance in the South". Meanwhile, a police commissioner named Bull Conner was becoming a hero with Southern bigots by his oppressive tactics and attacks on demonstrators with dogs and fire hoses. In 1963 white mobs roamed the city looking for trouble, and blacks responded with violence of their own; the climax came when a bomb at the Sixteenth Street Baptist Church killed four black girls and the black community exploded with riots. Only then did blacks and whites come together to talk about it. Since then some progress has been made, but Birmingham still has far to go.

The oldest parts of **downtown** can be found near Morris Avenue, now repaved in brick and with new shops and restaurants filling restored old warehouses and commercial blocks. From here 19th and 20th, respectively the major shopping and business streets, extend northwards to **Woodrow Wilson Park** surrounded by city and state offices, City Hall, and the courthouse. Between the park and the modern **Civic Center** stands the **Birmingham Museum of Art.** Founded in 1950 the museum has grown impressively adding to its original Kress collection of old masters more European and American painting, especially Western artists like Remington and Catlin as well as Inca and other Pre-Columbian art, Oriental Art and a collection from the ancient Near East (Tues-Sat 10-5, Thurs until 9 pm, Sun 2-6, donation).

Though much of downtown has turned into parking lots, a substantial number of buildings remain from the boom days, along First, Second and Third Avenues; some, like the recently restored Steiner Building at First and 21st Street, are delightfully gruesome in the way only neo-Romanesque American buildings of the 1880's and 90's can be. Along with a number of Art Deco skyscrapers from the 1920's, like the Watts Building on 21st Street, they give downtown more the appearance of a Northern city than one in the Deep South. South of downtown, at 331 Cotton Avenue, a restored mansion called **Arlington,** built in 1822, is all that remains of the original pre-Birmingham town of Elyton; Union troops used it as a headquarters in 1865 (Tues-Sat 9-5, Sun 1-6, adm.). East of downtown on First Avenue you can see the remains of one of the earliest Birmingham ironworks, the **Sloss Furnaces,** which are supposedly haunted. The city has plans to turn them into an industrial museum.

Further south is Red Mountain, still full of ore, which looms over the city to remind it of its origins. A few years ago the city sliced through it for the Red Mountain Expressway (US 280), revealing 500 million years of history including several layers of fossils in the rock, and attracting geologists and palaeontologists from all over. Now they've built the **Red Mountain Museum** right next to it, on 22nd Street off Arlington Avenue, where you can make that long trip through time yourself, on a walkway through the cut, and see exhibits not only on this, but all the sciences. The star of the show is the skeleton of a mosasaur excavated here, a kind of seagoing dinosaur of fearsome aspect (Tues-Sat 10-5, Sun 1-5, free). Also up here off US 31 is **Vulcan,** the Iron Man. An Italian-Alabamian sculptor named Giuseppe Moretti designed him, and before he was installed here in Vulcan Park he had to suffer the indignity of holding up advertisements for Heinz pickles at the 1904 St. Louis World's Fair. Now, even worse, they've given him a torch to hold that looks rather like a popsicle and glows red whenever Birmingham records a traffic fatality (the brochure calls Vulcan the "world's largest safety reminder"). Moretti's strange icon, uncanny like something dredged up from a lost continent, deserves better treatment. He's 55 feet high, on a 124-foot pedestal atop the 400-foot mountain, and there's a fine view of Birmingham from the **observation deck** recently built beneath his feet, reached by a glass-front elevator (daily 8:30-10 pm, adm.).

South of Red Mountain is where Birmingham keeps its better residential suburbs, like Mountain Brook and Homewood, and also two more attractions: the 70-acre **Birmingham Botanical Gardens** with lots of roses, a conservatory and a noted Japanese Garden with a tea house the Japanese built for the New York Worlds Fair (daily sunrise to sunset); and the **Jimmy Morgan Zoo** (named after a former mayor), the largest in the South, which has a white rhinoceros, a Siberian tiger and lots more (daily 9:30-5, adm.).

Around Birmingham there are a number of other industrial towns that grew up in the same period. **Bessemer,** named for the British inventor of the modern steelmaking process, is one of these just southwest of the city; here you may visit the **Bessemer Hall of History,** with fossils, local memorabilia from the pioneers and the industrialists and a "typewriter that once belonged to Adolf Hitler". On the way to another steel town, **Gadsden,** you'll pass an unusual rock formation atop Chandler Mountain. An early settler gave **Horse Pens 40** its name, because there are forty acres of it and some of the rocks form natural corrals where the Indians kept horses. Today it is a popular site for music and crafts festivals. Gadsden itself was the scene of a dramatic Civil War encounter when the Yankee raiders of Colonel A. D. Streight came through in 1863, a story that includes both a famous midnight ride, by a mail carrier named John Wisdom to warn the people of Rome, Georgia, 67 miles away, and the heroism of a 15-year-old girl named Emma Sansom, who showed Nathan Forest's irregulars shortcuts through the woods, occasionally coming under enemy fire, enabling Forrest to capture the raiders. There's a monument to Miss Sansom in a park on Broad Street at First. At the northern edge of town, off Route 227, a large city park has been established to show off the impressive 90-foot **Noccalula Falls;** there's also a botanical garden and a pioneer museum in a group of 200-year-old log cabins moved here from Tennessee (daily 8-sunset, adm.).

Anniston, one of Alabama's finer cities, owes much of its current felicity to the progressive industrialist who founded it in 1872, Samuel Noble. Its nickname "the Model City of the South," seems to reflect the pride of its early citizens in the exact rectangularity of their street plan. Noble named most of those streets for Episcopal bishops, and they survive today, lined with the spreading oaks that Noble planted, on both sides of Quintard Avenue, the main street, where a statue of the founder has been erected. Anniston is a progressive city, and the home of the **Alabama Shakespeare Festival.** Its good sense and racial tolerance make it a striking contrast to Birmingham. The city is proudest of its **Anniston Museum of Natural History** at 430 McClellan Boulevard, begun by local naturalist, H. Severn Regar; among the exhibits are life-size displays of wildlife and habitats from all over the world, an Ornithology Hall, and a native trail on the grounds (Tues-Fri 9-5, Sat 10-5, Sun 1-5, free). Another of Samuel Noble's contributions is the church of **St. Michael and All Angels** on Cobb Avenue at 17th (1890), a romantic-Romanesque work made entirely of Alabama stone and wood with a lovely interior.

North of the city, **Fort McClellan** contains the **Women's Army Corps Museum,** on one of the WAC's earliest bases from World War II (Mon-Fri 8-4, Sat & Sun 12-4, free). On the other side of this extensive military base, there's **Jacksonville,** the home of Jacksonville State University. Just off the town square the **Dr. Francis Museum** is recreated as an 1850's physician's office. In the Jacksonville cemetery there is a monument over the grave of John Pelham, one of the Confederacy's best-remembered heroes; when, after sixty battles, the young and gallant Pelham was killed, belles all over Alabama put on mourning. South of Anniston, the big **Talladega National Forest** stretches across four counties. **Talladega,** on its western edge, has the **Alabama International Motor Speedway,** one of the holy places of the Dixie cult of stock-car racing.

A look at a road map gives away the character of this part of Alabama; here in the southern reaches of the Appalachians, most roads run northeast to southwest, as they do in eastern Tennessee, following the valleys between the folded mountain ridges. The mountains promise some scenery and natural wonders and these can be found all over. Southwest of Talladega, near the small town of Childersburg, are found the truly spectacular **De Soto Caverns,** with "onyx curtains," 2000-year-old Indian burials and long stalactites; the main cavern, twelve storeys tall, is an incredible sight. To the Creek nation, this was an important religious site, and the mythical founding place of their people. Later, the whites came and mined it for saltpetre to make gunpowder (on Rt. 76; Mon-Sat 9-6, Sun 12:30-6, adm $3.75). Another cave, this one north of Birmingham off I-65, is over a mile in length, the **Rickwood Caverns State Park.**

In DeKalb County, north of Gadsden, **Lookout Mountain** stretches from that city to the Georgia line and beyond to Chattanooga. Here it offers two more waterfalls: 100-foot **De Soto Falls,** another state park (both the falls and the caves were visited by the Spanish explorer) and beautiful **Little River Falls** in Little River Canyon, the deepest gorge east of the Rocky Mountains. Both can be reached from the town of Fort Payne; the 1880 **Fort Payne Opera House** here is one of the oldest theaters in Alabama. The town fits snugly in one of the long narrow Appalachian valleys, with Lookout Mountain on one side and Sand Mountain on the other. On this mountain you can visit another rugged gorge, called **Buck's Pocket,** and nearby **Sequoyah Caverns,** with its "looking-glass lakes," is almost as good as De Soto (daily 8:30-5, summer 8-7 pm; adm $3.00). The entrepreneur who operates this cave is none other than the man who spent his life painting "See Rock City" on the roof of every barn, garage and birdhouse in the South. Now he has an attraction of his own. Sequoyah lived for a time in a Cherokee town near Fort Payne, and it was here that he completed his work on the Cherokee alphabet.

Tennessee Valley. From the northeast corner of Alabama to the northwest, the great river loops down, now backed up into three long lakes by TVA dams. As in Tennessee, TVA made all the difference, and it has created the paradox of this isolated, traditional, typically Appalachian region now being also the most modernized and forward-looking part of Alabama.

First, however, there are more caves to explore. Russell Cave, near the Tennessee border off Route 2, was known to early settlers, but it was not discovered until 1953 that the archaic Indian remains are among the oldest in the United States. The first prehistoric troglodytes turned up as early as 7,000 B.C., and the cave served as a shelter continuously for 8,000 years. Now, as the **Russell Cave National Monument** the results of thirty years of archaeological work can be seen in exhibits in the visitors center and the cave itself (daily 8-5, summer until 6, free). Further south off Route 2, near Woodville, **Cathedral Caverns** features some of the largest grottoes and stalagmites anywhere (daily 8-6 pm, summer 9-5, adm. $2.50). **Scottsboro,** the Jackson County seat, halfway between the caves, earned notoriety in the 1930's for the "Scottsboro Boys" case; now it must endure two big TVA nuclear power plants nearby. A four-building complex housing the **Scottsboro-Jackson Heritage Center,** an Appalachian pioneer museum, is scheduled to open in 1983. The town's courthouse square is the site of a popular crafts and curios market on the first Sunday and Monday of each month. **Guntersville Lake,** behind Guntersville Dam, is, like all TVA lakes, ringed with recreation areas and stocked with fish.

The first capital of Alabama was originally called Twickenham, after the home of the founder's favorite poet, Alexander Pope. Later on , when everyone was mad at the British just before the War of 1812, the town renamed itself **Huntsville,** after another early settler. Eventually the capital was moved to a more central location, and the city that once seemed to have great potential gradually found its level as a sleepy river town with a few textile mills. Then came TVA and the government facilities its cheap power attracted; during World War II thousands were employed at the hastily-built Redstone Arsenal. After the war Huntsville's life was changed forever when the Defense Department made Redstone the research and development center for all its rocketry programs and later for the space program. The government sent Dr. Werner von Braun and dozens of other German scientists; when von

Braun arrived in 1950, Huntsville's population was 16,000. Twenty years, untold billions of dollars, and several moon landings later, it had grown to 140,000. Alabama's instant city, with a cosmopolitan population of new arrivals from all over the U.S. and the world, isn't classic Alabama, but it's quite a town in its own right. Its growth has slowed as the space program has been cut back, but the boom years have left behind a new downtown, new parks and a wealth of cultural organizations including an art museum, three ballet companies, and a Civic Opera.

Downtown much of old Huntsville has made a graceful transition, restored in two residential historic districts: **Old Town,** just off Courthouse Square, and the **Twickenham Historic District,** with the largest collection of antebellum homes in the state. One of them, the **Weeden House,** built in 1819 at 300 Gates Avenue, can be toured (Tues-Sun 10-4, adm.). Two more restoration projects are underway: **Constitution Hall Park,** also on Gates, a group of early structures including the meeting hall where Alabama's constitution was adopted in 1819, and the **Depot Museum** in the old station on Church Street, planned as an exposition of the city's past in transportation and industry. New Huntsville has added to these, besides a clutch of skyscrapers, the **Von Braun Civic Center** that includes the **Huntsville Museum of Art** with a small collection of American artists and Oriental works and continuous exhibits from other museums (Tues-Sat 10-5, Thurs evening 7-9 pm, Sun 1-5, free). Nearby, a beautiful green setting for downtown has been created in the **Big Spring International Park,** with a lagoon crossed by decorative bridges. The park has been furnished with gifts from foreign nations—hence the name; there are park benches from Britain, cherry trees from Japan and a German sundial, among others.

To the west the Arsenal has now become the **Marshall Space Flight Center.** Adjacent to it on Governor's Drive, you can see what they have done at the **Alabama Space and Rocket Center,** with plenty of rockets, from the Redstones that launched the first satellites to the big Saturn V. All the gadgetry that goes with them is on display with Miss Baker, the famous "monkeynaut," and exhibits on current NASA activities, including a simulated ride on the Space Shuttle. Guided tours of the Marshall Center leave regularly from here (daily 9-5, summer 8-6, adm. $ 3.50). For something a little slower a riverboat called the *Alabama Star* offers cruises on the Tennessee River from the docks south of downtown. East of the city, on **Monte Sano Mountain,** there's a state park and one of the most curious buildings in Alabama; the white-columned **Burritt Museum** is only somewhat antebellum (it was built just before World War II). A local doctor had it constructed in the shape of a Maltese cross for his home, and later donated it to the city to house this collection of Indian relics and pioneer and Civil War memorabilia. The grounds which have a fine view of the city, contain a "pioneer village" of buildings brought from all over Alabama, and furnished to portray everyday life in the early days (Tues-Sun 1-6 pm,. adm. by donation).

West of Huntsville, **Athens College** at Athens is the state's oldest; its Greek Revival **Founders Hall** was completed in the 1840's. During the Civil War Athens was the first Alabama town to be captured, and the citizens suffered a very unpleasant occupation under a Union general named Ivan Vasilivitch Turchinev until Nathan Forrest came to boot him out in one of the last Confederate victories of the war. **Decatur** also had its troubles in the war; after the armies were through fighting over it only a few buildings were left standing. However Decatur was rebuilt and TVA turned it into a smaller Huntsville, packed with industry along its share of riverbank. Its restored downtown area, **Old Decatur,** stretches along Bank Street past the 1833 **State Bank Building.** Decatur is a city devoted to the outdoors; its attractions include **Cook's Natural History Museum,** with exhibits on wildlife in the Tennessee Valley (412 13th Street; Mon-Sat 9-noon & 1-5, Sun 2-5, free; it's run by a local exterminating firm); the **Wildlife Interpretive Center** of the Wheeler National Wildlife Refuge, is on an island created by Wheeler Dam (Wed-Sun 10-5, free); and an unusual park called **Point Mallard,** with all kinds of sports including ice skating, nature trails and a big swimming pool with mechanically created ocean waves (summer only; Sun-Wed 10-7, Thurs 10-9, Fri & Sat 10-8; adm. $3). Across the Tennessee from Decatur, there's a tiny village Alabamians are very fond of. **Mooresville** is one of the state's oldest towns, and it's often claimed to be the one that has changed the least.

South of Decatur, towards Birmingham, the town of **Cullman** was founded by German immigrants in the 1870's. The house of the founder, John Cullman, has now become the **Cullman County Museum** at 211 Second Avenue (Mon-Wed & Fri 9-noon & 1-4:30, Thurs 2-4:30, Sat and Sun 1-4:30, adm.) but the town's real attraction can be found across US 278 from St. Bernard College. **Ave Maria Grotto** was the life work of a Benedictine monk, Brother Joseph Zoettl. For over forty years, he spent whatever spare time a Benedictine has creating miniatures of famous churches of the world from local stone and whatever other materials people sent him. There are over 130 of them, arranged in a heavenly village on a landscaped hillside—St. Peter's, Lourdes Cathedral, and the others. Not all the buildings are religious; there's a Colosseum and an Alamo (daily 7-sunset, adm.).

Back on the river, the city of **Florence** has grown up where TVA began, with Wilson Dam and the nitrates plant at Muscle Shoals. The shoals were an impediment to navigation that Alabamians were petitioning Washington to do something about almost as soon as settlement commenced. A canal to circumvent them was not begun until 1890, and it was a young Alabama engineer named George Goethals who planned the job, giving him some good practice for the Panama Canal he was to build two decades later. Florence started out as a trading post in 1779. Its oldest structure, the 1811 **Pope's Tavern,** where Jackson once spent a night, is the town's museum, on Heritage Drive (Tues-Sat 9-noon & 1-4, adm.). The town's most famous son is commemorated at the **W. C. Handy Home and Museum** at 620 College Street. The "father of the blues" didn't stay long after he grew up; he had a Methodist minister for a father who disapproved of this sort of secular music, but his family has contributed much personal memorabilia for this museum (Tues-Sat 9-noon & 1-4, adm.). South of downtown along the riverfront—this part of the river is really TVA's **Pickwick Lake**—the **Indian Mound and Museum** marks an important site of the Mississippian Culture, the largest temple mound in the Tennessee Valley (Tues-Sat 9-noon & 1-4, adm.).

In this "tri-city area," Florence has two little sisters on the opposite shore: **Tuscumbia** and **Sheffield.** The latter, near Muscle Shoals, claims to have the largest recording studio in the world, equally popular with country and rock singers (tours available through the Muscle Shoals Music Association, 381-1442). It's here, of course, because many bands require the entire electrical output of a TVA dam to power their amplifiers, and one is at hand: **Wilson Dam,** the first and one of the biggest, begun as part of the Muscle Shoals project during World War I when TVA was still just a gleam in Senator Norris' eye. As in all the TVA installations, tours are available (off Rt. 133, daily 9-5, free). Tuscumbia's fame is the home of Helen Keller, **Ivy Green,** at 601 E. 5th Street. You'll find it just as it was portrayed in the famous movie, and a local theatre company does regular performances of *The Miracle Worker* here on summer evenings (Mon-Sat 8:30-4:30, Sun 1-4:30, adm.).

West of the tri-cities, the **Natchez Trace Parkway** cuts through a pretty corner of the state, following the pioneer's road through Mississippi from Tennessee. To the south, more Alabama mountain scenery awaits in a little-traveled part of the state. The **Natural Bridge,** two sixty-foot limestone spans, can be seen off U.S. 278 south of Haleyville (daily sunrise to sunset, adm. $2). Only in America, perhaps, have such natural wonders been transformed into profit-making enterprises. The Natural Bridge is in Winston County, now almost entirely within the **William B. Bankhead National Forest.** This isolated area was "free Winston" in the Civil War, the place where resistance to the Confederacy and its goals was the strongest. Another attraction, and a very peculiar one, can be found on U.S. 43 near the town of **Phil Campbell.** The steep, narrow canyon called **The Dismals** by the early settlers really isn't so dismal, but it contains an outlandish variety of flora, the biggest hemlock trees anywhere, caves, fissures, waterfalls and some unusual rock formations in which you may see the "Indian head." One of the falls has the gift of a permanent rainbow whenever the sun is shining. By request, you can drop in on a summer night to see the twinkling phosphorescent worms called "dismalites" (daily, sunrise to sunset, adm.). And finally, to bring Alabama to a fitting close with one of its fonder eccentricities, there's the **Coon Dog Memorial Park,** off Route 247 near Cherokee, where a hundred or so of the area's most mourned hounds have found eternal peace under such epitaphs as "Raleigh was his name, treeing coons was his game . . ."

Tourist Information. In **Huntsville's** Von Braun Civic Center at 700 Monroe Street, the city operates a Tourist Information Center, open Mon-Sat 9-5 (533-0125; for a recorded listing of events, call 533-5723).

Restaurants. *In Birmingham*: Burtscheins's Bavarian Gardens***, 1505 20th St. S.; Cane Break**, 1926 4th Ave. N.; Veneto's**, 1980 Hwy. 150 S.; Cathay Inn**, 1926 29th Ave. S.; Rod Tarter's Creole Room**, 2410 Canterbury Rd.; Down the Street Restaurant**, 414 21st St. S.; TS's**, 400½ 20th St. N.; Durante's**, 193 Vulcan Rd.; Sarris Seafood**, 600 31st St. N.; Burly Earl's*, 2109 7th Ave. S.; Carlile Bros. Barbeque*, 3510 6th Ave. S.; Waite's*, 2101 7th Ave. S. *In Bessemer*: Bright Star**, 304 19th St. *In Anniston*: Annistonian Restaurant**, 1709 Noble; De's**, 1411 Quintard. *In Jacksonville*: Village Inn*, 109 Clinton St. *In Huntsville*: Tony Mason's**, 1809 University Drive; Ike's**, 310 Governors Dr. S.E.;

Gibson's Barbeque*, 3319 Memorial Pkwy. *In Scottsboro*: Davis Restaurant*, 115 W. Willow Hwy.

Annual Events in Alabama

In February: Mardi Gras, in *Mobile* (late Feb. or early March).
In March: Azalea Trail Festival, in *Mobile*; Selma Pilgrimage in *Selma*; Arts and Crafts Festival, in *Fairhope*.
In April: *Birmingham* Festival of the Arts, each year honoring a different foreign country; Eufaula Pilgrimage, *Eufaula*; Dogwood Festival, in *Birmingham*.
In May. Montgomery Jubilee, and Seventeen Springs Craft and Hobby Fair, both in *Montgomery*; Alabama Jubilee, with balloon races, in *Decatur*.
In July: Alabama Shakespeare Festival, in *Anniston*; Blessing of the Shrimp Fleet, in *Bayou le Batre*; Alabama Deep-Sea Fishing Rodeo, on *Dauphin Island*: Talladega 500 Stock car race, at *Talladega*.
In October: Alabama State Fair, in *Birmingham*; National Peanut Festival, in *Dothan*; Shrimp Festival, at *Gulf Shores*; Tennessee Valley Old Time Fiddlers' Convention and Anvil Shoot, *Athens*.
In December: "Christmas on the River," in *Demopolis*.

Accommodation in Alabama (Area code 205)

Mobile and the Coast

Malaga Inn, 359 Church St., tel. 438-4701, *Mobile*. Fairly expensive, downtown.
Admiral Semmes Hotel, 251 Government St., tel. 433-2771, *Mobile*. Expensive, also downtown.
Cindy's Town House, 1061 Government St., tel. 438-4653, *Mobile*. Moderate expensive, in historical district.
Palms Motel, 3944 Government Blvd., tel. 666-7600, *Mobile*. Moderate.
Taylor Motel, 2598 Government Blvd., tel. 479-5481, *Mobile*. Moderate.
Beverly Motel, 5458 Government Blvd., tel. 661-0331, *Mobile*. Moderate, many facilities.
Bama Motel, 4012 Government Blvd., tel. 661-5734, *Mobile*. Inexpensive.
Grand Hotel, tel. 928-9201, *Point Clear*. The Grand old dame of the Alabama coast; modified American plan; expensive.
Paradise Inn, tel. 861-2812, *Dauphin Island*. Moderate-expensive.
Malbis Hotel Courts, Malbis Plantation, tel. 626-3050, *Daphne*. Moderate.
Gulf State Park Resort, tel. 263-5561, *Gulf Shores*. Moderate.
Baron's Motel, 701 S. Mobile St., tel. 928-2328, *Fairhope*. Inexpensive.

Montgomery and Central Alabama

Marion Motel, Hwy. 5 Bypass, tel. 683-9042, *Marion*. Inexpensive.
Dill's Motor Court, 521 E. University Blvd., tel. 758-7571, *Tuscaloosa*. Inexpensive.
Stafford Inn Downtown, 2209 9th Street, tel. 345-5800, *Tuscaloosa*. Moderate.

Travel Inn Motel, US 82 Bypass, tel. 339-3900, *Tuscaloosa*. Inexpensive.
Graystone Motel, US 80, tel. 874-6681, *Selma*. Inexpensive.
Governor's House Motor Inn, 2705 E. South Blvd., tel. 288-2800, *Montgomery*. Expensive.
Whitley Hotel, 231 Montgomery St., tel. 262-6461, *Montgomery*. Downtown, moderate.
St. Francis Hotel, 3102 Mobile Hwy., tel. 263-4421, *Montgomery*. Moderate.
Doby's Hotel Court, 3453 Mobile Hwy., tel. 288-8110, *Montgomery*. Near downtown, moderate.
Royal Inn, 3211 Mobile Rd., tel. 288-8760, *Montgomery*. Inexpensive.
Park Lane Motel, 970 W. South Boulevard, tel. 288-2600, *Montgomery*. Inexpensive.
Horseshoe Bend Motel, Hwy., 22 & 280 Bypass, tel. 234-6311, *Alexander City*.
Lakepoint State Park Resort, US 431 North, tel. 687-8011, *Eufaula*. Moderate.
Trojan Inn Motel, tel. 566-1630, *Troy*. Inexpensive.
Viking Motor Lodge, US 231 Bypass, tel. 566-4090, *Troy*. Inexpensive.
Town Line Motel, Hwy., 29 Bypass W., tel. 222-3191, *Andalusia*. Inexpensive.

Birmingham and Northern Alabama

Plaza Hotel-South, 808 20th Street S., tel. 933-9000, *Birmingham*. Moderate.
Motel Birmingham 7905 Crestwood Blvd., tel. 956-4440, *Birmingham*. Moderate.
Century Motel, 624 Decatur Highway, tel. 849-7431, *Birmingham*. Inexpensive.
Tara House, 2800 20th Street S., tel. 871-0343, *Birmingham*. Inexpensive.
Interstate Motel, 5921 1st Avenue N., tel. 595-4609, *Birmingham*. Inexpensive.
Cabana Motor Inn, 1631 2nd Avenue N., tel. 252-7141, *Birmingham*. Inexpensive.
Redwood Inn Motel, 205 Hood Ave., tel. 543-8410, *Gadsden*. Inexpensive.
Five Points Motel, 101 Tupelo Pike, tel. 574-3163, *Scottsboro*. Inexpensive.
Heart of Anniston Inn, 1301 Noble St., tel. 237-1661, *Anniston*. Moderate.
Vann Thomas Motel, 3002 McClellan Blvd., tel. 237-2861, *Anniston*. Inexpensive.
Gamecock Motel, S. Pelham Rd., tel. 435-3300, *Jacksonville*. Inexpensive.
Kelly's Economy Motel, Hwy. 280 & 231, tel. 378-6043, *Childersburg*. Inexpensive.
Barclay Motel, 2201 N. Memorial Pkwy., tel. 536-7441, *Huntsville*. Moderate.
University Plaza, 4212 Governors Dr., tel. 539-4421, *Huntsville*. Moderate.
Shelby Motel, 2209 N. Memorial Pkwy., tel. 534-2481, *Huntsville*. Moderate.
Frank-Ann Motel, 2101 Memorial Pkwy., tel. 536-8511, *Huntsville*. Inexpensive.

Catalina Motel, 5011 Governors Dr., tel. 837-2200, *Huntsville*. Inexpensive.
Park Valley Motel, 11821 S. Memorial Pkwy., tel. 881-3423, *Huntsville*. Inexpensive.
Athens Motel, Rt. 31 S., tel. 232-0131, *Athens*. Inexpensive.
Nitefall Motel, 2611 US 31 S., tel. 353-0481, *Decatur*. Inexpensive.
Anderson Motel, US 31 N., tel. 734-0122, *Cullman*. Moderate.
Cullman Motor Inn, US 31 N., tel. 734-2736, *Cullman*. Inexpensive.
Grant Hotel, 115 Montgomery Ave., tel. 383-1821, *Sheffield*. Moderate.

A new organization, the *Tennessee Valley B & B of Alabama* offers European style bed and breakfast in several homes in northern Alabama for a nominal fee. Advance reservations are required; write for a listing of homes at P.O. Box 1066, Scottsboro, AL., tel. 259-1298.

For more information on Alabama, write the Bureau of Publicity and Information, 532 South Perry St., Montgomery, AL 36130. Information on available camp sites in state park grounds is available from the Division of Parks, Dept. of Conservation and Natural Resources, 64 N. Union St., Montgomery, AL 36130. For fishing and hunting regulations, write the Division of Fish and Game, in the Department of Conservation.

Mississippi

I like Mississippi. This is the best state in the Union. The only thing is, I want to make it the best state for me and my people, too.

—Medgar Evers

Mississippi is the most lied about state in the nation.

—A Mississippi bumper sticker

Mississippi is a curious place. Its record in the 20th century and its hard statistics have given rise to its unenviable reputation as "The Worst State": its per capita income, welfare expenditures and public education often come out at the bottom of the national heap, its "Plane of living" is the lowest. For a century before and after the Civil War, two-thirds of all Mississippians were black and victims of some of America's worst Jim Crows, while white Missippians traditionally have "waved the bloody shirt" and pushed the panic button of White Supremacy whenever any social or economic reforms were proposed, for fear that they may benefit blacks as well as whites. White Mississippians elected one of the worst men ever to sit in the U.S. Senate, Theodore G. Bilbo, who in 1939 submitted to Congress the "Greater Liberia Act," a plan to resettle black Americans in Africa, who appointed a publicity agent of the Mississippi Power & Light Company to the office of presidency of the University of Mississippi, and who so ranted and raved that he finally died of cancer of the mouth. Even the land itself was cursed under the tyranny of King Cotton, which not only exhausted both the soil and its toilers, but impoverished them with its widely fluctuating market prices. For a hundred years Mississippi was a foreign country isolated in a forgotten corner of the Union. When it did return to the nation's attention during the Civil Rights movement in the 1960's, it only made its tarnished image worse.

And yet as poor and bigoted as Mississippi may have been, it proved to be culturally the most innovative state in the South, if not in the entire country, in the first half of the 20th century. A distinctive American form, the blues, was born in the shacks of Mississippi Delta sharecroppers around the turn of the century, while Faulkner, Richard Wright, Tennessee Williams and other Mississippians have changed the course of American literature.

The critics were dumbfounded. How could some of America's best writers come from a state that barely qualified as civilized? Such creativity never blooms in a vacuum. For one thing, the everyday speech of Mississippians is the most colorful in the country (people there aren't lazy: they have "the hookworm hustle"). But an even greater advantage Mississippians have over their fellow mobile, acquisitive Americans is a fundamental sense of place. Many were born in the same towns as their great-great-granddaddies and count half of the state's population as their kin; etiquette and manners as sweet as mint juleps still count for something, and the pace of life is slower. Both black and white Mississippians have an inordinate attachment to the physical land itself, the scent of the black soil, magnolias and verbena, the state's feverish, swollen summers and violent thunderstorms, its meandering country roads. This relationship with the land, so profoundly chronicled by Faulkner, is perhaps the most basic attraction of his novels.

What frightens Mississippi's intellectual community most these days is the dissolution of this sense of place; they look at Jackson and its deathly sprawl and despair. Economically, life has improved for both races since the Civil Rights Act, yet the very momentum that has brought Mississippi back to the Union threatens to undermine what many hold most dear, corroding that sense of place and community with junk T.V., junk department stores and fast food chains, junk architecture and, worst of all, junk ideas about progress (profits) ubber alles. One wonders what Faulkner would think of all this: would he curse the Snopses for destroying Mississippi's soul, or would he stand by the land, of which he wrote in his essay "Mississippi": "he knows now that you don't love because: you love despite; not for the virtues, but despite the faults."

Getting To and Around Mississippi

By Air. The major airport in Mississippi is at its capital, Jackson; other airports with commercial scheduled services are in Greenville, Natchez, Pascagoula, Gulfport, Meridian, Greenwood and Starkville; for northern Mississippi use Memphis airport.

By Train. Amtrak utilizes the rails of the Illinois Central Gulf Railroad connecting Chicago with New Orleans, with stations at Batesville, Grenada, Winona, Durant, Jackson, Hazelhurst and Brookhaven. Amtrak's Washington-New Orleans route stops at Meridian, Laurel, Hattiesburg and Poplarville. For information on routes and schedules, call toll free in Mississippi 800-874-2800, or in Jackson 969-4052.

By Car. The 450 mile **Natchez Trace Parkway,** operated by the National Park Service, is a non-commercial highway roughly following the famous Natchez Trace from Nashville to Natchez. The Trace began as a trail between Natchez, the French trading post on the Mississippi and Choctaw and Chickasaw Indian villages. "Kaintuck" flatboatmen who floated downstream to sell their wares in New Orleans widened the Trace into a rough road, on which they would return to the north in groups to combat the numerous bandits who lurked along the Trace. In 1808 Jefferson ordered the trail improved, and it became a major frontier route; after the Battle of New Orleans, Andrew Jackson and his victorious troops followed it north to their homes. Shortly thereafter, the introduction of steamboats on the Mississippi ended the need to travel north by land and the Natchez Trail was all but abandoned. Today only a few sections remain by the highway (which itself is not entirely complete at writing); highlights along the way include several prehistoric Indian mounds, hiking trails, historic sites, scenic overlooks and three campgrounds. For information, visit the Tupelo Visitor Center (Mile 266), or write to the superintendent, Rural Route 1, NT-143, Tupelo, MS 38801.

History

When the French decided to settle the Louisiana territory in 1699, they sent French Canadian Pierre Lemoyne d'Iberville and a contingent of soldiers and colonists to found a town at the mouth of Mississippi River, claimed for France by La Salle. D'Iberville mistook Biloxi Bay for the Mississippi's mouth and built a fort at the site of modern Ocean Springs. As was so often the case, the site chosen by the first colonists couldn't have been worse; the sand refused to respond to cultivation and most of the settlers died of fever. Eventually, under the leadership of d'Iberville's brother Jean Baptiste le Moyne, the Sieur de Bienville, the colony relocated to Mobile and then to Louisiana, where it took root as New Orleans.

In 1716 the French, eager to trade with the native Indians, set up a trading post and fort on the east bank of the Mississippi, which took the name Natchez from the dominant tribe in the area. Natchez prospered, and by 1720 it was almost as large as New Orleans. But disaster waited in the wings. The French had treated the Natchez Indians little better than slaves and on November 29, 1729, the Indians erupted, slaughtering almost every Frenchman in the Natchez district. After that, the fertile bluffs of the Mississippi seemed haunted and the French never returned.

After the French and Indian War (1763) the French ceded the Louisiana Territory to Spain, who in turn ceded all of the land east of the Mississippi River to Britain. Mississippi became part of East Florida and English settlers began to take up grants in the old Natchez district. During the Revolution the Mississippians of East Florida remained loyal to the British crown, only to wake up one day to find themselves turned into Spaniards when Governor Galvez of New Orleans captured the Mississippi Territory in 1781. For once Spanish rule was benign, as Spain bent over backwards to be liked by the great English majority, even permitting residents to worship in Protestant churches.

As Spain's international power waned the United States increasingly demanded free navigational rights on the Mississippi River and possession of the Natchez District, which it claimed by a 1783 treaty. Spain, distracted by the French Revolution, complied in 1798, and the Natchez District was renamed the Mississippi Territory (then including the present states of Mississippi and Alabama).

At the turn of the century the Mississippi Territory was an untamed frontier, where the invention of the cotton gin was beginning to make both large-scale farming and slavery extremely profitable. The perfectly flat, black, alluvial soil of the Delta was ideal for cotton and as word spread in the older Southern states, newcomers and speculators thronged into the territory.

One stranger, however, was highly suspect. In January 1807, former Vice President Aaron Burr (his political career ruined after he killed Alexander Hamilton in a duel) arrived in Bruinsburg north of Natchez with several boatloads of adventurers and a plot to capture New Orleans, to create an independent state in the west. One of his fellow conspirators, however, gave away the plot. Eventually Burr was sent to Richmond, Virginia, where Chief Justice John Marshall acquitted him in one of America's most famous trials.

In 1817, the Mississippi Territory was divided in half and Mississippi itself became a state, champing at the bit, on the verge of its famous "Flush Times". Natchez began taking on the airs of a planter aristocracy, credit and money were cheap. As prospective settlers thronged to the new state clamouring for land Andrew Jackson obliged them by wining and dining the Choctaw Indians and their chiefs at Doak's Stand, inveigling them to leave Mississippi. Some did and when Jackson became president the rest were "persuaded" to go west. The vast lands opened up by the Indian removal were quickly sold and soon the Natchez planters found themselves outnumbered by Jacksonian farmers in the east, who took control of the state's politics. Lawyers made more money than anybody else; Joseph Glover Baldwin, who dubbed the era "Flush Times" described Mississippi in the 1830's as "a legal Utopia, peopled by a race of eager litigants, only waiting for the lawyers to come on and divide out to them the shells of a bountiful system of squabbling".

Mississippi was the second state to secede from the Union and join the Confederacy. Oddly enough, few slave holders supported the move; they realized that it was Yankee money that purchased the cotton they grew, and hoped that Lincoln, a stalwart Free Soiler, would compromise with the South once in office. Hotheaded farmers in the eastern part of the state, however, could see little difference between Lincoln and radical John Brown. They feared immediate abolition and that Mississippi would be overrun by blacks, who outnumbered white Mississippians 3 to 2. One of the state's senators, Jefferson Davis, went on to become the president of the Confederacy.

U.S. Grant's siege of Vicksburg, one of the crucial battles of the Civil War, opened the Mississippi River up to Union navigation and greatly contributed to the North's eventual victory. At the end of the war, Mississippi found its institutions in total disarray, its capital Jackson decimated by fire, a veritable "Chimneyville". And yet, in the eyes of the North, Mississippi did not learn its lesson. The first state to hold a Reconstruction Convention and re-establish civil government in the South, it blithely ignored President Andrew Johnson's suggestions that it allow freedmen the vote and ratify the 13th Amendment abolishing slavery. Instead Mississippi reintroduced slavery under another name, the so-called "Black Code". As other Southern states hastened to enact their own Black Codes Northern Radicals screamed for blood. Johnson's plan for a nonpunitive Reconstruction failed utterly, and the South was divided into Military Districts. The black Republicans Mississippi then sent to Washington, despite the accepted Southern myth, were extremely able men. A senator later served as president of Mississippi's first black university, and a congressman went on to become a noted lawyer, author and Chicago Republican leader.

If antebellum Mississippi had paid homage to King Cotton, postwar Mississippi grovelled at his feet, producing eventually twice as many bales as it had before the war. And the more powerful cotton became, the harder life was for the State's impoverished black and white sharecroppers, de facto slaves to a one-crop economy. In 1890 Mississippi held a Constitutional Convention to decide how to disenfranchize blacks, both politically and economically, without inciting the wrath of Uncle Sam. After pondering this delicate question, Democrats came up with the

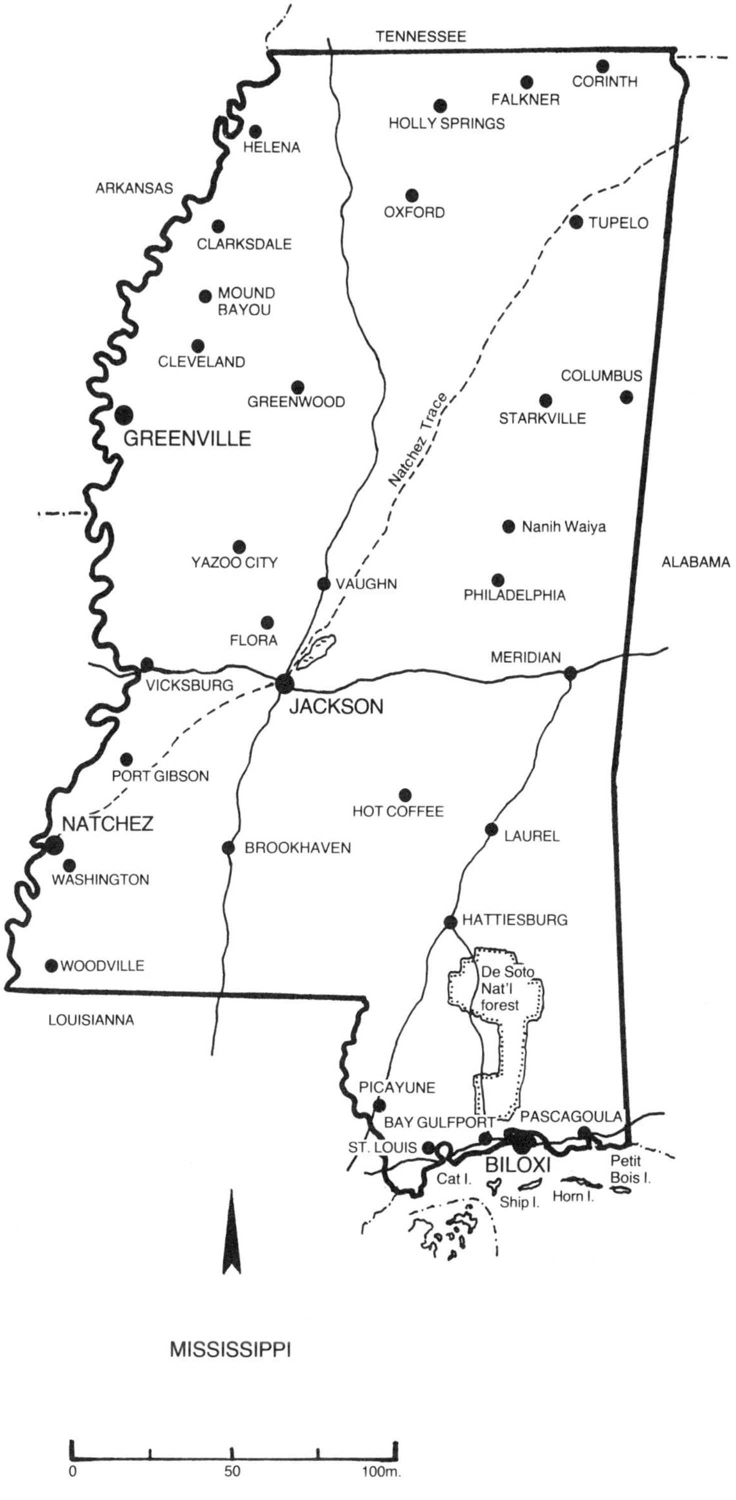

TENNESSEE
CORINTH
FALKNER
HOLLY SPRINGS
HELENA
ARKANSAS
OXFORD
TUPELO
CLARKSDALE
MOUND BAYOU
CLEVELAND
COLUMBUS
GREENWOOD
STARKVILLE
GREENVILLE
Natchez Trace
Nanih Waiya
YAZOO CITY
ALABAMA
VAUGHN
PHILADELPHIA
FLORA
MERIDIAN
VICKSBURG
JACKSON
PORT GIBSON
HOT COFFEE
NATCHEZ
LAUREL
BROOKHAVEN
WASHINGTON
HATTIESBURG
WOODVILLE
De Soto Nat'l forest
LOUISIANNA
PICAYUNE
BAY GULFPORT
PASCAGOULA
ST. LOUIS
BILOXI
Petit Bois I.
Cat I.
Ship I.
Horn I.

MISSISSIPPI

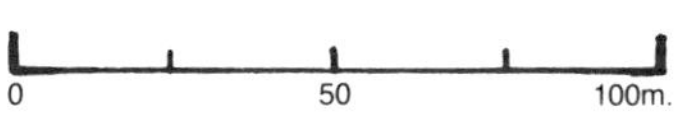

"Mississippi Plan," requiring a complex poll tax and a duplicitous literacy test, making it all but impossible for a black (or many poor whites) to vote. When the United States Supreme Court upheld the Mississippi Plan, other Southern states quickly adopted their own versions of it.

In the first decade of the 20th century, America's greatest Progressive era, Mississippi produced as its governor and then U.S. senator James K. Vardaman, a racist of the worst stripe and at the same time a liberal and idealist, who reformed the state's deplorable convict-lease system, and consistently voted against big business. Called the "White Chief" by his redneck supporters, he committed political suicide by voting against the declaration of World War I.

Vardaman, bigot that he was, was at least honest; his ideaological successor, Theodore G. Bilbo, euphemistically known as "The Man," was not, and several times was investigated on bribery charges while in office. Bilbo, too much of a buffoon for even Huey Long to take seriously, was an even worse racist than Vardaman, and during his long, foul-mouthed career acted as a malignant tumor on Mississippi's body politic. Bilbo first came to power when Vardaman fell from grace and stayed in office until his death in 1947.

Mississippi was the first state to ratify the 18th Amendment (Prohibition) and the last to repeal it, when it allowed counties to vote wet in 1966. Yet even during that long dry period, Mississippi had one of the highest rates of alcoholic consumption in the U.S. It even issued licenses to dealers to sell the illicit liquor, so the state could get its share of the profits. Along with Bilbo, Mississippi's version of Prohibition made it a national joke. Will Rogers quipped: "Mississippi will drink wet and vote dry—as long as any citizens can stagger to the polls."

World War II proved to be a turning point for Mississippi blacks as thousands caught the Illinois Central to jobs in northern war industries, away from the bitterness of Jim Crow. Few ever returned. White housewives panicked to rumors that Eleanor Roosevelt had formed secret "Eleanor Clubs" to deprive their homes and kitchens of low-paid black labor by sending black women into the factories and shipyards.

By the time the Supreme Court outlawed segregation in public schools in 1954, Mississippi's black population had declined dramatically; for the fiirst time in a century blacks were a numerical minority in the state. Even so, white Mississippians were not going to take integration gracefully by any means. Citizens' Councils formed in the early 1960's accused anyone "soft" on desegregation of Communism. Tempers flared when James Meredith broke the racial barrier at the University of Mississippi. A small army of U.S. Marshals had to protect him; one of the lighter moments in the history of the Civil Rights movement occurred when Governor Ross Barnett met the black student and the all-white Marshals at the entrance to Ole Miss and inquired: "Now, which one of you is James Meredith?" One of the more tragic moments occurred shortly thereafter, when Medgar Evers, head of the Mississippi NAACP and a leading supporter of Meredith, was shot in the back in his own driveway. In 1964 three young Civil Rights workers were murdered by the Ku Klux Klan.

Enough people were sickened by these killings to put an end to most of the resistance to desegregation and the Voting Rights Act. Blacks now occupy many elective offices in the state, including Medgar Evers' brother

Charles, mayor of Meridian. It would be premature to state that racism has been totally eradicated in the state, but the state has improved to the extent that many blacks who migrated to Chicago and Detroit in previous decades are now returning to the magnetic Mississippi countryside, to escape the same urban headaches that gave rise to the "back to the land" movement among whites.

Southern Mississippi and the Gulf Coast

The lower half of Mississippi is the state's tourist mecca, especially along the 65-mile Gulf Coast, the world's longest manmade beach. Off the coast are three barrier islands forming part of the **Gulf Islands National Seashore,** headquartered in the **visitor center** on Davis Bayou in Ocean Springs. Located about ten miles offshore, two of the islands, Horn and Petit Bois, are wildlife sanctuaries, home to colonies of raccoons, alligators and migratory birds, while **Ship Island,** the smallest of the three, is the site of horseshoe shaped **Fort Massachusettes.** Begun in the 1850's, the Confederacy tried unsuccessfully to complete the fort before it was captured by the Yankees, who used it as a base for their naval blockade of the South and for the attack of New Orleans. While Horn and Petit Bois Islands are accessible only by private or charter boats, two excursion boats sail to Ship Island: the **Pan American Clipper** from Gulfport leaves daily at 9 and 2:30 from March-Labor Day, and the **Pan American** from Biloxi departs daily at 9 and 2:30 from April-September.

Pascagoula, near the Alabama border, lies at the mouth of the Pascagoula, or "Singing River," named for the strange humming noise the river makes as it flows into the Gulf. According to legend, a Biloxi Indian chieftain was slighted when the princess he planned to marry fell in love with a member of the Pascagoula tribe. The Biloxi attacked the Pascagoula, who were soon defeated, but refused to surrender. The whole tribe instead sang their death song and, children and old people first, marched into the river to drown. The hum of the river is the haunting melody of their song, and the best place to hear it is in **Gautier** from August to October. An old sternwheeler travels up the river from Gautier's Plantation Home (US 90) daily in the summer.

Pascagoula, a shipbuilding center since the early 18th century, was once one of the leading lumber ports in the world. In 1718, a Frenchman designed the **Old Spanish Fort** (200 Fort Street) of great pine timbers and a mixture of rock-hard mud and shells. Said to be the oldest structure still standing in the Mississippi Valley, it is now a historical museum housing a prototype cotton gin, a plaque from d'Iberville's 1699 French colony, a few relics from the Conquistadors and much more (open daily 9-4:30, adm.). At the **Longfellow House** (3401 Beach Boulevard), Longfellow supposedly wrote "The Building of the Ship," mentioning "Pascagoula's sunny bay". Today Ingalls Shipbuilding in Pascagoula is Mississippi's largest industrial employer.

Ocean Springs to the west was the site of d'Iberville's 1699 settlement, the first white colony in the Mississippi Valley. Named for the springs once worshipped by the Indians (since then all but one has dried up) it is now a center for coastal craftsmen.

Biloxi, one of Mississippi's prettiest towns, occupies a narrow peninsula with a 25-mile coastline. When the colony d'Iberville planted near Ocean Springs refused to take, the French replanted it here in 1719. Biloxi (Indian for "first people") was the capital of French Louisiana until 1723. To give the capital an air of permanency French orphans, or "casket girls" (named for the wicker caskets in which they carried all their worldly goods) who volunteered to marry pioneer settlers were sent to Biloxi. Today the major industry in this lazy, Spanish-moss laden town is shrimp and oyster packing; the open trolley **Shrimp Tour Train** takes visitors on tours of the city and its waterfront, departing from Biloxi's landmark, the **Old Lighthouse** on West Beach Boulevard (Easter-Labor Day, daily at 10:30, 12, 1:30 and 3). The Old Lighthouse, built in 1848, was painted black when news reached town of Lincoln's assassination; since then it has been repainted white and was run for many years by a mother-daughter team (daily 9-5). **Beauvoir,** Jefferson Davis' home for the last 12 years of his life, is on US 90 west of Biloxi. Built in 1853, the ex-President of the Confederacy wrote his *Rise and Fall of the Confederate Government* here; many Davis family possessions remain throughout (open daily 8:30-5, adm.). In the late 19th century Biloxi was a popular resort for Northerners in the winter, as well as for Delta planters, who flocked to the **Magnolia Hotel** on Rue Magnolia, damaged in the 1969 Hurricane Camille and moved to its present location in Biloxi's "Vieux Marche" of historic structures. Today the Magnolia Hotel houses an historical museum and art gallery, open Tues-Sat 10:30-5:30, free.

Another resort, **Gulfport** was planned as an industrial and shipping center, which it still is, with its busy "banana terminal" unloading tropical produce. The **Harbor Tour Train** takes visitors past the banana terminal and the harbor, departing after every show at the **Marine Life Aquadome** (US 90 & 25th Ave.) where six times a day proficient porpoises, skindivers, seals and others go through their paces (open Easter-Labor Day, 9-6; rest of the year 10-4, adm.). **Pass Christian** to the west claims the loveliest homes on the Gulf Coast.

The Pearl River is the boundary line between Southern Mississippi and Louisiana; several miles up river the town of **Picayune** was named for New Orleans' most famous newspaper, the *Times-Picayune* in honour of a local woman, Eliza Jane Poitevent, who inherited the then bankrupt newspaper and turned it into a highly successful publication. She wrote under the name of Pearl Rivers and did much to launch the career of Dorothy Dix. Today Picayune is the home of **NASA National Space Technology Laboratories,** located south of town on Rt. 607. Here space shuttle engines and rocket boosters were tested; today the laboratories' main project is applying space technology to more earthly needs. Tours are available weekdays at 1 o'clock from the visitor center.

In **Lucedale,** north of Pascagoula, the **Palestinian Gardens** (US 98) is an outdoor model of the Holy Land laid out on a scale of one yard to the mile, complete with a mini Dead Sea, Golgotha and Jerusalem (open daily 8-5, adm.). **Hattiesburg** is an overgrown railroad town, the home of the University of Southern Mississippi. On campus the McCain Graduate Library contains one of the largest selections in the world of children's books, manuscripts and illustrations in the **Lena Y. de Grummond Collection of Children's Literature.** North and south of Hattiesburg stretches the 501,200 acre **De Soto National Forest,** part of the old longleaf pine belt that supplied the great lumber boom in the late 19th and early 20th centuries. The lumber boom fizzled in the 1920's, although timber and naval stores are still produced in the area.

Laurel, north of Hattiesburg, challenges anyone's preconception of Mississippian cultural backwardness with its **Lauren Rogers Library and Museum of Art** on Fifth Avenue, with a collection of 19th century American paintings by the Hudson River School, Homer, Whistler, Sloan and Innes; 19th century European art by Daumier, Millet and Constable; and an extensive collection of baskets (open Tues-Sat 10-12 & 1-5, Sun 2-5, free). Laurel is in **Jones County,** famous for its opposition to the Civil War. While there were patches of resistance to the war in Alabama and Tennessee, the farmers of Jones County burned in effigy the delegate they elected to the constitutional convention for voting for Secession, then actively waged a guerrilla war to sabotage the Confederacy. In adjacent Covington County, the hamlet of **Hot Coffee** received its name from the coffee pot a local entrepreneur hung over his door to advertize his thick, molasses sweetened brew; before long travelers in the region were estimating distances in miles to "hot coffee".

Meridian was the hometown of Medgar Evers and the "father of country music," "the Singing Brakeman," Jimmie Rodgers, who perfected the Blue Yodel and sang the "T.B. Blues" until he succumbed to the disease at age 35. Jimmie was buried in Meridian's Bonita Cemetery; his admirers in town built the **Jimmie Rodgers Memorial and Museum** in an old train depot at 39th Avenue, containing both personal and railroading memorabilia, a bright red locomotive and a carved memorial depicting Jimmie in his brakeman's cap (open Mon-Sat 10-4, Sun 12-6, adm.). The museum is located in lush **Highland Park,** where a structure houses the city's antique carousel, open on special occasions for the children to take turns riding "the horse with the lavender eyes".

A lavender-eyed horse is only one of Meridian's eccentricities; an Egyptian Revival Temple of Isis (actually the **Scottish Rite Cathedral**) stands at 23rd Avenue and 11th Street, adorned with a sphinx, an obelisk, multi-colored terra cotta and imposing columns. **Rose Hill Cemetery** contains the graves of a King and Queen of the gypsies, buried with so many jewels and gold coins that their tombs are encased in reinforced concrete to thwart grave robbers. At 203 22nd Avenue there is a medieval-style structure housing **Weidmann's Restaurant,** the oldest in Mississippi (1870). If its address is hard to find, it is because Meridian was built on two different town plans. For many years the city fathers could not agree on the name Meridian; half of the citizens preferred "Sowashee". Everyday the signs at the town's entrance would be changed, while each side developed its own town plan with somewhat chaotic results.

Meridian also has a small **Museum of Art** at 25th Avenue and 7th Street (August-June, Tues-Sun 1-5, free) and an antebellum museum home, **Merrehope** at 905 31st Avenue, built in the Academic Revival style (Mon-Sat 9-5, Sun 1-5, adm.).

Mississippi's largest city and its capital, **Jackson,** lies near the geographic center of the state, on the west bank of the Pearl River. Before selected as the site of the capital, the settlement here was known as Le

Fleur's Bluff, for a French Canadian's trading post. After the Treaty of Doak's Stand the legislature decided to move from Columbia to a more central location. Le Fleur's Bluff was renamed Jackson in honor of the man who rid the state of its Indians, and the first legislative session was held in Jackson's new state house in 1822.

Jackson was a railroad center during the Civil War, and as such became a Union target after the Siege of Vicksburg. The task of taking the city fell on the shoulders of General Sherman, who bombarded it into submission, then turned it into a blazing torch, saving only the governor's mansion, where he was lodged, and a few other residences. On July 18, 1863 he informed General Grant: "We have made fine progress today in the work of destruction". Indeed, only the brick chimneys remained giving Jackson the nickname "Chimneyville." After the war the city rebuilt and re-established its railroad links, attracted some industry, and grew into a fairly typical, pleasant state capital, its accents and mannerisms made famous in the novels of Jacksonian Eudora Welty. In the past twenty years, however, Jackson'a own citizens have razed large sections of the city, both healthy neighborhoods and slums, in favor of parking lots and highways.

At the head of Jackson's main thoroughfare, Capitol Street, stands the **Old Capitol,** today the **Mississippi State Historical Museum.** The Old Capitol, handsome Greek Revival structure, served as the seat of legislature from its construction in 1842 until deemed unsafe in 1903. Since restored, the building contains exhibits from Mississippi's prehistoric Indians, its frontier days, the Civil War, dioramas and more (open Mon-Fri 8-5, Sat 9:30-4:30, Sun 12:30-4:30, free). Mississippi's **New State Capitol,** modelled after the national capitol in Washington, is on Mississippi Street. Built in 1903, it is presently undergoing restoration—in the evenings its eagle-topped dome is illuminated. The state's **Governor's Mansion,** at 300 Capitol Street, is the second oldest still in use in the United States. Designed by William Nichols and completed in 1842, the mansion was the scene of Sherman's victory dinner celebrating the fall of Vicksburg. When the 1908 Legislature considered demolishing the mansion for commercial development, the cry went up across the state: "Will Mississippi destroy that which Sherman would not burn?" Of course not; the mansion was saved, and in 1975 it was designated a National Historic Landmark. Tours of the home are available for free Tuesday through Friday 9:30-11:30.

Next to the Old Capitol is a marble pile called the **War Memorial Building;** behind it, the **Mississippi Museum of Natural Science** has an aquarium, a biological pit and exhibits on the state's ecological communities (open Mon-Fri 8-5, free). The new **Mississippi Museum of Art,** within walking distance at 201 E. Pascagoula Street, houses four galleries of mainly contemporary art (Tues-Sun 10-4). The adjacent **Davis Planetarium** features an atmospherium to give its star shows an all-encompassing effect (shows daily except Monday, adm.). Nearby **City Hall** was spared the wrath of Sherman supposedly because his fraternal order of Masons used it as their meeting hall. On the City Hall grounds the **Josh Halbert Gardens** add a note of color to downtown.

Other things to see in Jackson are on the periphery, like the **Jackson Zoological Park,** a fine little zoo in a landscaped setting, at 2918 W.

Capitol Street (open daily, small adm.) and the **Mynelle Gardens** at 4736 Clinton Boulevard, with thousands of azaleas, camellias, and flowering trees (daily 8-dusk, adm.). East of Jackson, on Lakeland Drive, sports fans may want to seek out the **Dizzy Dean Museum,** with memorabilia of the Hall of Famer's career with the St. Louis Cardinals Gas House Gang. Adjacent to Smith-Wills Stadium, the museum is open during the baseball season from 10-7, Sat & Sun 1-7; other times daily 1-5, adm. In **Flora,** northwest on US 49, the **Mississippi Petrified Forest** was formed approximately 30 million years ago when driftwood logs floating on a primeval sea ended up here in an immense logjam. The logs that sank into the sand were preserved, and may be seen along a nature trail. An earth science museum on the site displays fossils and minerals found in the forest (open daily 9-5, til 7 from Memorial Day to Labor Day, adm.).

West of Jackson on the Mississippi River, **Vicksburg** was the scene of the pivotal Civil War battle for control of the Mississippi River. Early in the war the Confederacy recognized its location, on a steep bluff overlooking a great hairpin bend in the Mississippi, as strategically invaluable, as did President Lincoln, who declared, "Vicksburg is the key". If the Union could capture the city it could control the entire river and split the Confederacy in two.

The battle for Vicksburg, begun in the winter of 1862, pitted Confederate General John C. Pemberton against General Ulysses S. Grant, who was ordered to open the Mississippi up for Northern shipping. Based in Memphis, Grant spent the first few months of the campaign slogging through the swamps around Vicksburg with nothing to show for his efforts except a lengthening list of casualties. By springtime Lincoln's advisors were clamouring for his dismissal, and Grant decided to go all out in his attempt to take the city. He led his army through Louisiana to a point twenty-five miles south of Vicksburg, while Admiral David D. Porter, on the nights of April 16 and 22, ran fifteen gun and transport boats right past the deadly Vicksburg batteries, losing only two vessels. At Bruinsburg the Navy transported Grant's army across the river.

Grant's first thoughts were not to attack Vicksburg, but to go after Pemberton's army in the Mississippi hinterlands. He captured Jackson, then sqeezed the remaining Confederate forces towards Vicksburg. By mid-May, Grant had defeated the rebels at Champion Hill and Big Black Bridge, and decided to move in for the kill, storming Vicksburg on May 19 and 22, both times without success. Reluctantly, Grant began siege operations.

The Siege of Vicksburg lasted six weeks, as Grant loosed artillery shells on the 27,000 soldiers and 3,000 noncombatants holed up in the city's well-fortified positions. The latter took refuge in small caves dug in the sides of Vicksburg's clay cliffs. Mark Twain, in *Life on the Mississippi,* described the boredom of the besieged, cut off from the rest of the world, when

> "all in a moment come ground-shaking thunder-crashes of artillery, the sky is cobwebbed with the crisscrossing red lines streaming from soaring bombshells, and a rain of iron fragments descend upon the . . . empty streets: streets which are not empty a moment later, but mottled with the dim figures of

frantic women and children scurrying from home and bed toward the cave dungeons—encouraged by the humorous grim soldiery who shout 'Rats, to your holes!' and laugh."

Finally, on July 3, 1863, on the same day that Lee withdrew from disaster at Gettysberg, Vicksburg surrendered to Grant. The Lost Cause had entered its terminal stage.

The Union lines and Confederate strongholds around the city are preserved in **Vicksburg National Military Park.** The Visitor Center, on US 80, contains a film, exhibits from the siege, and a diorama of cave life (open daily 8-5, from 7-7 in the summer, free). From here you can take a 16-mile self-guided tour of the park, which encompasses monuments erected by the various states, the Vicksburg National Cemetery containing the graves of 17,000 soldiers, nine major Confederate forts and miles of breastworks, rifle pits and trenches, all strangely soft and undulating under the green grass. The *U.S.S. Cairo,* the first Union ironclad to meet misfortune by means of an electrically detonated mine (one of an amazing list of technological "firsts" bequeathed by the Civil War), has recently been raised from the Yazoo River and is being restored near the cemetery.

Vicksburg itself is a pretty, if somewhat genteely shabby town, with several historic homes that managed to survive the brutal shelling. The city's first bank, **Planters Hall** at 822 Main Street, also served as the home of the bank president, and as such contains both wine cellar and bank vault. The bank failed when President Andrew Jackson ordered that bank notes were no longer valid for the purchase of public land (open Mon-Fri 9-3, adm.). The **Old Court House,** on Grove Street, the tallest building during the siege, somehow managed to escape relatively unscathed, except for the cupola, which Admiral Farragut's gunboats turned into a sieve; the modern one is a replacement. Today the Court House, now a museum, houses a large and diverse collection of Civil War relics, steamboat memorabilia, a pipe collection, possessions of Jefferson Davis, and Grant's field chair (open Mon-Sat 8:30-4:30, Sun 1:30-4:30, adm.). A Vicksburg attraction that has nothing to do with the Civil War is the **Waterways Experiment Station** on Halls Ferry Road, an instructive toy belonging to the Army Corps of Engineers. The station is a scale model of the bottom half of the Mississippi River, and of Niagara Falls, where the engineers cause floods, explode miniature replicas of nuclear bombs, and play with little tug boats and dams to study the ecology of waterways, navigation, soil conservation, hydraulics, and new weapons systems. Free guided tours are available Mon-Fri at 10 and 2.

South of Vicksburg is the pleasant town of **Port Gibson,** on the Bayou Pierre. Port Gibson claimed it survived the Civil War because Grant thought it too pretty to burn; among its pretty white frame homes is the **Temple Gemiluth Chassed** on Church Street, an old Moorish style temple that houses the smallest Jewish congregation in the country. Across the street, the **First Presbyterian Church** has, instead of the usual cross on top of its steeple, a hand and finger pointing towards heaven, in memory of the congregation's first minister, who often emphasized points in his sermon with the gesture. Inside the church are chandeliers from the renowned steamboat *Robert E. Lee.* South of Port Gibson on Rt. 552 are the picturesque **Ruins of Windsor,** the ruins of one of the greatest Southern plantations, built in 1861 and burned during a party in 1890. Windsor stood five storeys high, as the massive twenty-two columns that remain attest; instead of a portico, the capitals support trees and other plants that have mistook them for giant planters. As a river pilot, Mark Twain used the observatory on top of Windsor as a navigational landmark.

The **Old Country Store** in nearby **Lorman** (Rt. 61) opened its doors in 1890 and has changed almost nothing since that day. It is one of the oldest general merchandise stores in continual operation in the United States, still making use of its old cheese cutter and tobacco cutter and wind-up display case for shoes. The store is open Mon-Sat 8:30-6, Sunday and holidays 12-5.

The site of **Natchez,** one of the oldest towns on the Mississippi River, was selected by La Salle in 1682 as the most desirable for a settlement. Unfortunately, the Natchez Indians had had the same idea many years before the French: their Grand Village stood on the banks of St. Catherine Creek in the present city limits. The Natchez were the last mound building tribe encountered by Europeans in North America, culturally more akin to the Aztecs than to their neighbors the Choctaws. Fervent sun worshippers, they believed their leader, who called himself the Great Sun, was born of its rays. In front of the main temple mound, facing the setting sun, burned an eternal flame, symbolic of the Great Sun's lineage. Every morning the Great Sun greeted the first beams of the dawn with a howl and three puffs of his sacred calumet.

The Natchez divided themselves into two great castes, the Aristocrats and the Stinkards, each with its own language. The Great Sun, however, could only marry Stinkards, although all the children they had were considered noble. When a Great Sun died, his wives and followers would be ceremoniously strangled. (The mounds and foundations that remain of the **Grand Village of the Natchez** may be toured at 400 Jefferson Davis Boulevard, Mon-Sat 9-5, Sun 1:30-5, free).

Relations between the Natchez and the French were anything but cordial. When Bienville and a contingent of soldiers arrived in 1716, their first act was to surround and surprise the Natchez village in retaliation for the murders of several French traders in 1702. The French forced the Indians to build Fort Rosalie (a trading post that mainly dealt in bear grease), and to supply food to them every month. The Natchez grudgingly complied, but when the French demanded their village of White Apple, they revolted, and in November, 1729, systematically massacred 712 men, women and children inside and outside Fort Rosalie. The French, under LeSeur, and their Choctaw allies, exacted revenge a few months later, selling the surviving Natchez as slaves, including the Great Sun, to the Spanish on Santo Domingo.

Abandoned until 1763, Natchez became the Mississippi River outpost of British West Florida. When the Spanish took the city, Governor Don Gayoso de Lemos brought the city its first rumblings of prosperity, and laid out its streets and squares. Under American pressure, Spain ceded the Natchez district to the United States in 1797, but had second thoughts about giving it up. Andrew Ellicot, the Quaker surveyor sent by President Adams to survey the district had to spend a year in his tent trying to get Governor Gayoso to leave. The Spanish abruptly pulled out at midnight,

March 30, 1798, and Natchez became the capital of the new Mississippi Territory.

The opening of the Mississippi River and the rich cotton lands of the Delta made Natchez the boom town of the early 19th century, a town at once sophisticated and savage. Flatboatmen who sailed their wares down Ol' Man Ribba to New Orleans would return to Natchez to begin the long trek home on the Natchez Trace (see "Getting Around") towards Nashville and points north. Soon a collection of saloons and bordellos known as Natchez Under the Hill lined the steep tier of streets on the city bluffs to serve the needs and desires of the rivermen and of the outlaws who preyed upon them; the saying that "the only thing cheaper in Natchez than a woman's body is a man's life" was confirmed by the trap doors in the rear of many establishments, not always used for the disposal of garbage.

Natchez not only attracted flatboatmen, but farmers as well who had heard tales of its nine month growing season and fertile soil. It wasn't long before the introduction of slavery and the cotton gin into the Mississippi Territory combined to elevate these farmers into "planters." Although Natchez suffered a loss of prestige when the assembly moved the capital of Mississippi to Washington, a few miles inland, it regained and surpassed its old status when the arrival of steamboats on the Mississippi River made it one of the world's premier cotton ports. In an amazingly short time the planters were building fantastic palaces commensurate with their new wealth (at one time half of the millionaires in the U.S. lived in Natchez), while they created a cultured leisure society reminiscent of Old Charleston, filling their homes with extensive libraries and art collections. Yet the frontier mentality always simmered beneath the surface of gracious Natchez. The slightest personal offense often demanded to be righted on the "field of honor". Speculation in land and slaves was rife.

The swiftness with which the Civil War destroyed the planters' society encased Natchez in a kind of time capsule; the city, failing to thrive, never bothered to knock down any of the beautiful homes in the name of progress, because there wasn't any progress. In the 30's when oil was discovered and a few industries began to open in the city, a group of local ladies had the idea of conducting "pilgrimages" for tourists to some of Natchez's sumptuous antebellum mansions, to encourage their restoration. As the pilgrimages met with surprising success, the rivalry between two of the ladies' clubs, the Pilgrimage Garden Club and the Natchez Garden Club, heated up. Home owners had to decide which "pilgrimage" to belong to, and genteel ladies in hoop skirts and parasols almost came to blows over prospective pilgrims until they made a truce under the banner of **The Natchez Pilgrimage,** which is held with great hoopla every spring and fall. Six sets of five homes apiece are shown morning and afternoons; two homes are available for candlelight tours, on nights alternating with the Confederate Pageant of antebellum costumes, music, and dance. (For information on the pilgrimage, visit Pilgrimage Headquarters, Stanton Hall Grounds, 410 N. Commerce Street, or write P.O. Box 347, Natchez, MS 39120, tel. toll free (800) 647-6742.)

If you can't make the pilgrimage but still want a taste of antebellum Natchez, six sites remain open all year, daily from 9-5, with separate admissions. These include the exotic, octagonal **Longwood** on Lower

Woodville Road, where tools and building supplies remain untouched since the Civil War halted construction; Longwood's owner, Dr. Haller Nutt, was an avid Union sympathizer who actively supplied Federal troops in the area, only to watch them burn his plantations and cotton gin, after Confederate soldiers had already burned all his cotton. Dr. Nutt died shortly afterwards, reputedly of a broken heart. The seventeen room basement, the only finished section of Longwood, is furnished with antiques. At Pearl and Monroe, **Stanton Hall,** the lavish headquarters of the Natchez Pilgrimage, is open on a daily basis; with its European furnishings and large ballroom it is considered the most ornate of the mansions. A Greek Revival mansion, **The Burn,** at 712 N. Union Street, was used as a Federal hospital during the war, and features fine gardens and antiques; it is one of many antebellum homes in Natchez that take overnight guests as well (Pilgrimage Headquarters has a list of them). **Melrose,** on Melrose Avenue, is considered to be the architectural gem of Natchez, housing early 19th century furnishings and adorned by beautiful gardens. At the terminus of the Natchez Trace, on Ellicott Hill, **Connelly's Tavern** built in 1798 is one of the oldest and most interesting structures in the city; its list of rules include "No more than five to sleep in one bed" and "Organ grinders to sleep in the washhouse." Another home open year round, **The Briars,** is located a little ways outside Natchez on Canal Street behind the Ramada Inn. Here Jefferson Davis married Varina Howell in 1845; European and Oriental antiques grace the interior.

Once nefarious **Natchez Under the Hill,** has been spruced up with trendy bars and restaurants. Only a small part of the district remains, most of the structures having fallen into the Mississippi River in landslides. When John James Audubon painted a landscape of Natchez in the early 19th century, the prominent landmark was **Trinity Episcopal Church,** on Washington Street; two other historic churches in Natchez are **St. Mary's Cathedral** on Union and Main, Mississipi's first cathedral, with an exceptionally lovely interior, and the **First Presbyterian Church** on South Pearl and State Street, built in 1829.

Just north of Natchez are the steep embankments of the **Devil's Punch Bowl,** a mysterious crater engulfing many acres near Clermont Plantation. In the 18th and 19th centuries, Devil's Punch Bowl was associated with tales of runaway slaves, pirates, and master criminals like John A. Murrell, who used it as a rendezvous. **Washington** nearby became the capital of the Mississippi Territory in 1802, the same year in which Jefferson College was founded, the first institution of higher learning in Mississippi.

At Jefferson College the state's first constitutional convention convened; here Aaron Burr was arraigned for treason under the "Burr Oaks" when no room could be found large enough to hold all of the spectators the event attracted. The college closed its doors in 1964, but the state has since restored its main buildings, set up several historical displays, and turned the old campus into a park. On the Natchez Trace near here, signs point the way past numerous pig farms to the **Emerald Mound** (1300-1600) one of the largest mounds in the country, believed to have been built by immediate ancestors of the Natchez Indians.

Harvard University called **Woodville** the best example of an antebellum Southern town. It is Mississippi's third oldest town, located some twenty miles south of Natchez. Woodville was the boyhood home of Jefferson Davis, who grew up at **Rosemont Plantation** (Rt. 24) which was built in 1810 in the typical Southern Planter's style. It contains many original furnishings and every few years attracts a reunion of Davis descendants (open March-December, Mon-Fri 9-5, adm.). Woodville boasts two historic districts, one around its Courthouse, the other on Church Street.

Restaurants. *In Pascagoula*: The Longfellow House**, 3401 Beach Blvd.; La Font Inn**, US 90 E. *In Biloxi*: White Pillars***, 100 Rodenburg Ave.; Mary Mahoney's Old French House***, 138 Rue Magnolia; Baricev's**, 633 Central Beach Blvd.; The Long House*, Dubuys Rd. *In Pass Christian*: Annie's**, Henderson Point. *In Gulfport*: Angelo's**, 3206 W. Beach Blvd. *In Hattiesburg* : Mrs Twilley's Boarding House*, 923 N. Main St. *In Meridian*: Weidmann's**, 203 22nd Ave. *In Jackson*: Le Fleur's***, 4800 I-55 N.; Mayflower*, Capitol Street; *In Mendenhall*: Mendenhall Hotel Revolving Tables**, 100 E. South St.; *In Vicksburg*: Tuminello's**, 500 Speed Street. *In Natchez*: The Carriage House**, High & Pearl Streets; King's Tavern**, 613 Jefferson; Cock of the Walk*, Natchez Under the Hill; Mammy's Cupboard*, Rt. 61 S.

Northern Mississippi

For many people, Mississippi north of Vicksburg, Jackson and Meridian is a miasma of pine forests, red clay, kudzu, and the smouldering passions of Yoknapatawpha. The last of Mississippi's Choctaw Indians live here, on reservations around **Philadelphia** in Neshoba County; west of town the Indians operate the **Choctaw Crafts Center,** where they sell beautiful double-weave baskets and other handicrafts (Mon-Fri 8-4:30). On Rt. 21 the Neshoba County Fair takes place for a week every August. It is the last county campground fête in the country, where visitors stay in cabins they own on the actual fairgrounds. Religious orations, political speeches, cow shows, harness racing, and carnival amusements combine to make the fair popular among rural Mississippians and among those who regard it as a last vestige of an ancient American ritual.

To the north, on Rt. 39 near Noxapater, the Choctaws consider **Nanih Waiya Mound** to be the sacred birthplace of their people, the great mother mound from where the first Indians emerged, glistening wet, and where they laid themselves to dry in the sun. An old swinging bridge leads to a cave beneath the mound (open daily 5 am-10 pm). Mississippi State University is to the north in **Starkville,** on the other side of a section of the Tombigbee National Forest and the Noxubee National Wildlife Refuge. On campus there are two museums, the **Cobb Institute of Archaeology** with artifacts from ancient civilizations in Europe, Asia, and Mississippi (open Mon-Fri 10-4, Sat & Sun 12-4, free), and the **Dunn-Seiler Museum** specializing in paleontology, mineralogy, and Indian archaeology (Mon-Fri, 8-5, free).

Columbus, east of Starkville, is a leisurely, antebellum town spread around the confluence of the Tombigbee and Luxapala Rivers. Hernando de Soto wandered through this part of Mississippi in 1540, but the first permanent settlers were a trader named Thomas Thomas and a tavern keeper named Spirus Roach, who resembled an opposum, giving rise to the Indian name of the settlement, Possum Town. Later cotton planters from the east lacked the Indians' sense of humor and renamed the town Columbus in 1821. Columbus grew as a trade center, located on the only navigable river in the area, and on the Washington-New Orleans military highway (Rt. 12) built by Andrew Jackson after the War of 1812. Columbus escaped destruction in the Civil War, and served as the Confederate capital of the state after Sherman turned Jackson into "Chimneyville." It has always been one of Mississippi's leading educational centers; in 1885 its Mississippi University for Women became the first state supported college for women in the U.S. Playwright Tennessee Williams grew up in the local Episcopal Rectory.

Many of Columbus' elegant homes are open for tours during the springtime Columbus Pilgrimage. Open year round, however, is the **Columbus and Lowndes County Museum** at 316 Seventh Street N., in an antebellum mansion, featuring a collection of local decorative arts and wedding dresses (open Tues-Thurs 1-4, free). **Waverly,** one of Mississippi's finest plantation homes, is northwest of Columbus on Rt. 50; built in the 1850's, its outstanding feature, a lofty rotunda, is topped by a sixteen windowed dome and adorned with four spiral staircases and cantilevered balconies. The numerous pieces of built-in furniture are another unusual feature (open daily dawn to dusk, adm.)

North of Jackson on US 55, the tiny town of **Vaughn** witnessed a legendary moment in American folklore, when the Illinois Central's Cannonball Express, driven by Casey Jones, collided with a freight train on April 29, 1900. Casey Jones had volunteered to make the run to Canton, Mississippi from Memphis when the regular engineer fell ill. Although the Cannonball Express left the Memphis station 90 minutes late, Casey had gunned the locomotive down the track, going at times over a 100 miles an hour to make up for lost time. By the time he reached the big curve in the tracks at Vaughn, the train was almost on schedule—when the red lights of a caboose loomed ahead. Shouting for his assistant to bail out, Casey put on the brakes, blew the whistle, and pulled the reverse lever. The crash splintered the locomotive to pieces, but because Casey had heroically stayed at the controls he was the only one to die in the ear-shattering collision. In his memory an illiterate black engine wiper named Wallace Saunders composed the famous Ballad of Casey Jones and received a bottle of gin for the song, which made others who copied it wealthy. The **Casey Jones Museum** in Vaughn is in the village restored depot and contains railroad memorabilia (open Wed-Sat 9:30-5:30, Sun 1:30-5:30, adm.50¢).

In **Greenwood** further north, **Florewood River Plantation** on US 82 is a reconstruction of a typical antebellum Delta plantation, with outbuildings and in the summer, living history demonstrations by costumed guides. An audio-visual program on cotton is presented and visitors are invited to try their hand at picking cotton. (Open Tues-Sat 9:30-5, Sun 1-5, adm.) Nearby, **Cottonlandia** focuses on the history of life in the Delta, containing a mastadon skeleton, Indian artifacts, a diorama of the natural history of the Delta region, a wildflower garden, and temporary art exhibits (open Mon-Fri 9-5, Sat & Sun 2-5, adm.).

Greenville on the Mississippi is a cradle of literati, counting among its natives the crusading editor of the *Delta Democrat-Times,* Hodding Carter, who wrote a number of books on the South, including *Southern Legacy;* famed Civil War historian Shelby Foote; and William Alexander Percy, author of the classic *Lanterns on the Levee* (1941), an autobiographical account of life in the Delta. Greenville's port is one of the busiest along the Mississippi, with an eleven mile slack water harbor formed by Lake Ferguson. Greenville is a pleasant, small city, indeed, a Soviet delegation touring the country in 1972 chose it as their favorite American city, dealing Greenville a real left-handed compliment when they claimed "here we feel absolutely at home!" Just north of Greenville on Rt. 1 are the **Winterville Mounds and Museum.** Built by the Mississippi Valley Indians around the year 1300, the civilization at Winterville had reached its peak when de Soto passed through in 1540. The seventeen small and large mounds that make up the site are thought to have been part of a major ceremonial center in the lower Mississippi Valley. A museum on the site, built to resemble a mound itself, houses some of the many relics excavated on the site. (Open Mon-Fri 9-12 and 1-5, Sat & Sun 1-5 adm; mounds open during daylight hours.)

Mound Bayou to the north was founded as an all black town for ex-slaves by Isaiah Montgomery, who purchased the land from a railroad in 1887. The land was cheap because it was swampy and uncleared and infested with malarial mosquitos; Montgomery, realizing that his pioneer settlers could not live or sleep in such conditions, made an arrangement with the railroad, which would pick up the settlers in the evening, letting them sleep on the train to Memphis, where they'd catch another train to sleep on returning to Mound Bayou in the morning. This unusual sleeping arrangement continued until cabins were erected on the cleared land. Mound Bayou, named for two bayous surrounding an Indian mound, was incorporated in 1898. Former residents still return on July 12 (Founders Day) in honor of Isaiah Montgomery.

Tunica County, near the Tennessee border, has the unpleasant distinction of being the poorest county in the U.S. To the east in Lafayette (Yoknapatawpha) County, and its county seat **Oxford** (Jefferson), the sagas of the Sartorises and Snopses were played out under the watchful eye of William Faulkner, whose 1840 plantation home, **Rowan Oak** is now a literary shrine. After Faulkner's death in 1962 it was purchased by the University of Mississippi, which has done an excellent job of maintaining it as it was during Faulkner's lifetime; no signs point the way to the house at 900 Garfield Street, hidden behind massive cedars adjacent to the university. Faulkner bought the home in 1930 and did much of the restoration work on it himself; he named it because of a Scottish belief that a branch of rowan wood wards off evil spirits and other unwanted guests. Tours of Rowan Oak are conducted by Ole Miss graduate students, who show visitors Faulkner's inner sanctum, where his rickety portable typewriter still sits by his day bed, and where the outline of *A Fable* is written on one wall in eight columns. (Rowan Oak is open whenever Ole Miss is in session, Mon-Fri 10-12 and 2-4, Sat 10-12, closed Sundays. To make sure the house is open, call ahead, 232-7318.) Faulkner is buried in St. Peter's Cemetery, at Jefferson and North 16th Street.

Ole Miss opened its doors in 1848. The presence of its first president,

Augustus B. Longstreet, author of the humorous **Georgia Scenes,** attracted other members of the Southern intelligentsia to Oxford. The most famous building on campus, the great brick **Barnard Observatory,** modelled after the Poulkova Observatory in the U.S.S.R., is now the Center for the Study of Southern Culture. Ole Miss's library contains a collection of Faulkner's first editions, his Nobel Prize medal, and recordings of the Mississippi blues. The **University Museums** on University Avenue and Fifth Street, feature Classical antiquities, Civil War relics, exhibits on physical sciences, and the **Mary Buie Museum of Dolls** (open Tues-Sat 10-4, Sun 1-4, free). In Oxford itself, note the **Lafayette County Courthouse** (1871) the setting for several scenes in Faulkner's novels, and the elegant Italianate mansion **Ammadelle** at 627 N. Lamar, designed in 1859 by Calvert Vaux.

Holly Springs north of Oxford, is another pretty antebellum town that grew up under the reign of King Cotton. Founded in 1835 by Virginian William Randolph, a descendant of John Randolf, it grew into a miniature Tidewater community, a town of lawyers, nouveau riche planters and slaves imported from Virginia. During the Civil War Grant made Holly Springs his supply base for his attempt on Vicksburg; Confederate General Van Dorn captured the town and the supplies by surprise, delaying in effect the fall of Vicksburg for a year. Yellow fever epidemics and widespread erosion of the once rich cotton lands destroyed Holly Spring's economy, but not the antebellum homes or the **Courthouse Square Historic District,** which retains its late 19th century appearance.

Falkner, east of Holly Springs, is a small town named for Col. William C. Falkner, great-grandfather of the novelist (who added the "u" to the family name). A hero of the Mexican and Civil Wars, railroad baron, author, founder of a college and a politician, Col. Falkner was one of the most colorful men of his day, and the inspiration for some of the characters in his grandson's novels, particularly in *Sartoris* and *The Unvanquished.* General Beauregard and his army retreated to **Corinth** in the east after the Battle of Shiloh, fought twenty miles to the north. Pursued by Federal forces, Beauregard retreated once more, and Corinth was occupied by the Union army for the rest of the war. Just south of Corinth, in the all but abandoned town of Jacinto, the **Jacinto Courthouse,** a fine example of late Federal architecture built in 1854, has recently been preserved as a historical museum (open Tues-Sat 10-5, Sun 1-5, adm.).

In **Tupelo,** a two day blood soaked battle took place on July 14-15, 1864, between Confederate General Nathan B. Forrest and Union General Andrew J. Smith, sent to Tupelo by Sherman to defend the railroad from Louisville, his major supply line. The battle fought at **Tupelo National Battlefield** was a draw; the site is on Rt. 6. In Tupelo the **Natchez Trace Visitor Center** has information on the famous frontier road, a small museum of artifacts, and a film, the *Path of Empire.* The two room "shotgun" style house where Elvis was born and spent his first thirteen years has been restored to its Depression era appearance; humble as it is, the house was repossessed when the Presleys could not make payments on it. Today you can tour the **Elvis Presley Birthplace,** on Elvis Presley Drive, next to Elvis Presley Park (open Mon-Sat 10-5, Sun 2-5, adm.).

Restaurants. *In Starkville*: Starkville Cafe*, Main Street. *In Greenwood*: Giardina's**, 314 W. Park; Murphee's Museum & Health Food*, Humphrey Hwy. *In Greenville*: How Joy**, 1939 Hwy. 82 E.; Doe's Eat Place*, 502 Nelson. *In Clarksdale*: Delta Warehouse**, 232 Sunflower Ave. *In Oxford*: The Warehouse**, 1402 Jackson Ave. *In Corinth*: Thurston's**, 1519 Polk. Gurley's Village Inn**, N. Gloster St.

Annual Events in Mississippi

In February: Dixie National Livestock Show, *Jackson State Fairgrounds*; in late February or March, Mardi Gras, in *Biloxi*.
In March: Natchez Pilgrimage and Confederate Pageant, *Natchez*; other antebellum pilgrimages in *Vicksburg, Woodville* and on the *Gulf Coast*.
In April: World Catfish Festival, *Belzoni*; pilgrimages in *Port Gibson, Holly Springs* and *Columbus*.
In May: Gum Tree Festival, *Tupelo*; Landing of D'Iberville festival, *Ocean Springs*; Blessing of the Fleet, *Pass Christian*; Annual Commemorative Battle of Champion Hill, *Vicksburg*; Jimmie Rodgers Festival, *Meridian*.
In June: Pecan Grove Festival, *Batesville*; Blessing of the Shrimp Fleet, *Biloxi*.
In July: Choctaw Indian Fair, *Philadelphia*; Mississippi Deep-Sea Fishing Rodeo, *Gulfport*; National Tobacco Spit, *Raleigh*.
In August: Neshoba County Fair, *Philadelphia*.
In September: Delta Blues Festival, *Greenville*.
In October: Gumbo Festival of the Universe, *Necaise Crossing* (Bay St. Louis); Fall Pilgrimage Tours, *Natchez*; Gateway to the Delta Festival, *Yazoo City*; Mississippi State Fair, *Jackson*; Gulf Coast Oktoberfest, *Biloxi*.
In December: Chimneyville Crafts Festival, *Jackson*; Merrehope Plantation's Trees of Christmas, *Meridian*.

Accommodation in Mississippi (Area Code 601)

Southern Mississippi and the Gulf Coast

Longfellow House, 3401 Beach Blvd., tel. 762-1122, *Pascagoula*. Moderate cottages.
La Font Inn, 2703 Denny Ave., tel. 762-7111, *Pascagoula*. Moderate.
American Motor Inn, Rt. 90 E. & 63, tel. 769-6200, *Pascagoula*. Moderate-inexpensive.
Broadwater Beach Hotel, US 90, tel. 388-2211, *Biloxi*. Expensive resort hotel, near beach.
Biloxi Beach Motor Inn, 115 W. Beach Blvd., tel. 388-3310, *Biloxi*. Moderate.
Balmoral Apartment Motel, 200 Balmoral, tel. 388-1481, *Biloxi*. Inexpensive.
Sea Gull Motel, US 90, tel. 896-4211, *Biloxi*. Inexpensive.
Twin Star Motel, US 90, tel. 388-2610, *Biloxi*. Fairly inexpensive.
Gulf Hills Inn & Golf Club, tel. 875-4211, or (800) 647-3962, *Ocean Springs*; expensive golf resort.
Fountainhead Motel, US 90, tel. 864-1381, *Gulfport*. Moderate.

Fairchilds Motel, US 90, tel. 896-7515, *Gulfport.* Inexpensiv
packages available.
Carriage Inn, 914 Broadway, tel. 544-5100, *Hattiesburg.* Moderate.
Broadway Inn, 1818 Broadway, tel. 584-6201, *Hattiesburg.* Inexper
Town House Motor Hotel, 340 Beacon St., tel. 428-1527,
Moderate.
Virginia Court Motel, South Frontage Rd., tel. 482-2487, *M*
Inexpensive.
Jacksonian Inn, Northside Drive (I-55N.), tel. 981-2345, *J*
Moderate; good restaurant.
Bill Will Motel, US 80 tel. 924-5313, *Jackson.* Moderate-inexpensi
Esquire Inn, Washington Street, tel. 638-5750, *Vicksburg.* Inexpen
YMCA, 821, Clay St., tel. 638-1071, *Vicksburg.* Inexpensive; men
Silver Street Inn, One Silver Street, tel. 442-4221, *Natchez.* Expen
Natchez Under the Hill.
The Burn, 712 N. Union St., tel. 445-8566, *Natchez.* Expens
antebellum home furnished with antiques.
Monmouth, 36 Melrose St., tel. 442-5852, *Natchez.* Expensive; ante
accommodations similar to The Burn.
Prentiss Motel, US 61, tel. 442-1691, *Natchez.* Moderate.
Dumas Riverview Motel, 218 John R. Junken Dr., tel. 442-0221,
Moderate.

Northern Mississippi

Columbus Motel, Hwy. 82 at 24th St., tel. 328-2551, *Columbus.* Mo
YMCA, 602 Second Ave. N., tel. 328-7696, *Columbus.* Men only; c
Yazoo Motel, Hwys. 49 & 16, tel. 746-2161, *Yazoo City.* Inexpensi
Travel Inn Motel, Hwys. 49 & 82, tel. 453-8810, *Greenwood.* Inexp
Gilhara Motor Hotel, Hwy. 82E., tel. 332-1527, *Greenville.* Inexpe
Azar Motel, Hwys 82E. & 1, tel. 332-1511, *Greenville.* Inexpensive
Plantation Inn, 420 S. State Hwy., tel. 624-6541, *Clarksdale.* Mode
Ole Miss Motel, 1517 East University, tel. 234-2424, *Oxford.* Inexp
Holly Springs Motel, Hwy. 78 N., tel. 252-3381, *Holly*
Inexpensive.
Rex Plaza Motor Inn, Hwys. 45 & 78, tel. 842-2911, *Tupelo.* Mode
Trace Inn, 3400 W. Main, tel. 842-5555, *Tupelo.* Moderate-inexp
on Natchez Trace.
Motel Carro, 708 N. Gloster St., tel. 842-1213, *Tepelo.* Inexpensiv

For more information on Mississippi, write to the Departm Economic Development, Division of Tourism, P.O. Box 22825, J MS 39205, or call them toll free outside the state 800-647-2290 Mississippi 800-962-2346. Information on camping in Mississippi parks is available from the Bureau of Parks and Recreation, Depa of Natural Resources, 717 Robert E. Lee Bldg., Jackson MS Hunting and Fishing regulations in the state are available fr Department of Wildlife Conservation, Box 451, Jackson, MS 3920

Louisiana

Louisiana, the 18th state admitted to the Union and the only banana republic north of the Rio Grande, has an area of 50,820 square miles—3,100 are water and approximately 7,000 are gumbo. The state motto is "If you ain't goin' to shake it, why'd you bring it?" The state animals are the Kingfish and the mudfish (along with the Cajun, this is one of the few species to adapt itself completely to Louisiana; farmers sometimes plow them up in their fields). The state flower is the fleur-de-lis, the state bird, the mosquito.

The truth sounds just as odd. The highest point in this state is the Shell Oil Building in New Orleans, a good 150 feet higher than "Driskill Mountain" (535 feet) in Bienville Parish. The lowest point would be the ground beneath it; the state's largest city exists quite comfortably five feet below sea level. Louisiana has two state songs, one of them being "You Are My Sunshine." A country singer named Jimmie Davis wrote it, and an adoring Louisiana elected him governor. Consider some Louisiana place names. Near the Mississippi, you can motor from Archie to Archibald, taking a moral route from Port Necessity through Extension to Enterprise, and if you Aimwell and follow the path of Duty, not dallying on that broad road that leads to Eros, you'll greet the New Era at Acme of success. Down in Cajun country there's Bayou Bonne Idee and Lake Misère, Lake Felicity and Chauvin, whose French-speaking citizens are of course Chauvinistes.

Given, says Georgia, that a logician could easily posit Mississippi, there is nothing in the rest of the South that would allow you to imagine such a place as Louisiana. The terrain, with its abundance of bayous and swamps, makes a difference (it swims over strata of equally abundant oil and natural gas, for which the Louisianians are grateful), but the state really owes most of its distinctiveness to the presence of the French. These come in two varieties: Creoles, from French-Spanish culture of New Orleans, and Cajuns, involuntarily relocated from Canada, who are on the whole country folk. (There are also black Creoles and black Cajuns, as well as sprinklings of Italians, Canary Islanders, Croatians, Filipinos and Indians who fit right in.) Thanks to the French, Louisiana doesn't have counties, but parishes, in which all these peoples, along with the Anglo-Southerners who occupy the other half of the state, have combined to make a history, an outlook, and a way of life that leave the state a strange orphan child in the family of the Solid South, sometimes disapproved of, but usually envied. Of course there's New Orleans, of all America's cities the one that has suffered least from the disintegrating and homogenizing effects of contemporary American yahooism, but the rest of Louisiana does its best to be worthy of her. This means not only that reality is occasionally stranger than fiction, but that for both casual vacationers and studious travelers, the state has something unique to offer.

Getting Around in Louisiana

Chances are you'll be heading first for New Orleans, Louisiana's metropolis, which is very well served by air and bus lines and even Amtrak; if so, refer to the section **Getting to New Orleans** under that city. Otherwise:

By Air. The state's other major airports are at Baton Rouge, Shreveport, Alexandria, Lake Charles and Monroe. Delta or Texas International can take you to these. Southern and Frontier also serve the state and a small line called Commuter Airways connects many of the larger cities. Baton Rouge's **Ryan Airport** is on Plank Road, six miles north of downtown and the **Greater Shreveport Municipal Airport** can be reached by Interstate 20, southwest of the city.

By Train. Because New Orleans is a major terminus, Amtrak serves Louisiana well. *The City of New Orleans* passes through Hammond on its way to Jackson, Mississippi and Chicago; the *Crescent,* to Atlanta and New York, stops at Slidell; and Lake Charles, Lafayette, New Iberia and Schriever are served by the *Sunset Limited* on its way to Houston and Los Angeles. The toll free number in the state is (800) 874-2800, and the local number in New Orleans is 525-1179.

History

There is a bend in the Mississippi, just a few miles below New Orleans, whose name commemorates the little-known event that made Louisiana a French possession and not just another part of British North America. In the tremendous Imperial competition for control of the lower Mississippi in the late 19th century, it appeared the French, through government indifference and occasionally through lack of government (during the regencies) would lose the head start that intrepid explorers like La Salle had given them. In 1699, however, an expedition under Jean Baptiste Le Moyne, Sieur de Bienville, was looking over the prospects for settlement along the Mississippi when, to everyone's consternation, a squadron of British ships came sailing up the river. The resourceful Bienville received them warmly and told his old friend Captain Banks all about the string of forts he had been establishing along the Mississippi, and how it really wasn't worth their while exploring the place when the French had beaten him to it. Banks believed all those bald-faced lies and turned his ships about at the spot known today as *English Turn,* unwittingly saving Louisiana (as La Salle had named it, for Louis XIV) from the fate of becoming another Mississippi or Alabama, with no jazz, no fais-dodo and no hot sauce.

In fact it was neither France nor Britain, but the Spanish who had the inside track on Louisiana. Hernando de Soto discovered the Mississippi in 1542, and some of his countrymen may have been there decades earlier. The voyages of other conquistadores gave Spain a fairly good idea of the territory, but Spain was never interested in long-term investments; instead of the legendary Seven Cities of Cibola, with limitless gold for the greedy and strong, they found only steamy bayous, mosquitoes and the thoroughly discouraging Choctaw Indians, a people whom the ethnologists with unconscious humour refer to as "semi-sedentary," who hadn't any clothes save the feathers they wore over their buttocks, let alone golden jewelry, and whose only talent seemed to be internecine warfare. The conquistadores moved on.

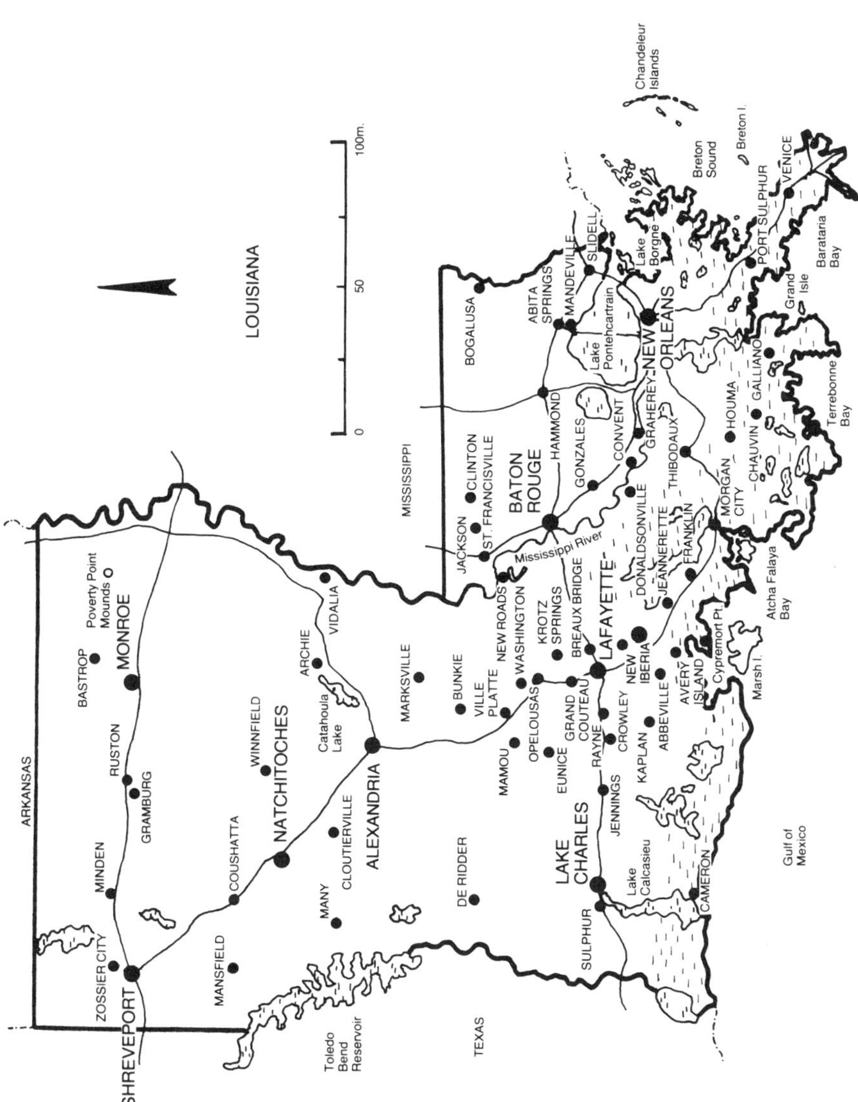
LOUISIANA
0
50
100m.
ARKANSAS
MISSISSIPPI
TEXAS
Gulf of Mexico
SHREVEPORT
ZOSSIER CITY
MANSFIELD
MINDEN
GRAMBURG
RUSTON
BASTROP
MONROE
Poverty Point Mounds
COUSHATTA
NATCHITOCHES
WINNFIELD
MANY
CLOUTIERVILLE
ALEXANDRIA
Catahoula Lake
ARCHIE
VIDALIA
DE RIDDER
MARKSVILLE
BUNKIE
VILLE PLATTE
MAMOU
OPELOUSAS
WASHINGTON
NEW ROADS
KROTZ SPRINGS
BREAUX BRIDGE
EUNICE
GRAND COTEAU
LAFAYETTE
RAYNE
CROWLEY
JENNINGS
LAKE CHARLES
SULPHUR
Lake Calcasieu
CAMERON
KAPLAN
ABBEVILLE
NEW IBERIA
JEANNERETTE
AVERY ISLAND
Cypremort Pt.
Marsh I.
Atcha Falaya Bay
FRANKLIN
MORGAN CITY
DONALDSONVILLE
THIBODAUX
HOUMA
CHAUVIN
GALLIANO
Terrebonne Bay
Grand Isle
Barataria Bay
PORT SULPHUR
VENICE
Breton I.
Breton Sound
Chandeleur Islands
Lake Borgne
NEW ORLEANS
GRAHEREY
CONVENT
GONZALES
BATON ROUGE
Mississippi River
JACKSON
ST. FRANCISVILLE
CLINTON
HAMMOND
Lake Pontchartrain
MANDEVILLE
ABITA SPRINGS
SLIDELL
BOGALUSA
Toledo Bend Reservoir

La Salle paddled down the Mississippi from the Great Lakes in 1682, and Bienville's brother, Sieur D'Iberville, helped to solidify France's claim with a voyage in 1699. The party landed on the banks of the river, appropriately on Shrove Tuesday, Mardi Gras day, and visited the site of New Orleans a few days later. Further upstream they noted the red pole that marked an Indian hunting boundary—where Baton Rouge is today—and split up, Iberville trying his luck with the bayous back towards the gulf and Bienville returning downriver towards the episode at English Turn. After this, France persevered in consolidating its hold. Its missionaries, trappers and traders spread throughout the territory; Natchitoches was established in 1714 and New Orleans, the city that would be the key to the entire Mississippi Valley, four years later. Still, serious colonization did not happen until the Regent, the Duke of Orleans, turned the project over to private enterprise in the person of the Scottish economist and speculator John Law. Law, "the man who invented inflation," tried to create value in Louisiana land by making everyone want some and the result of his speculation, the bursting of the "Mississippi Bubble" in 1820, not only created a financial panic and a lasting depression in Europe, but gave the new colony a bad reputation and seriously retarded its growth.

Louisiana became a persistent drain on the French treasury. That, and trouble with the Natchez Indians upriver, made Louis XV anxious to rid himself of it. The British gave him the opportunity by defeating him soundly in the Seven Years War (or French and Indian War, as it is known in America); they seemed to imply at the peace conference in Paris that they didn't mean to let Louis keep Louisiana, and the King obligingly passed the colony over to his Bourbon cousin, Charles III of Spain. The Louisianians didn't like it—particularly the citizens of New Orleans, who rebelled—but business with the Spanish Indies was good and they soon learned to live with the new dispensation. Curiously, the aftermath of the war had the effect of making Louisiana, though lost to France, more French than ever. Thousands of French Acadian refugees, victims of a brutal British dispersal from their Canadian homelands, found their way to the only place in America they were welcome in odysseys that lasted years, coming individually or in small groups to Louisiana by way of the thirteen colonies, the West Indies, the Mississippi, or even France. They received land grants in the forests and bayous of southern Louisiana, and their descendants are the Cajuns.

Louisiana played a small role in the American revolution. As Spain supported the colonists against its old enemy England, New Orleans became an important center for transmitting money and supplies for the American cause; probably the furthest western battles of the war were combined actions of the Americans and the Spanish under Governor Bernando de Galvez (for whom Galveston, Texas, is named) against British-held West Florida and the east bank of the Mississippi, successfully booting the redcoats out of Baton Rouge and Natchez in 1779. After the war, the rapid settlement of the territories along the Ohio River made Louisiana an important part of the young republic's geopolitical considerations. The river route down to New Orleans was the only possible trade outlet for the new lands and an American presence began to be felt, as U.S. and Spanish authorities negotiated almost continuously over the intricacies of trading rights. In 1801, Louisiana again came under French rule, thanks to the conquests of Napoleon, but the French never asserted themselves until 1803.

With the task of conquering Europe on their hands, they naturally weren't much interested in North America, and when President Jefferson's ministers went to buy New Orleans, Napoleon, receiving them in his bathtub, astounded them by offering the entire Louisiana territory, 827,000 square miles as far north as Saskatchewan, for about the same price; his army needed the money. Congress was just as surprised as the ambassadors and the Louisiana Purchase was almost voted down. Good sense prevailed, however, and authority was formally turned over to the U.S. in December of that year. In 1812, Louisiana became the first state to be carved from the territory and the first state west of the Mississippi.

In that same year, an event occurred that reflected the great changes and economic growth that was finally making Louisiana a place of some importance in the world. The first steamboat on the Mississippi, the Pittsburgh-built *New Orleans,* appeared amid great celebrations in the city it was named for. The old flatboats that had carried the river trade up to that date were slow and clumsy; they had to be poled upstream by hand and the trip could take as long as four months. Now, it would not be long before New Orleans was the second largest port of the nation, a position it still enjoys today. Agriculture was booming on the plantations along Louisiana's rivers and bayous. The process for refining sugar had been invented in the state in the 1790's, a year after Eli Whitney made his cotton gin; both transformed the state's economy and where once only indigo and onions grew, now fortunes did. In the decades before the Civil War, Louisiana was enjoying a golden age, even more so than the rest of the South; the mansions of New Orleans' Garden District, and the string of plantations along the Mississippi, unmatched in splendour by anything else in Dixie, testify to the special world of aristocratic refinement the state's Creole-American elite had created for itself.

On January 26, 1861, Louisiana became the seventh state of the Union to secede, spending a month and a half as an independent republic before deciding to join the Confederacy. Its adventure did not last long. To cut off the major outlet for southern trade, Lincoln sent gruff old Admiral David G. Farragut, the son of a Minorcan immigrant in Tennessee, who had lived for a while in Louisiana but remained loyal to the Union. Farragut wasn't about to be dismayed by the guns of Fort Jackson and Fort St. Philip at the mouth of the Mississippi; he sailed right by, losing only a few ships and occupied New Orleans, Baton Rouge, and the rest of the parishes along the river. For the remainder of the war the Confederates kept their capital at Opelousas, and later Shreveport, and were able to hold northern and western Louisiana against the Yankees without any major engagements. The Union forces had what they wanted, though, and the capture of New Orleans was the first step towards control of the entire Mississippi and the beginning of the end for the South. During Reconstruction, Louisiana had a black lieutenant governor, Oscar Dunn, and it also had a carpetbag administration that was perhaps more venal than the average. Riots against it occurred in New Orleans and other towns, and the White League and a local version of the Klan called the "Knights of the White Camellia" were founded to murder and terrorize blacks, with great success. Federal troops went home in 1877, and Louisiana returned to normal, if somewhat poorer and meaner.

Evidence for calling Louisiana the United States' only banana republic is not hard to uncover; this state has had no less than nine constitutions in its 160 year history and even today politics are a lively exercise in feudal intrigue, with power concentrated in closely-run baronies by courthouse gangs, old warhorses and city machines. Things have changed a little: currently there's a Republican in the governor's chair and a black mayor in New Orleans, but back in the 1920's monolithic Democracy ran the state like any pack of Central American padrones. What happened in that decade amounted to nothing less than a popular revolution, something no one could have predicted and no one could explain, engineered by the alarming rhetoric of one man—Huey Long, the Kingfish. When Louisiana woke up one morning in 1928 to find that this short, florid, homely creature in a pink suit had been elected its governor, the immediate reaction of many was to wonder just who he was, and where he came from. The answer would be Winnfield, a sad little town that time forgot near Alexandria, in the center of the state. Huey grew up here reading everything he could lay his hands on and emerged as a travelling salesman for patent medicines and lard substitutes before working his way through law school—in half the usual time—and making the easy transition from drumming up business to drumming up votes with an engaging spiel and a stock of back-country jokes. Somewhere along the road he picked up an ideology. It isn't clear just how, but resentment of the rich and their kept politicians, and of the lack of opportunity for everyone else, was evident enough in places like Winn Parish, and it remained only for someone as clever as Huey to turn it into a cause.

No doubt about it, Huey was a revolutionary. The rich got soaked, and particularly the big corporations and out-of-state interests; the governor fought them time and again in the legislature to increase their taxes and narrow their fields of influence, and he won almost every round. When Standard Oil tried to get him impeached by purchasing legislators, he raised enough money to buy some of them back, and won again. In his term, coinciding with the onset of the depression, Long began a tremendous public works program, building bridges, constructing a highway system, where almost none had existed before, creating his own personal monument, the skyscraper State Capitol, and turning little LSU into a major state university. His development agenda was the issue of the day and it served to make him even more popular, along with such symbolically important acts as making schoolbooks free to all the state's children, and abolishing the poll tax to give some blacks the vote. At the same time, however, he was subverting the state constitution in a thousand ingenious ways to make Louisiana into America's first bonafide dictatorship, with the politically controlled State Police acting as his Praetorian guard on motorcycles.

While governor, Huey built a new Governor's Mansion in Baton Rouge, a scaled-down model of the White House designed, as he joked to reporters, so that when he got to be the real thing he would know where the light switches were. The next logical step towards the presidential ambition that occupied most of his adult life was to the Senate, a place where his ideas and oratory could reach every corner of the nation. The 1930 Democratic primary—the only election that counted in an era when Republicans hardly ever bothered to put up candidates—saw Huey, still in the governor's chair, facing an aged conservative supported by the only effective opposition left in the state, the beleaguered New Orleans machine. The highlight of the campaign, just a few days before election day, saw the Kingfish kidnapping a former friend who was threatening to tell the press about corruption in the Highway Department, and about Huey's mistress, and then talking the man into delivering a radio address denying the whole thing. Huey won again, and left the state's affairs in the hands of a handsome non-entity appropriately named O. K. Allen, while still returning from Washington whenever an important bill came up in Baton Rouge to cuss at his legislators, tell them how to vote, and occasionally kick them in the pants.

While the Depression raged, Huey locked himself in a hotel room for a few weeks and came out with his political testament, a book called *Every Man a King* that translated his Louisiana populism to a national scope. He had a plan, called "Share the Wealth," proposing confiscatory taxes on the rich to provide an extensive social welfare scheme, a 30-hour week, a few thousand bucks off the top for everybody and a guaranteed income. Soon, from coast to coast, everybody knew who Huey was, and no one was more aware of him then President Roosevelt; during FDR's first term, the two men conducted one of the great political feuds of the century, leaving Louisiana a battleground of patronage wars and court investigations. As the New Deal faltered, it appeared that Huey could actually win the 1936 presidential election, or at least draw off enough votes as a third-party candidate to defeat Roosevelt. Many Americans began to consider the threat of fascism in their own country; Sinclair Lewis wrote a somewhat hysterical novel called *It Can't Happen Here,* in which it did happen, and a character modeled after Huey became an American dictator, only to be overthrown by an even blacker scoundrel modeled after Douglas MacArthur.

Instead, what happened was that Huey got himself shot. The professional mythographers of political assassinations have done as thorough a job on what happened that hot Sunday evening in 1935, in a corridor off the State Capitol lobby, as they did on the case of President Kennedy. There have been claims that a conspiracy was at work (it wouldn't have been the first), or that Huey was accidently shot by one of his own guards. It seems, however, that young Carl Weiss, a brilliant doctor and a quiet, intellectual member of Louisiana's old aristocracy whose father-in-law was a judge and a Long enemy, was both sane and alone when he decided to become a martyr for liberty. He never did get a chance to explain; seconds after he pulled the trigger, Long's bodyguard pumped either forty-five or seventy bullets into him. The accounts differ.

Even though the last remnants of the Long machine were suffering an epidemic of court convictions by 1940, the family name was carried on in state politics by several other Longs, including one named Speedy O., and Russell Long, who sits in the U.S. Senate today, working for the big oil interests his father slapped down so often. Huey's bumptious little brother, whom nobody ever took very seriously, hit his stride in the 1950's, an era when Huey's memory was still the dividing line of political loyalties. Earl Long— picture him telling off-color jokes to the crowds while continually mopping his brow with a handkerchief soaked in Coca-Cola—makes even a better story than Huey. Without much of his brother's ferocious energy, and none of his ambition, Governor Earl (1948-52 and 1956-60) had a high time becoming a genuine Southern folk hero, the only successful Southern progressive politician of the 50's,a good ol' boy who had to admit, at least in private, that Lincoln was right. Earl got back many of the social programs and stiff corporate taxes that had gone out after Huey's assassination, and he battled, quixotically though fitfully, against the segregationist cranks and the politicians who succumbed to their brand of what Earl called "skingameism," like the country crooner-turned-Governor Jimmy Davis.

What really endeared Earl to the people of Louisiana, however, was his lively eccentricity, stoutly upheld against the shocked proprieties of all the state's bluenoses and hypocrites—not least of whom was his wife, who twice had him kidnapped and committed to mental institutions during his second term. Earl talked his way out on both occasions. He had gotten himself into this fix with such stunts as once lecturing the state legislature on the Negro problem: "You the people that sleep with 'em at night and kick 'em in the street in the daytime . . ." and spending more time making a spectacle of himself in Bourbon Street strip joints than he did in Baton Rouge. When General De Gaulle visited Louisiana, Earl diverted the motorcade down Bourbon so that the girls could see him, and at the end of his term, he had all of them over to the Governor's Mansion for a little celebration. One of those girls was the famous Blaze Starr, later to become a fixture on the "Block" in Baltimore, and who had once played house with the chieftain of another banana republic, Philadelphia Mayor Frank Rizzo, back when he was still a cop. Blaze and Earl were carrying on a torrid affair until Earl's death in 1960, a few days after an election in which he had won his final vindication at the polls by winning the Democratic nomination for Congress from Winn Parish.

Things in Louisiana have quietened down considerably since then (though the current leading light of state politics, the once and future Cajun governor Edwin Edwards, is a colorful character in his own right). The state, awash in a sea of oil and natural gas, hasn't known such prosperity since the Flush Times before the Civil War. In the South, only Virginia and Florida have higher average incomes. All of the cities, and even many of the rural districts, are doing well, and as the population inches up to five million, Louisiana still does a good job of absorbing its newcomers; it's a state that is tenacious in its differences.

New Orleans

> "Great Babylon is come up before me. Oh, the wickedness, the idolatry of this place! . . . Oh, farewell. Pray for your sister in a heathen land."
>
> —Rachel Jackson

Tennessee, in 1814, was itself no placid garden of culture and piety, and for Old Hickory's wife to have written these words back home while accompanying her husband to the turkey shoot at Chalmette, she must have seen something that really opened her eyes. She probably wasn't around for Mardi Gras, and she didn't come into contact with the keelboatmen, many from her own state, whose carryings-on here offended New Orleans as much as New Orleans offended Rachel, but perhaps word reached her ears of the strange Sunday parties in Congo Square, where the slaves performed their African dances to the pounding of drums, or of the "quadroon balls" where wealthy men selected their mistresses. It could have been a servant girl discreetly offering knowledge of some powerful *gris-gris*—a voodoo charm—that would make Old Hickory livelier in the sack, something to do with locks of hair, johnswort or dead chickens. Maybe it was just that everyone seemed to be having such a good time.

Now, you can start from the suburbs of anywhere and say you are going "into town," but if you are a state or two away and you are going to "the City," in all the U.S.A. you can only be talking about New York, San Francisco or New Orleans. It is a title of the most profound honor and respect. Even if New Orleans weren't a booming commercial center, and even if its port didn't ship 167,135,226 tons of cargo last year, this city could claim it. People are still having a good time in New Orleans, and that has more than a little to do with it. With its tolerance, its humanity born of a rich history and cultural diversity, and its amused distaste for the morbid passions of the rest of the South, New Orleans is a breath of fresh air, a place that has as little to do with the South of the Bible Belt and the hookworm belt as it possibly can. New Orleans is a city of jazz funerals, pink houses and toy shops; it has things other American towns have thrown away, like carousels in the parks and streetcars and things they never had, like sidewalk cafés. It has the prettiest houses, the most interesting cemeteries, the finest square and the best stories to tell. Its most ingratiating surprise is that, while full of tourists, it is not a tourist city. There isn't a touch of Disneyland in it; New Orleaneans are rather too mature to allow much tackiness, and they have a happy convergence of interests with their millions of guests to keep their city unaffected, comfortable, accessible and always true to itself.

Don't expect to hear any creamy Southern accents ("It sounds ignorant here," as one New Orleanean explained it). The city will most likely address you in standard American, the way you hear it on the radio, but you may catch a trace of the old argot of the working-class districts, which will make you think you're in Brooklyn. All those songs written about the city since:

> "Sadie Green, the vamp of New Orleans,
> Got more beaux than the Navy's got marines . . ."

will mislead you as to the correct pronunciation: she is "New Orlyuns" to new acquaintances, and "N'orlins" when you get to know her really well.

Some Distinctions. For a city that has always existed on the fringes of the national consciousness—some Americans believe it to be purely mythical—N'orlins has had a surprisingly deep influence on the American culture and language. To mention jazz would be too easy, but you are probably not aware that the city invented the free lunch (in a bar on Exchange Alley) and the cocktail (the druggist Peychaud first served them in egg cups or "coquetiers"), following up the discovery with such renowned intoxicants as the Sazerac and the Ramos gin fizz. Volumes could be written on the subject of New Orleans and money. The appelation "Dixie" has nothing to do with the Mason-Dixon line, but instead with the ten dollar bills printed by the Bank of Louisiana, common currency along the Mississippi, engraved in French—DIX. "Two bits" means a quarter today because Spanish New Orleans cut up its silver pesos into eighths for change, and a half of a bit was a "picayune," a word that found its way into the language, and into the city's leading newspaper, the *Times-Picayune,* which today costs fifteen cents. Another word the Spaniards contributed during their brief stay is calaboose, a jail, from their *calabozo* just around the corner from Jackson Square.

Getting to New Orleans

By Air. Almost every major airline comes to **New Orleans International Airport,** in the suburb of Kenner about twelve miles from the central business district. Because the city is such a popular tourist spot, most U.S. lines occasionally offer discount fares. To get to the airport most inexpensively, take the bus from the corner of Tulane Avenue and Elk Place in the business district; otherwise there are airport limos (about $5 per person) and taxis (a $15 trip).

By Train. Union Terminal is in the Civic Center, at 1001 Loyola Avenue, where the information number is 525-1179. The Amtrak descendent of that famous train, The City of New Orleans, comes down from Chicago and Memphis and there are also services to New York-Washington-Atlanta and Houston-Phoenix-Los Angeles.

By Bus. Both Greyhound and Trailways have their stations in the Union Terminal.

Getting Around

New Orleans Public Service. That's the name of the city's public transportation, probably the only big city bus line in America to be a private corporation (they supply New Orleans with its electricity, too). The streetcar named Desire, the ones named Elysian Fields, Calliope and Cemeteries and all the others as well, are now no-nonsense green buses in this efficient and relatively inexpensive system; only one streetcar line remains, and that one is a National Historic Landmark and a tourist attraction in itself. The **St. Charles Avenue line** also gives you a lesson in the city's development, passing from the business district through Irish Channel, the Garden District and the newer neighborhoods around Audubon Park. Catch the trolley at Common and St. Charles for one of the truly pleasant experiences New Orleans has to offer.

You'll be interested in two more of Public Service's loop routes: the **Vieux Carré Mini-bus,** which wanders through the French Quarter along Iberville, Chartres, Esplanade and Dauphine (except during rush hours, when it travels down Bourbon and back up Royal) and the **Business District Shuttle Line,** a loop between Rivergate and the Superdome around Canal, LaSalle and Paydras Streets. Schedules and

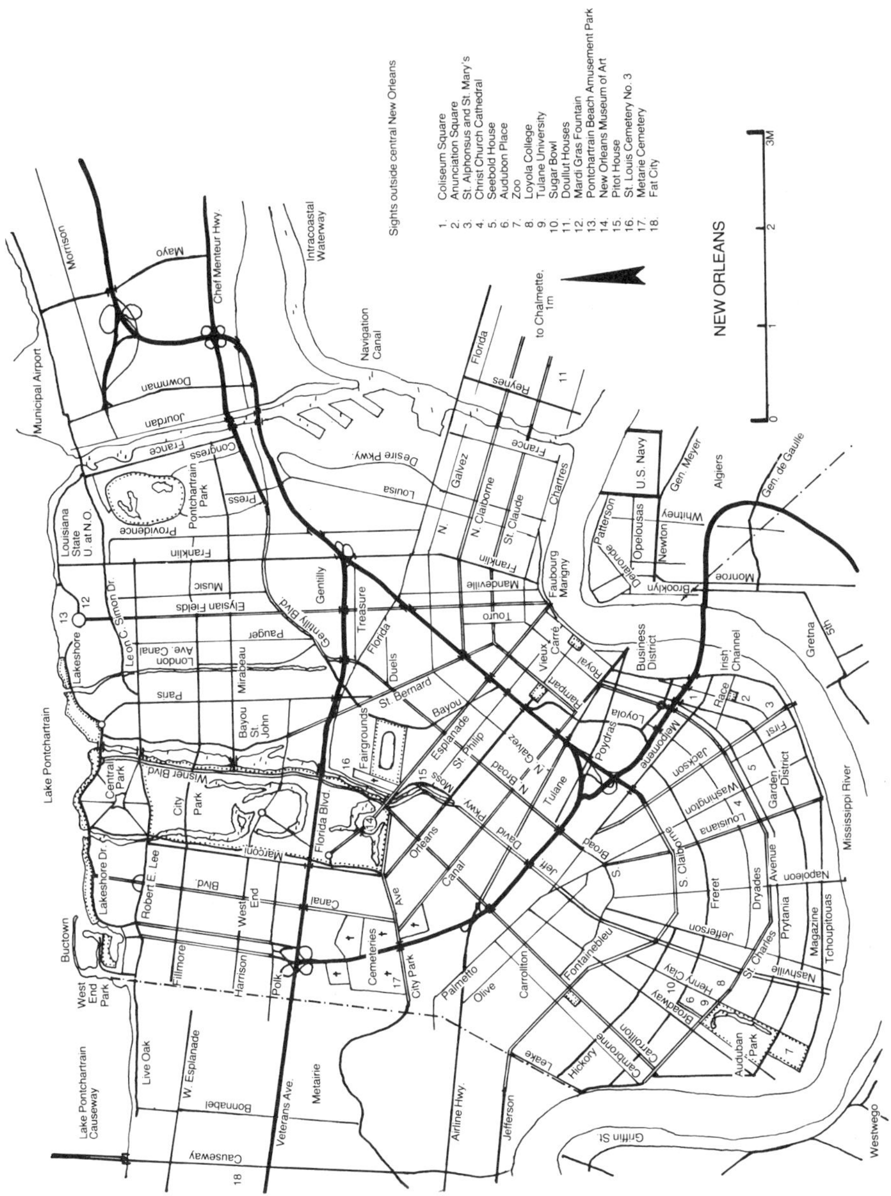
NEW ORLEANS
Sights outside central New Orleans
1. Coliseum Square
2. Anunciation Square
3. St. Alphonsus and St. Mary's
4. Christ Church Cathedral
5. Seebold House
6. Audubon Place
7. Zoo
8. Loyola College
9. Tulane University
10. Sugar Bowl
11. Doullut Houses
12. Mardi Gras Fountain
13. Pontchartrain Beach Amusement Park
14. New Orleans Museum of Art
15. Pitot House
16. St. Louis Cemetery No. 3
17. Metarie Cemetery
18. Fat City

information on all Public Service's lines can be obtained at their office, 317 Baronne Street, or call 595-2192.

By Taxi. In the central city you can usually hail a cab from the street; otherwise, telephone. There are several companies, all radio dispatched. Rates are more expensive than in New York, but cheaper, slightly, than most other cities.

By Car. In general, New Orleans' traffic is formidable, but not impossible. It's no fun seeing this city through the windshield, but if you must, street parking is found never in the business district, occasionally in the Vieux Carré (where there are, by the way, no traffic lights), and easily enough in the rest of town. Bourbon, Royal and the streets around Jackson Square except Decatur are closed to traffic most of the day. You might try parking at the Superdome and taking the Business District Shuttle Line to Canal Street; rates there are cheaper than most other garages when there are no events taking place.

By Boat. There's a free ferry crossing the Mississippi every twelve minutes, from the foot of Canal Street to Algiers, and another from Jackson Avenue in the Irish Channel district to Huey P. Long Avenue in the suburb of Gretna; both are interesting ways to see the working side of New Orleans along the docks and riverside industrial areas.

Otherwise, you can spend a few hours on one of the cruise ships, old-fashioned—though not old—steamboats that ply the Mississippi through the port to Chalmette or to Audubon Park (tickets about $7). The *Natchez* sails three times daily from a wharf in front of Jackson Square, and the *President* and the *Mark Twain* start from Canal Street by the ferry.

By Carriage. On the Decatur Street side of Jackson Square you'll find a queue of gaily decorated old buggies, whose drivers would be delighted to show you around the French Quarter for about $5 per person.

A Brief Note on Orientation. The way the New Orleaneans have arranged their city, the usual locational terminology is meaningless, and a compass will only tell you lies; thanks to the bends of the Mississippi, the presence of Lake Pontchartrain, and the resistance of the inhabitants to any kind of facile systems, no American city looks so inscrutable on the map. Canal Street is the prime meridian; everything upriver is **Uptown,** like the Garden District, and everything downriver, **Downtown,** like the Faubourg Marigny. That's why New Orleans talks about its "Central Business District," or "CBD." If they wanted to call it "downtown," they would have to move it.

Vieux Carré streets change their name when they cross Canal, a relic from the days when the French and American zones were doing their best to be two separate cities. For those beyond the old town, Canal divides them into North and South (such as Rampart, Claiborne and Broad Streets). That doesn't mean they really are North and South, but it would have been neither more nor less inaccurate and confusing to call them East and West; "Downriver" and "Upriver" is what they mean to say. The grid of streets adapts itself to follow the river as it curves and so, now and then, South Claiborne Street is north of North Claiborne. Then there's the **West Bank,** the part of town across the river that includes

Algiers and Gretna; it's really south of the city proper—and don't confuse it with the **West End,** up on the lakeshore by City Park, which lies north-northwest of the business district. The space in between is still often called "Back of town". Perhaps the best-named street in New Orleans can sometimes be found here; Perdido (lost) Street was so dubbed by the Spanish for its habit of wandering off into the swamps and disappearing. The swamps, at least, were drained long ago, but somewhere between Elysian Fields and Felicity Street you can still get Perdido.

Tourist Information. The place to start is the **Visitor Information Center,** at 334 Royal Street, home of both the State Office of Tourism and the Greater New Orleans Tourist and Convention Commission, which between the two of them can answer any question (566-5011; they're open daily 9-5 pm). Also, you are bound to run across one of the dozen or so weekly publications like *Go* and *This Week in New Orleans,* or even *Nueva Orleans Internacional* that can tell you something about events, nightlife and restaurants. For cultural events, there are listings in the *Times-Picayune,* the monthly *New Orleans Magazine,* and an interesting weekly paper called *Gambit.*

History

It is quite fitting, somehow, that the original population of New Orleans was made up largely of jailbirds. The city had been founded by Bienville in 1718, and his engineer de Pauger had immediately laid out the Place D'Armes and the streets of the Vieux Carré—the "old square" that makes up today's French Quarter—but the government at first had a hard time getting anyone to live there, especially after the collapse of the "Mississippi Bubble". The royal prisons being full, as usual, it wasn't long before a boatload of debtors and smugglers and another of wayward Parisian ladies, appeared at the new settlement. Under French and, after 1763, Spanish rule, the town was already acquiring a reputation as a gay and worldly place.

The French got along fine with the Spaniards; in fact, they quickly integrated their societies and used the word "Creole," meaning "native" as it did all over the West Indies, to describe the culture that resulted. The Spanish government, however, wasn't as warmly received; in 1768 New Orleans rose up and booted them out, declaring an independent city-state in the first anti-colonial rebellion anywhere in North America. It couldn't last. The Escorial responded by sending a good Spaniard by the name of Don Alexander O'Reilly with three thousand men and orders for a not too selective use of the firing squad. "Bloody O'Reilly" easily subdued the city and executed the leaders of the revolt. Despite this calamity, as well as the uncertainties of war when New Orleans served as a base for assisting the American revolutionaries, and great fires in 1788 and 1794 that destroyed much of the Vieux Carré, the city prospered as commerce on the Mississippi gradually increased. Reflecting this new wealth, the city acquired its first civic ornaments, the St. Louis Cathedral, the Presbytère and the Cabildo (the Spanish governing council that met there was really the Very Illustrious Cabildo) all on Jackson Square.

In 1803, the Cabildo returned authority in New Orleans to the French, and twenty days later, the French flag came down and the stars and stripes went up. The Creoles, to put it mildly, were shocked. They had already met some Americans, and unfortunately for first impressions they were the Kentucky and Tennessee boatmen who brought the expanding West's commerce down the river, hail fellows who boasted they were "half horse and half alligator" and liked nothing better than to tear up river towns at the end of their journeys. They had to be tough—the Mississippi was in those days a gauntlet of murderers and pirates—but this did nothing to endear them to the civilized New Orleaneans. Creole mothers threatened to feed unruly children to these "Kaintocks," a word the city eventually applied to Americans in general.

The river, and the city with it, entered a boom era under American rule, and as a slightly less monstrous variety of Kaintock arrived—businessmen, planters and speculators— the natives still wouldn't have anything to do with them, this in spite of the efforts of the First American governor, William C. C. Claiborne, a capable and sympathetic man who learned French and married a Creole girl. The Americans built their own city next to the Vieux Carré, in the Faubourg Ste. Marie, and the two halves of town existed in relative isolation, a Berlin with a wall of mutual cultural pretensions running down what is now Canal Street. Not to be outdone, the Americans, with money to burn, tried to act refined too, and endowed their quarter with some magnificent Greek Revival architecture, notably the old City Hall still standing on Lafayette Square. In truth, both sides had something to learn from each other, though it took them years to find it out. The Americans made New Orleans a great city, and the Creoles made it interesting.

A brief interlude of co-operation came in 1814 when the British, whom both sides disliked more than they did each other, threatened the city with a force of veterans of the Napoleonic campaigns under the Duke of Wellington's brother-in-law, Sir Edward Pakenham. When General Andrew Jackson arrived with thousands of those same Kentuckians and Tennesseans to defend the city, the Creoles didn't complain at all. Hundreds even joined up, along with blacks, Cajuns, Indians and pirates. Down in the marshes around Barataria Bay, the legendary Jean Lafitte and his band of buccaneers had been foiling American and British attempts to catch them for years. While the British were coming, however, Lafitte and his Baratarians offered their services out of a sincere wish to help save New Orleans; Jackson, at first, disdained them as common criminals, and only accepted their aid at the last minute. The Battle of New Orleans, fought east of the city at Chalmette plantation on January 8, 1815, after a month of manoeuverings, wasn't much of a battle from the British point of view. Packenham went in with twice as many men as Jackson, and came out of it two thousand short while the Americans lost only thirteen; General Pakenham himself was killed, and Jackson gained the fame that resulted in his election as President in 1828. Most accounts relate how New Orleans idolized the stern general, and the city did indeed eventually erect the equestrian statue with Jackson gallantly tipping his hat to passersby in the square they renamed for him. However, what really happened, right after the battle, was that the Creoles hauled Jackson into a city court and fined him a thousand dollars for infringing on the freedom of the local press and abusing martial law—thus giving the future President a good lesson in democracy.

With the war past, New Orleans went back to business, sharing fully in the South's antebellum golden age as the region's financial center and leading port. Wealth and leisure allowed the city to indulge its passions and idiosyncracies. One of these, after Waterloo, was Napoleon; plots were hatched almost continuously to bring him to New Orleans, or help restore his throne, and at the time of his death a cabal of Creole adventurers was all set to sail for St. Helena. New Orleans finally had to be content with naming a dozen streets after Napoleon and his battles. Other free spirits were using the city as a base for what used to be called "filibusters". In an age when the nation's citizens were even more imperialistically inclined than its government, schemes to seize Texas, Cuba, Santo Domingo and anything else within reach were common. William Walker, the greatest filibuster of them all, who ran Nicaragua as a feudal principality for two years in the 1850's, was acquitted in a sensational trial here upon his return to the U.S.

More peaceful New Orleaneans had their fancies too. The theatre (both in French and English) prospered here with a greater degree of sophistication than elsewhere in America, as did the opera. Continental singers often made their U.S. debuts in the great opera house that once stood on Bourbon Street, and particularly after the Civil War their arrivals were the highest moments for New Orleans high society. The Flush Times were the great age for city folklore. Every old house in the Vieux Carré sooner or later had a story attached to it; when you pass the Le Prêtre Mansion, at 716 Dauphine, think of the mysterious Turk—a master thief or the brother of Sultan himself—who lived here in the 1790's with his harem, throwing lavish parties for society, then suddenly turning up murdered—his ladies and servants completely disappeared. Or else, consider the Orleans Ballroom, just around the corner, site of the "quadroon balls" where light-skinned slave girls could win their freedom the hard way, before a free black man named Thomy Lafon put an end to it by buying the place and giving it to an order of black Catholic sisters for use as an orphanage. Then there are such characters as Marie Laveau, the most famous of the voodoo queens, in a time when voodoo was still more religious ritual than sympathetic magic. She was real, but Annie Christmas, the seven-foot mustachioed woman who they say ruled the waterfront in the 1820's and could carry three barrels of flour at once, probably wasn't.

Harsh reality finally found its way to New Orleans in 1862, in the company of General Ben Butler. The South's metropolis had been its third city to fall to the Yankees, a blow from which the Confederacy really never recovered, and to guard it Lincoln sent his pet bulldog Butler, who had just done a masterful job of intimidating Baltimore into submission, and now repeated his triumph here. In return for his skill at appropriating their property, particularly precious metals, for the Union cause, the citizens gave Butler his nickname: "Old Silver Spoons".

Only a few years after Appomattox, however, New Orleans was back to its old tricks. Mardi Gras made its reappearance with tableaux mocking Reconstruction that made even the North laugh, and the still-busy port ensured that the city would recover quickly from the war's disturbances. At the turn of the century, New Orleans was adding to its store of history with the beginnings of jazz in Storyville, the most illustrious red-light district of all time (see under Basin Street). In the 1930's, the city got itself into trouble by opposing Huey Long; his organization and the city's Democratic machine couldn't cut a deal, and consequently Huey began expressing his dismay at what a sinful place New Orleans was, while doing his best to "restore order" by taking over the city police and subverting its courts. Long did give the city its first bridge over the Mississippi, which still bears his name (just across the parish boundary), but for a while all state funds to the city were choked off. President Roosevelt, Huey's great enemy, came to its rescue; the WPA gave the city jobs to hand out while restoring everything in town, including the French Market and every building on Jackson Square. Still, Huey weakened the machine enough for a patrician reformer named de Lesseps "Chep" Morrison to finish it off in the 1940's, bringing the Crescent City some Atlanta-style New South boosterism and downtown development.

This new age—in a way the final triumph of the Kaintocks—didn't do too much damage. There was one unfortunate freeway, and another one that was supposed to go right past Jackson Square, but instead turned out to be the first place in America where the highwaymen were successfully resisted, after a long battle that attracted nationwide attention. Somehow, New Orleans managed the trick of staying prosperous without becoming another Atlanta, and this engaging, only semi-mythical community currently lives quite well on tourism, the port, finance and oil, with a black Creole mayor named Dutch Morial, a Mardi Gras as good as it ever was, a historic center devoutly protected by the Vieux Carré Commission, a cultural life unmatched in the South and a legion of friends and well-wishers all over the world. Everyone who's ever been there, in fact.

New Orleans Houses. They come in all shapes and all colors, and as tricked up with decorations as some of them are, none are ever lacking in tastefulness or grace. The oldest buildings in the Vieux Carré, simple stucco facades with shutters and perhaps a small balcony and a distinctively French roofline, like the Napoleon House on Chartres Street, gave way as the city waxed in prosperity and importance to more pretentious constructions. Under Spanish rule, town mansions of the Spanish style, with beautiful enclosed courtyards as their main feature, appeared along Royal Street and elsewhere in the old quarter. A little later on, in the early decades of the 19th century, houses of both influences were transformed by New Orleans' love affair with the cast iron railing. Even if these weren't a New Orleans invention—most came from foundries in Philadelphia or Baltimore, which both have some fine examples of their own—the city's wealthy adapted them to their own fancies, and ordered them by the boatload. Both in the French Quarter, and in the Americans' Garden District, you will see lovely ironwork in designs of morning-glories, bows and arrows, lyres, owner's initials, cornstalks, grapevines and every sort of flowery arabesque. These are what come to most peoples' minds when they think of New Orleans; they make the city a garden in iron.

New Orleans Streets. The best travel poster this city's convention bureau could ever produce would be its own street map. Where else could you find a street corner of Desire and Abundance, or Telemachus and

Euphrosine, Providence and Madmen, Treasure and Rabbits, Law and Music, Mystery and Ponce de Leon, Fig and Fern, Pocahontas and Buick, Piety and Humanity, Gayoso and Perdido, Socrates and Brooklyn?

De Pauger, at the behest of his client John Law, named the streets of the Vieux Carré quite expediently for everyone at the French court whose influence could possibly help the new colony along; in the new subdivisions of the American city, however, the pattern for fantastical names was set when the streets beyond Lee Circle were called after the nine Muses—Calliope, Erato, Thalia, Melpomene, Terpsichore, Euterpe, Polyhymnia, Urania and Clio, if you've forgotton, with Nayades and Dryades to keep them company. Calliope, of course, is pronounced cally-ope, like the steam organs that used to delight New Orleans' children at circuses and on the riverboats. Since then, developers and landowners have dubbed new streets as their whims demanded, after fruit trees, their girlfriends, Spanish governors, French and classical themes, automobiles, or Napoleon's battles. There's a General Diaz, for the Mexican tyrant, a Stephen Girard, for the great Philadelphia financier, and in one section, off Elysian Fields Avenue, a group of streets called Pleasure, Humanity, Abundance, Agriculture, Industry, Hope, and Duels.

And then there's Tchoupitoulas, the dockside thoroughfare that skirts the uptown neighborhoods as far as Audubon Park. Its name, which you may pronounce as you see fit, may have something to do with mudfish or with the local flock of Choctaw. They tell a story in New Orleans about a policeman of the old days who found a dead horse at the corner of Common and Tchoupitoulas while making his rounds. After several attempts at recording it in his notebook, "Dead horse at Ch . . ." he took the horse by the tail and dragged it to the corner of Common and Magazine.

Whatever their names, New Orleans streets do not often fail to live up to them; be they rich or poor, business or residential, sedate or full of life, each is interesting in its own way. And one more thing; you will learn that New Orleaneans still call their sidewalks "banquettes," as the French did. The city's soggy setting necessitated that it become the first in America to pave its streets, but before the first Belgian blocks were laid, the Vieux Carrés *rues* and *calles* were often swamps and occasionally rivers. Logically, the French began to call their city blocks *islèts,* and the sidewalks were their "little banks".

Mardi Gras. If you want to attend this spectacular party New Orleans throws for itself, you had better plan ahead; it's so popular that room reservations even a few months in advance might be hard to find. The word means "fat Tuesday," the last day before Lent, and it has seen Carnival festivities in New Orleans since the city's founding. By the 1850's, however, things seemed to be getting out of hand in the wild, spontaneous, celebrations, and the city officials were on the verge of banning Mardi Gras altogether when a group of leading citizens met in the Gem Bar on Royal Street to found the "Mystick Krewe of Comus," a carnival society patterned after the Cowbellians of Mobile, Alabama. Their purpose, to provide a parade and a masked ball featuring a tableau, was copied by other "krewes", notably Rex, and a more organized and less dangerous Mardi Gras assumed the form it still has today.

Carnival season begins on Epiphany, with the ball of the Krewe of Twelfth Night Revelers, and other krewes' masked balls continue on for a month or so, the expense of attending these events often drives New Orleaneans cheerfully mad, if they are fortunate to be invited to more than a few. Most of these are society affairs, and it's very difficult to scare up an invitation unless you know someone; only the krewe of Bacchus' ball, an extravaganza held at the Rivergate exhibition hall, is open to the public. The last two weeks before the fatal Tuesday the season heats up, as each krewe's parade passes down St. Charles Avenue and Canal Street, with as many as twenty-five elaborate and expensive floats, each illustrating some part of the parade's theme. The climax, Mardi Gras Day itself, is opened by the "walking clubs," mostly from Uptown neighborhoods, stopping at as many bars as they can before converging on St. Charles Avenue ahead of the grand Rex parade. This krewe's leader is the King of Carnival, usually a prominent businessman, and the parade behind him includes the "fatted calf" and members dressed as butchers. Countless informal carnival societies have their own floats following Rex; as in all the parades, there are "throws" for the crowd, all sorts of trinkets, gaudy plastic jewelry and aluminium "doubloons," a recent addition. Most krewes mint them each year, and some New Orleaneans collect then for a hobby. Meanwhile, somewhere in the city the black krewe of Zulu is parading, led by a King and a "Big Shot of Africa," tossing not doubloons but gilded coconuts. At night comes the final parade, that of Comus, illuminated by torch-carrying "flambeaux". While Rex and Comus hold their balls in the Municipal Auditorium, the streets of the French Quarter are packed with revelers, lasting all through the night. By morning,however, calm reigns, and the streetcleaners are busy effacing every trace of the celebrations. While everyone is sleeping it off, Carnival ends and Lent begins, definitively.

There are enough interesting sidelights about Mardi Gras to fill a book, endless charming details of tradition and protocol; anecdotes, such as the story of how "If Ever I Cease to Love" became the Mardi Gras song, a story involving a certain Grand Duke Alexis of Russia and an American opera singer; side shows like the clubs of black "Indians" and the he-she costume contests. Though much remains the same, each year's Mardi Gras is unique, with different parade themes, a few thousand costumes no one had thought of before and perhaps some new twist that will become a tradition in years to come. Guides and schedules are available everywhere for Mardi Gras, but really you're on your own, to have a good time at the biggest and best party in all the U.S.A.

The **Vieux Carré,** or **French Quarter,** looks bigger than it really is—only seven blocks by twelve. The long, straight streets and low buildings trick the eye. Bourbon Street is here, along with the French Market, the famous restaurants and historic buildings. Tourists poke their noses everywhere, but the Vieux Carré is neither a museum nor an amusement park—if indeed a little, at least, of both; New Orleaneans of every sort still live here, and there are churches and grocery stores in equal number to the bars and hotels. Most of the old Creoles are long gone; migrated out to Gentilly and beyond. After the turn of the century, the section was

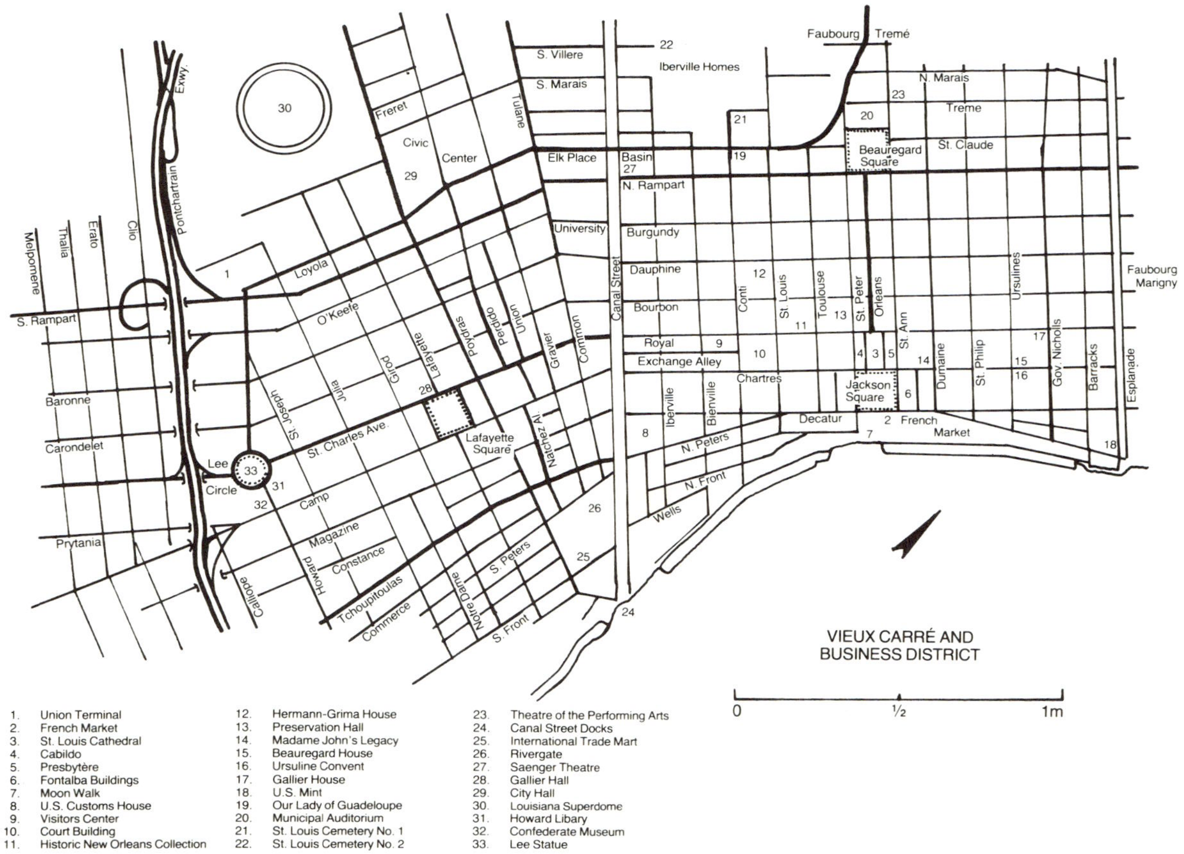
VIEUX CARRÉ AND
BUSINESS DISTRICT
0
½
1m
1. Union Terminal
2. French Market
3. St. Louis Cathedral
4. Cabildo
5. Presbytère
6. Fontalba Buildings
7. Moon Walk
8. U.S. Customs House
9. Visitors Center
10. Court Building
11. Historic New Orleans Collection
12. Hermann-Grima House
13. Preservation Hall
14. Madame John's Legacy
15. Beauregard House
16. Ursuline Convent
17. Gallier House
18. U.S. Mint
19. Our Lady of Guadeloupe
20. Municipal Auditorium
21. St. Louis Cemetery No. 1
22. St. Louis Cemetery No. 2
23. Theatre of the Performing Arts
24. Canal Street Docks
25. International Trade Mart
26. Rivergate
27. Saenger Theatre
28. Gallier Hall
29. City Hall
30. Louisiana Superdome
31. Howard Libary
32. Confederate Museum
33. Lee Statue
Faubourg Tremé
Faubourg Marigny
Iberville Homes
S. Villere
S. Marais
N. Marais
Treme
St. Claude
Beauregard Square
Elk Place
Basin
N. Rampart
University
Burgundy
Dauphine
Bourbon
Royal
Exchange Alley
Chartres
Decatur
N. Peters
N. Front
Wells
Canal Street
Iberville
Bienville
Conti
St. Louis
Toulouse
St. Peter
Orleans
St. Ann
Jackson Square
French Market
Dumaine
St. Philip
Ursulines
Gov. Nicholls
Barracks
Esplanade
Tulane
Freret
Civic Center
Loyola
O'Keefe
S. Rampart
Pontchartrain Exwy.
Melpomene
Thalia
Erato
Clio
Baronne
Carondelet
Prytania
St. Joseph
Julia
Girod
Lafayette
Poydras
Perdido
Union
Gravier
Common
Natchez Al.
Lafayette Square
St. Charles Ave.
Lee Circle
Camp
Magazine
Constance
Howard
Calliope
Tchoupitoulas
Commerce
Notre Dame
S. Peters
S. Front

predominantly Italian, and like that other Italian neighborhood in New York—Greenwich Village—it began to attract writers and artists, who wandered into town from the Southern hinterlands. Faulkner, for one, lived on Pirate's Alley in the 1920's, and Walker Percy wrote a manifesto urging his fellows throughout the South to live and work together in the Quarter. A rediscovery of the old center, and some new money, wasn't long to follow; restoration on a large scale began in the 40's, and continues today.

Jackson Square: You will probably begin your circumnavigation of the French Quarter with cafe au lait and those rectilinear Creole doughnuts—*beignets*—at the Cafe Du Monde, (open 24 hrs.) looking out over the beautiful square the French called Place D'Armes. Most visitors do; they're easy to pick out, brushing heaps of powdered sugar from the beignets off their clothes as they go. Before you lies America's finest square, a part of de Pauger's original plan whose borders were lovingly cultivated by two generations of a single family to grow five exquisite buildings, in a perfectly symmetrical arrangement that would warm any French heart. The square itself, laid out as a lush garden with broad pedestrian streets on three sides, has as its centerpiece the equestrian statue of Andrew Jackson by Clark Mills. The inscription: "The Union must and shall be preserved," was added by Old Silver Spoons, head of the Union occupation forces General Ben Butler, in 1862. It's a paraphrase of Jackson himself, at the famous "Battle of the Toasts" with John C. Calhoun. The streets on the edges of the garden provide a permanent carnival for residents and tourists alike. Artists hang their works on every foot of the garden's iron fence; some are quite good, some awful and some will do your portrait in twenty minutes. Musicians are always present—medieval troubadours, leftover hippie guitarists, classical guitarists, woodwind trios, the ineffable glass harmonica man, or whoever else is in town at the moment, not to mention balloon and hot dog vendors.

There has been a church on the site of **St. Louis Cathedral** ever since the founding of New Orleans. The first was swept away in the hurricane of 1723, and the second burned, setting the stage for Don Almonester y Roxas to make his grand act of philanthropy, contributing the funds not only for the cathedral you see today, but also for the Presbytere and the Cabildo flanking it. In return for his generosity, Don Almonester received the title of Perpetual Commissioner and Royal Ensign of the Illustrous Cabildo (which sounds like a position expressly designed for civic benefactors), and also had arrangements made for masses to be said in perpetuity for his undoubtedly worthy soul. The facade was entirely rebuilt in the 1840's, when the ward of the Cathedral decided that the gracefully proportioned bastard-architecture of the Spanish original wouldn't do; they replaced it with equally graceful French bastard-architecture—half Romanesque, half Baroque, with three tall steeples, the memorable silhouette of today's Vieux Carré skyline, replacing three low cupolas. Inside, ceiling paintings commemorate past bishops, and among the stained glass windows are several presented by the Spanish government in 1962. Volunteer guides give tours of the cathedral, with donations requested. Alleys on both sides of the cathedral connect Jackson Square with Royal Street, passing the **Cathedral Garden** in back. **Pirate's Alley,** which apparently never knew Jean Lafitte or any other pirate and **Antoine Alley** are both as picturesque as anything in the city.

The **Cabildo,** known then as the Casa Capitular, was completed in 1795, a year after the dedication of the cathedral, as the seat of government for both city and colony. Eight years later, however, the building witnessed the formal transmission of authority first from Spain to France, and then from France to the U.S. only twenty days later. The Americans chiseled the arms of Spain from the pediment and put up their own eagle and shield, decorated with emblems, banners and cannonballs. The Cabildo's twin opposite the cathedral, the **Presbytère,** was also designed by the Spanish architect Don Gilberto Guilleman; both had their Mansard roofs added in the 1840's. This Presbytère never fulfilled its original purpose, but served as a courthouse until recent years; now both buildings are part of the **Louisiana State Museum** (Tues-Sun, 9-5, separate admission for both). In the Cabildo exhibits detail the colonial history of Louisiana and the Mississippi River, with relics, documents, portraits, ship models, a two-hundred-year old pirogue, a reconstruction of the earliest French colonial council room and even Napoleon's death mask (one of a dozen, at least!). The Presbytère offers temporary exhibits of the decorative arts and other subjects and a permanent collection of costumes, toys, Mardi Gras and a section devoted to New Orleans' own lovely contribution to Art Nouveau; glass pottery of the "Newcomb Style"; perhaps the most interesting object sits under the arcade by the entrance—it's the world's oldest submarine, the *Pioneer,* pride of the Confederate Navy in 1861. Unfortunately, with the northern capture of New Orleans imminent, she had to be scuttled before she ever saw action; it was probably just as well, though, for her successor, the *Hunley,* drowned three crews before ever reaching the open sea.

The ambitious Louisiana State Museum has grand plans for expansion. Besides owning the old U.S. Mint and "Madame John's Legacy" (see below), it has acquired three buildings behind the Cabildo with plans for restoring them. **The Arsenal,** on St. Peter St. (1839), intended as a military museum, **Jackson House** and **Creole House,** both on Cabildo Alley, and both constructed in 1842.

Micaela Leonarda Antonia Almonester y Roxas y Broutin, daughter of the first great benefactor, is one of the grand ladies of New Orleans history. Disdaining the suits of nearly every well-heeled bachelor in town, she went to France and became the Baroness de Pontalba, in a convoluted love story that included getting her shot, almost fatally, by her father-in-law. The 1848 Revolution sent her home again to New Orleans, where she began to play an active role in the city's quiet Creole-American civil war. In particular, she turned her attention to Jackson Square, then a dusty parade ground; her wealth paved and landscaped it and helped pay for Jackson's statue. And to counter the drift of business and fashion away from the Vieux Carré, she hired architect James Gallier to design the **Pontalba Buildings** (1850), two matching jewels, to cover the uptown and downtown sides of the square. New Orleans likes to call these America's first apartment blocks; they are really glorified row houses in brick with the necessary cast iron balconies (note the Baroness' initials in script) running their length, a Creole adaptation of the residential terraces popular in London and New York. Although the Upper Pontalba now belongs to the city and the Lower to the state, both continue their original functions: shops below and apartments with the longest waiting lists in town above. The State Museum has restored one of the Lower Pontalba's apartments to its original splendor—the **1850 House** (no. 529 on the St. Anne Street side, open daily except Mon 9-5, adm.). In the same building, at no. 527, the National Park Service people (looking very out of place in their woodsy green uniforms) will be glad to tell you about the embryonic **Jean Lafitte National Historical Park.** The government is still acquiring sites for this one and in the meantime they operate this Visitor's Center, with a gallery of historical exhibits, and offer walking tours through the Vieux Carré (daily 9-5, free).

On the side of the square facing the river, we are back at the Café du Monde and the **French Market,** of which the café is one of the oldest tenants. Fruits and vegetables, these days, have been exiled to the back sheds on North Peters St. (where the city's very popular flea market also occurs on weekends). The original main buildings have been gussied up for trendy shops and restaurants, an ice cream parlor and a candy factory. Like everything else on Jackson Square except the cathedral, the French Market was restored in the 30's by the WPA. The Mississippi flows only a few yards away from here, though you can't see it. In another of that river's persistent oddities, here its level is actually higher than the ground on both sides; the silt it carries builds up natural levées on the banks, and the government has piled them higher to prevent Jackson from drowning and to keep Illinois topsoil out of the café au lait during the spring floods. From Jackson Square, a stairway over the levée leads to the **Moon Walk,** a riverfront promenade named after former mayor Moon Landrieu, who built it. From here you can look across to Algiers and watch the freighters and tankers from all over the world churn up to America's second port.

Upriver from Jackson Square on Decatur Street, you pass immediately the monumental, abandoned pile of thc old Jax brewery and Wilkinson Court, an old commercial alley now undergoing restoration. Further south, Decatur runs into the Greek quarter of the French quarter, replete with restaurants, import shops and bouzouki music spilling into the street. When the **U.S. Customs House** was begun in 1846, the docks and the river were right behind it, where S. Peter Street runs now; since then, it has receded about four blocks. This Egyptian revival extravaganza was not completed until the 1880's; now undergoing restoration, its glass and marble business hall is one of the finest rooms in New Orleans. The Civil War, of course, retarded the building's completion. Even before hostilities began the man in charge of the work—later Confederate General Pierre Beauregard—had left to take his post at Charleston where he was fated to fire the opening shot of the war at Fort Sumter.

As many French survivals as there are in the Vieux Carré, **Chartres Street** isn't one of them. It's pronounced "charters" now (similarly, sound a grating long "i" in I-berville and Cont-I). Two old buildings on Chartres carry the name **Napoleon House.** The first, at no. 500, owns a somewhat discredited legend that Mayor Girod, who lived here, planned to put the old emperor up in his own house after his fellow conspirators sprung him from St. Helena. This one is now a bar and the other, at no.

514, has an origin even cloudier. For decades New Orleaneans knew it better as the Pharacie Dufilho, and now the city and Tulane University have recreated this old-fashioned drugstore as the **Historical Pharmaceutical Museum** (Tues-Sun 10-5, adm.). A block away at no. 440, **Maspero's Exchange** (1788) is probably the oldest building in this part of the Vieux Carré, begun right after the great fire of that year. Maspero ran it as a coffee house for the shippers and businessmen, but it gained its fame in 1814. With the British sighted in the Gulf, the citizens founded their Committee for Public Safety here and used it as headquarters for organizing the defense. When Jackson arrived he found New Orleans disciplined and ready. Maspero's too, like so many of the city's historic sites, now houses a bar; that's one of the things that makes sightseeing in the French Quarter so agreeable.

Around the corner at 615 Toulouse, the **Toulouse Street Theatre** will be presenting a concert or play. New Orleans has a good reputation for theatre; the productions here are one reason, and another is a block away at 616 St. Peter: **Le Petit Theatre du Vieux Carré,** a repertory group that has been around since 1922.

Royal Street, throughout the city's history, has been the elegant main stem of Creoledom, lined with mansions and commercial buildings that strive to look like mansions. The city has it closed to traffic most of the day, so that window shoppers may stroll peacefully past the antique shops, bijouteries, and other exclusive establishments.

Before the Americans came in force and vacuumed all the money in town across Canal Street into the new business district, the bankers' corner in New Orleans was at Royal and Conti. At 403 Royal, the delicate script "LSB" on the iron railings belonged to the Louisiana State Bank, in this building designed for them by Benjamin Latrobe. No. 343 across the street was the city branch of the Bank of the United States, which Andrew Jackson, in his presidency, was to squash as thoroughly as he did the British at Chalmette. On the third corner, at no. 334, the 1826 Bank of Louisiana has now become the **Visitor's Center** for both the city and state tourist agencies, the necessary first stop for every visitor in New Orleans. Somehow, in a rare lapse of judgement, the city allowed the destruction of one entire fine block of Royal Street for the 1909 **New Orleans Court Building.** Such an injudicious decision could never go unpunished in New Orleans, and now the judges have been squeezed upstairs and forced to share their building with the numberless squadrons of stuffed birds in the **Louisiana Wildlife Museum,** along with turtles, fish and snakes that now slither where once lawyers did. It may be the only chance you'll ever have to see a passenger pigeon (open Mon-Fri 8:30-3:45, free).

417 Royal, a mansion of the early 1800's, now is Brennan's famous restaurant, where crowds line up for breakfast every morning. Don Jose Faurie, who built it, was the grandfather of painter Edgar Degas, but the house is better known as the home of Paul Morphy, the child prodigy who became America's first international chess champion at the age of 21. Morphy—originally O'Murphy—was the name of an Irish-Spanish family that had already distinguished itself in the city's public life. Judge Morphy's son Paul, born in 1837, achieved celebrity in America and Europe with such stunts as defeating eight grandmasters simultaneously

while blindfolded, and winning three games behind his back while performing a piano recital in a crowded concert hall. Burned out at an early age, though apparently happy, Morphy botched his career as a lawyer largely through indifference, and died in 1884 from taking a cold bath on a hot day. At 534 Royal, the 1792 Merieult House, one of the two survivors of the fire of 1974, now houses the **Historic New Orleans Collection** with both a permanent collection and temporary exhibitions of paintings, prints and maps, antiques, and memorabilia from the city's past (open Tues-Sun 10-5, free). Behind its courtyard, another house is tucked away, the 1888 **Williams Residence,** decorated to that period and open to visitors (same hours, admission). Across the street, the 1816 **Maison Seignouret,** now the studios of a television station, has one of the city's loveliest courtyards, the "Brulatour Court." New Orleans likes to joke that the **Maison le Monnier,** Royal at St. Peter, was "the city's first skyscraper," all of four storeys tall.

Bourbon Street. Every city should have one, but only New Orleans does. This celebrated address of bars, jazz clubs and girlie shows bears no resemblance to the seedy strips of any other American town. One hates to use such a word for a place synonymous throughout the world with every kind of jolly naughtiness, but Bourbon Street, the mecca of the tourist and conventioneer, is as wholesome a place to get tanked-up as you'll find. That doesn't mean it is ever dull. Like Royal Street, Bourbon banishes automobiles all day except for the rush hours, for the protection of the shambling merrymakers, and also to keep the cars from drowning out the jazz that pours forth from places like the Maison Bourbon and the Famous Door. As you do your own shambling down Bourbon Street, you'll have your senses assaulted in another way too; some of the strip joints employ gentlemen whose job it is to open the door and give a peek to likely customers passing by.

Just as the Vieux Carré has two Napoleon Houses, there are also two **Old Absinthe Houses.** In the 1806 original, at 238 Bourbon, Andrew Jackson and Jean Lafitte supposedly planned the embarrassment of the British while lingering over the age's intoxicant of choice. They probably didn't, but you may search for Lafitte's business card, if you wish, among the thousands that visitors have pinned to the walls. Wormwood, which has the twin virtues of being addictive and dissolving your brain cells, is illegal in the United States, and even in New Orleans, so you will find it neither here nor in the other Old Absinthe House at 400 Bourbon, which earned its name by snapping up the ancient bar fixtures of the other when Prohibition struck. The absinthe dripper is now only a relic, and the secret of the last century's decadent poets is lost to us forever.

At St. Louis Street, where the activity along Bourbon begins to get intense, you may take time out to visit two historic houses on the side streets. 820 St. Louis is the **Hermann-Grima House** (1831), probably the only Georgian-style aberration in the French Quarter—a Philadelphia house with a Creole balcony, restored with period furnishings (Mon-Sat, except Wednesday, 10-3:30, Sun, 1-4:30, adm.). **Casa Hove,** at 723 Toulouse, may be as old as 1740; today it is a perfume shop downstairs, and furnished with antiques upstairs (Mon-Sat 10-4:30, adm.).

If, for you, looking at antiques would only be a waste of a good drink, try the **Voodoo Museum,** at 739 Bourbon, for a historical excursion into New Orleans' own particular twilight zone. There are resident palmists and tarot readers, also a resident boa constrictor, and a gift shop with "a wide assortment of specialized gris-gris" (daily 10 am-midnight, adm.). Where St. Peter Street crosses Bourbon is America's Jazz Corner, as your ears will inform you, and fittingly, just around the corner stands **Preservation Hall,** 726 St. Peter (shows nightly at 8 pm). The musicians, some of whom probably remember Storyville, are as well preserved as the jazz. They make a little money off requests; on the wall behind them a dusty old sign declares one dollar for traditional tunes (that might be Royal Garden Blues or South Rampart Street Parade), two for others and five for "When the Saints Go Marching In." They must be damnably tired of it. Dusty and old describes the Preservation Hall itself. You may not get a seat, but the floor is considerably more comfortable anyhow. The music never disappoints—you may even get to see the legendary Sweet Emma—and the audiences are a treat to observe in themselves.

West of Bourbon, where most tourists never penetrate, the more determinedly residential parts of the quarter stretch along **Burgundy** and **Dauphine Streets,** where a few old mansions rub shoulders with less pretentious and more numerous old apartments, Louisiana "shotgun" houses, garages and neighborhood shops. **Buster Holmes' Restaurant** is here, at 721 Burgundy, the citadel of red beans and rice where the locals hang out.

Downriver from Jackson Square. Like the blocks west of Bourbon Street, those north of Orleans are the quieter parts of the Vieux Carré being furthest from Canal Street. Because the conflagrations of the 18th century never reached this far, some of the city's oldest homes can be found here.

The downtown side of **Decatur Street,** alongside the French Market, is seeing as much change as the uptown; no longer a drab waterfront district, now it spawns bright shops, restaurants and toy stores while new residents reclaim buildings that had declined into garages or warehouses. At this end of the quarter, **Royal Street** is still the main stem. From the corner of Dumaine you can observe the fanciest and simplest extremes of Creole architecture: the **Miltenberger Houses,** at 900-10 Royal, three storeys of cast iron confection built for one of the city's leading families in 1838, and at 632 Dumaine, the house that has acquired the name **"Madame John's Legacy"** since George Washington Cable called it that as the setting for his story "Tite Poulette." It is simple because it was one of the first. All or part of it may date back to 1726, making it the oldest structure in the Mississippi Valley; local historians like to argue about it. Madame John may be fictional, but her house has belonged at different times to both a ship's captain and a pirate—among a score of others in the old records. The Louisiana State Museum has it fixed up with bright green shutters, and they use it as an annex to the Presbytère to display the decorative arts of colonial Louisiana (Tues-Sun 9-5, adm.). Further down Royal, where some of the older Creole houses have been replaced by Americanized cottages with front yards, and where some excellent bookstores can be found, one plain structure at no. 915 is ornamented by the Vieux Carré's favorite cast iron bagatelle, the **"Cornstalk Fence."** Made in

Philadelphia in the grand days of the 1830's, there's only one other like it, on Prytania Street in the Garden District.

By the time Bourbon Street reaches this far, the strip is already slowing down a bit. **Lafitte's Blacksmith Shop,** at St. Peter Street, anchors its downtown end; there is little documentary evidence one way or the other, but New Orleaneans have always kept alive the story that the honorable brothers Lafitte set up shop here as a front—the French probably had a more elegant word for it—for liquidating their piratical profits. Built in 1772, it has been altered little since and naturally it's now a bar. Back towards the river, at 1113 Chartres, you may pay your respects to the memory of three famous New Orleaneans at one blow at the 1826 Greek Revival **Beauregard House.** Paul Morphy was born here, General Pierre spent time here as a lodger when he was down and out after the Civil War and novelist Frances Parkinson Keyes moved in for the winters starting in 1944; she financed the restoration of both the house and its formal garden and since her death both have been opened to the public (Mon-Sat, guided tours—by volunteers in period costume—on the hour from 10-4, adm. $2.50). Across the street, another claimant for the oldest building title is the lovely 1745 **Ursuline Convent.** The good sisters no longer abide here, but the Diocese has gone to great expense to restore both the convent and the adjacent **Our Lady of Victory Church,** built in 1846 (tours of both on Fridays at 1, 2 and 3 pm, adm. $2.50).

Sons of two famous architects proved their worth in this end of the quarter. Henry Latrobe, whose father Benjamin designed much of the U.S. Capital and several buildings in New Orleans before succumbing to the Louisiana mosquito, gets credit for introducing the Greek Revival to this city with his 1814 **Thierry House,** at 721 Governor Nicholls Street, which he built at the age of nineteen. James Gallier, probably the best known local architect, gave us the exquisite Pontalba Buildings and James Gallier Jr., among his many works around New Orleans, built himself a fine house at 1132 Royal. As beautifully restored and sumptuously furnished as the **Gallier House** its real attraction is the exposition of the craft work in iron, wood and plaster that made such a house possible; there are short films on these subjects, a small museum and even complimentary coffee and dessert at the end of the tour (guided tours Mon-Sat 10-3:45, adm.). Two doors down, at the corner of Governor Nicholls St., the cruelty of a woman, and one of the leading high society figures at that, gave the Vieux Carré what is very surprisingly its only certified haunted house. Madame Delphine La Laurie was apparently even fonder of torturing her slaves than attending parties. When a small fire occurred in her house, in 1834, she was found out, and soon after made a dramatic midnight exit whilst a mob of outraged citizens tore her doors down. All this has become an elaborate legend, but Delphine's descendants insist the poor girl was framed, and it isn't really clear who is doing the haunting, Delphine or the slaves.

Esplanade Street, or just the Esplanade, the downriver limit of the quarter, was once the most desirable address on the Creole side of town. It is nothing at all like Canal Street; its mansions of the 1830's have resisted the encroachments of commerce (there are a few restaurants though) and its neutral ground is crowded with all the big old trees the rest of the Vieux Carré doesn't have. There's something to see at either end and a pleasant walk between. On the river, Esplanade at Decatur, the Louisiana State Museum is busy restoring the imposing 1835 **U.S. Mint.** Nothing has been minted here since 1909 and coins stamped with "O" for New Orleans are rare indeed. For the brief period when the city was in the hands of the Confederacy, all the rebel change and blueback notes were issued here. When the state is finished, in 1982 or 83, the Mint will contain yet more Louisiana history and art, including the presently homeless **Jazz Museum,** and the **Mardi Gras Museum.** Up at the western end of Esplanade, really around the corner at 1218 Burgundy, there's the **Cabrini Doll Museum,** in a children's art center operated by the city (Mon-Fri 1:30-6, Sat 9:30-5, free).

Rampart Street, the western limit of the Vieux Carré, took its name from the Spanish fortifications. Until recently, as demolition and renewal projects took their toll, this was New Orleans teeming black Broadway and a major commercial thoroughfare. At Conti Street, **Our Lady of Guadeloupe** was built in 1826 as a mortuary chapel—to keep malaria and yellow fever out of the Cathedral. It's the policemen's and firemen's chapel now, but best known in local folklore for the two saints' shrines next to the altar. When the local faithful need help with an impossible problem, they ask St. Jude; his companion also has his share of devotees. St. Expedite? The story is that the statue came in a crate marked EXPEDITE, and stranger still, that story appears to be true. He does have a reputation for responding to all supplicants expeditiously. Four blocks west, the quiet and somewhat neglected **Beauregard Square** now serves mainly as a welcome mat for the ponderous **Municipal Auditorium,** the site of most Mardi Gras balls. It isn't the 19th century work it appears to be—the WPA did it in the 1930's.

Until this patch of ground found a hometown Confederate general to be renamed for, it was known as Congo Square—Champs Congo—a spot of magical associations for the history of black America, the place where the transmission of African culture into the country was most evident and best chronicled. In the early 19th century, Congo Square lay just outside town, and on Sundays, slaves from the surrounding plantations would gather to make music, dance and re-enact the religious rituals of their homelands, each tribe or nation in its own corner of the square. Only the slaves of the Creoles would be present, as they were in similar Sunday gatherings throughout the French and Spanish West Indies; none of the Americans would permit their chattels to indulge in such heathen business. Until the 1840's, when they were suppressed, the dances were becoming gradually more social, less elemental—the voodoo rituals and snake-worshiping ceased, as did the tribal divisions, and equally wild and enthusiastic dances were performed to popular airs with African rhythms and words in Creole French. Congo Square was a rather well-known cultural phenomenon; the New York Tribune music critic, H. E. Krehbeil, came down to transcribe many of the tunes and the New Orleans Creole composer Gottschalk incorporated them in his music. George Washington Cable, who found the whole thing un-Christian and repugnant, was nevertheless fascinated enough to write extensively about the frenzied, half-naked blacks with their homemade string and reed instruments, their dances—the Counjaille, the Calinda and the Congo, "to describe which would not be pleasant". The scene, filtered through

Cable's Puritan sensibilities, is hard to picture, but it would help to consider that jazz was born just a few decades later and a few blocks away.

The end of a long-ago canal gave **Basin Street** its name; its immortality came at the turn of the century, courtesy of a well-intentioned city alderman named Sidney Story. The question of how to manage its courtesans, and where to put them, had troubled New Orleans for years. Mr. Story made the issue his own and after an examination of red-light districts in European cities—just how he did this is unclear—his proposal for a restricted good-time district seemed the perfect solution. Perfect, that is, except for Story. The new district grew up almost overnight and right from the start, everybody called it Storyville. Basin Street—"that's the street where the light and dark folks meet," according to the old jazz number—was its grand boulevard, where veritable palaces, sumptuously appointed with stained glass, gilt and marble in rooms decorated to various exotic themes, appeared for the pleasure of the city's elite, created by a long list of colorful madams—like the one who had a music box in her mattress—with endless lines of credit from their Business District clientele. On the back streets, more modest brothels and saloons served the less opulent and on the alleys behind these, vice showed no allure but considerable degradation, in dim shacks where customers were more likely to be rolled than gratified. All this forty-block Babylon was presided over by a saloonkeeper and politician named Tom Anderson, the "Mayor of Storyville". For the edification of visiting salesmen and lodge brothers, the mayor published a directory called the Blue Book, covering all the major attractions in properly purple prose. (Like the Sears catalogues of the day, it's been reprinted for nostalgia's sake, and you might find one in a New Orleans bookstore.)

Of course there was a musical accompaniment. Storyville's prosperity created employment for hundreds of musicians and gave many aspirants the wherewithal to buy a cornet, clarinet, banjo or saxophone, for which they proceeded to invent new tricks, while unknown geniuses added figures from ragtime, syncopation, improvisation, polyphony. The name for it may have derived from the Creole slang verb *jaser,* to gab or chatter, or some etymologically obscure sexual suggestion and jazz appeared so quickly and naturally that its long gestation was temporarily forgotten. Now, however, the musicologists have traced such a tune as the Tiger Rag to an old French quadrille, hiding in the back rooms of New Orleans all that time. Most, though not all, of these musicians were black; in New Orleans, neither that nor their accustomed surroundings in Storyville kept their music from overflowing the district into the more genteel quarters. Everyone heard jazz from the black funeral processions. Opera patrons, after performances, found teenage bands with improvised instruments serenading them for coins from the steps. The city's sophisticates even began to import jazz for their private parties. Even so, Storyville was the place where the true art was evolving.

Even in New Orleans, a place like Storyville couldn't have lasted too long. Its demise came, however, from an outside force—the U.S. Navy. If New Orleans was not degenerating into an age of intolerant prudery, the rest of the nation was and with the righteous Wilson leading America into a clean, wholesome war, the government decided it didn't want its innocent sailor boys exposed to something they wouldn't even see in

France. Somehow, in 1917, they managed to get Storyville shut down. The district died even more quickly than it first appeared, in a kind of painted Götterdämmerung of melodramatic despair, memorable last binges, arson and mass liquidations of ornate furniture and gilt-framed Bouguereaus. The musicians, carrying with them Storyville's imperishable legacy, bolted for Chicago, Kansas City or even New York, where their talents were already much in demand. Within ten years, the area around Basin Street declined into the city's worst slum and in the late 30's, for one of the New Deal's first and biggest housing projects, the city tore every bit of it down. The enormous Iberville Homes complex that replaced it remains today, in better shape than most of its counterparts across the country. The architects built it with front stoops and balconies, so that New Orleans people would feel at home.

About the only thing left, on the widened, asphalt Basin Street of today that deals death to all but the most nimble pedestrians, is another city-within-a-city, older and more enduring than Storyville: a city of the dead. The **St. Louis Cemetery No. 1,** which you may have seen in the movie *Easy Rider,* is a major element in the legendary, fantastical side of New Orleans. It should be evident why people cannot be buried in this city, five feet below sea level. The water table is just below the surface; the coffins might not sink even if holes were drilled in them and they would have a habit of working their way back up to the surface. Consequently, New Orleaneans are deposited in tombs or crypts above ground, made of brick covered with plaster and set in rows, presenting the curious picture of some ancient Greek city done in miniature. There is even a kind of acropolis, in the lofty marble sepulchres of the mutual burial societies, Italian, Portuguese and French among them. Here and in the family vaults, bodies are not embalmed; when new tenants arrive, the old bones are pushed to the floor to make room. Many of the city's poorer citizens have vaults built into the walls called "ovens" from their shape.

Among famous New Orleaneans buried here are the two wives of Governor Claiborne. The governor, always a man of few words, gave them both the same inscription. Two tombs are credited with the remains of the celebrated voodoo queen Marie Laveau. True believers and dilettantes alike visit them for favors; besides the strange offerings—paper and plastic flower constructions and small change in multiples of two or eleven cents, both tombs are covered with x-marks of brick dust; each one records a wish. This oldest surviving New Orleans cemetery, romantically dilapidated as it is, has become one of the city's attractions; there's an attendant on hand who knows every bone and sells a little booklet about the place published by the Diocese. St. Louis No. 2, much the same, lies across the projects on Iberville Street. We should mention that all this part of town north of Rampart is the old **Faubourg Treme.** It may seem to have more past than present and the city is demolishing most of what remains to construct **Louis Armstrong Park** next to Beauregard Square and the new **New Orleans Theatre of the Performing Arts.** Near the park, on St. Philip Street, you can see the opinion of the displaced black neighborhood on all this in one of the most arresting protest murals to be seen on any American wall, portraying the neighborhood's past and its destruction.

Canal Street. In the beginning, this was the city's "common," just outside the walls, but after 1803, with the coming of the Americans it became a kind of cultural border, crossed only on business; in fact, the median strips of New Orleans' boulevards are still called "neutral grounds" after the original here, dividing one of the city's broadest streets. A canal planned in the 1850's that was never built gave it its name, as well as its width. Such a location made Canal the city's shopping street at an early date and you can still see several ornate examples of 19th century commercial blocks among its shops, hotels and department stores (D. H. Holmes, Maison Blanche and Godcheaux).

At the foot of Canal Street, one way to see the city and its port is to take the free ferry ride across to the old neighborhood called Algiers; more luxurious tours are available on two steamboats, the *President* and the *Mark Twain.* New Orleans has made this strategic corner of town, in the angle of Canal and Poydras Streets, its major redevelopment area, with new hotels and offices in what was once the busiest part of the docks. The cross-shaped tower with the spinning top is the **International Trade Mart,** a city landmark visible from all over. It's nothing but a bar revolving up there; two floors below, an Observation Deck offers the second-best view of New Orleans (daily 8-10 pm, adm., a separate admission for the outside glass-front elevator to the top, 407 feet above Canal Street). The **Louisiana Maritime Museum,** on the same floor, tells the story of the city's port and its long-ago love affair with the Mississippi steamboat with a small collection of ship models, maps, charts and other memorabilia. Behind the Mart, **Rivergate** is the name the city has given to its sprawling, ultra-modern exhibition hall with its slender columns and swirling, free-form roof. The Bacchus krewe throws its Mardi Gras ball here because it's big enough to get their floats inside. Since Rivergate was built in 1968, new developments have been planned for the entire area, and a number of glossy new hotels have gone up.

Further up Canal, older buildings reassert themselves over the brash newcomers, among the neon, flags and ornamental lights, the stores and the colorful crowds that make up this one of America's great downtown streets. Most of the uptown bus routes begin here, as well as the streetcar down St. Charles. At North Rampart the city has restored one of those magnificent movie palaces from the 1920's, the **Saenger Theater,** and they presently use it for touring Broadway shows and other prestige attractions.

The Central Business District. One of the striking contrasts in New Orleans, as you'll notice on your way from the Vieux Carré to the Garden District, is between the human scale and nonchalant beauty of those older parts of town and the desperate clumsiness of the really dismal quarter where the city conducts its business. In the South, only Atlanta has a larger collection of monolithic faceless skyscrapers and like Atlanta's they are surrounded by streets roaring with traffic, endless parking lots and little else. The buildings look as if they were designed by a computer and one actually was (the Latter Center on Common Street). Common and Gravier, the streets closest to Canal, are decent and interesting enough, with some comfortable old shops and restaurants, and relics of earlier commercial architecture, but beyond these the Business District isn't much fun for the sightseer on foot.

It wasn't always this way; back in the early 1800's the Americans were determined to make their city, growing up on streets laid out under the Spanish as the Faubourg Ste Marie, the equal of Creole New Orleans in every respect, and they lined St. Charles Avenue with such impressive structures as the famous St. Charles Hotel, a marble edifice with Corinthian columns that was probably the grandest establishment in the world in its day. Some reminders of this era remain around **Lafayette Square,** center of the American city. The new Federal Reserve Bank and other government buildings have appeared here in recent years, only to be upstaged by the oldest building on the square, **Gallier Hall** (1845), the masterpiece of architect James Gallier, Sr. and one of the finest Greek Revival buildings in the United States. Once the City Hall, this is now the home of the Recreation Department and some of the city's cultural organizations. Note the sculptural group on the pediment, where Liberty, Justice and Commerce look like they are joyfully exchanging gossip while the American eagle listens in. The square itself, sadly, has become the Alsatia of the city's bums, who spend their nights under the indifferent gaze of statues of Henry Clay, Benjamin Franklin and John McDonough, a philanthropist of the last century, who gave away schools the way Andrew Carnegie did libraries—there are a dozen named for him here, and more in Baltimore. Recently a good deal of renovation has been done around here, on once-proud streets like Camp, Julia and Magazine; the Lafayette Square area seems to have a bright future.

One block away on Poydras Street, **One Shell Square** is the city's tallest skyscraper; distinguished only by its size, it looms over the nearby Vieux Carré like a threat. Perdido Street, if you haven't found it yet, starts here, and it will take you up to Loyola Avenue and the **Civic Center,** the monument of Mayor Chep Morrison and the progressive, everything up-to-date atmosphere of the 1950's. Among the squat, International-style government buildings is the **City Hall,** a sorry replacement for Gallier's original; they've tacked a big sign on it that says "City Hall" so people will know what it is. For decoration there's a floral clock, across from the new aluminium main library, and statues of Latin American heroes along Loyola. You can also find the **Union Terminal** here, and among the acres of train tracks behind it, Louisiana's astounding "Eighth Wonder of the World," the **Superdome.** Actually you can't miss it; the complex covers about the space of twenty-four Vieux Carré blocks and in the dome itself, the largest sports stadium in the South peers over the tops of buildings all over central New Orleans. It's an unsettling presence, gold in color with a shape suggesting a flattened nuclear power plant. At night, illuminated with a faint ruddy glow, it is pure science fiction. They are so proud of it in New Orleans that they offer tours (daily 9:30-3:30 except during events, adm. $3.00) to point out all the buildings superlatives—and any place with 8,000 tons of air conditioning could hardly be called anything else but the Superdome. To what end, you may ask, is this prodigy devoted? Well, New Orleans has a football team called the Saints that has been so consistently awful that its fans have renamed them the Aints, and they are given to attending the games with paper bags over their heads in shame. Occasionally the Super Bowl takes place in the Superdome, as well as other events big enough to afford the rent; Muhammad Ali won his last title bout here.

Back towards the river, Lee Circle is the uptown boundary of the Business District. Once this was the most fashionable corner of the city but now General Lee, standing with a grim look atop his tall column, has two gas stations staring him in the face. A few steps away at 601 Howard Street, is the city's only work of Louisiana native H. H. Richardson, and one of its greatest architectual treasures, the **Howard Library** (1887), preserving its ivy-covered academic demeanor despite transformation into lawyers' offices. Around the corner, the **Confederate Museum** has kept alive the sacred memory of Lee and his rebel cronies since 1891. Torn and bloody battle flags of the Lost Cause, uniforms, guns, portraits and battle scenes and all kinds of wartime artifacts fill this dim, medieval hall (929 Camp Street, open Mon-Sat 10-4, adm.).

Irish Channel. Because New Orleans offered both tolerance and opportunity immigrants from Europe made it one of their prime destinations in the boom years before the Civil War. Many of them, predominantly the Irish and Germans, settled in this district between St. Charles and the river, from Howard to Jackson Street. Often down but never out, this area is now undergoing a revival with the help of an influx of new residents—Cuban immigrants among them. The best kept parts are those closest to St. Charles; along Tchoupitaulas housing projects have replaced much of the decayed waterfront district, only to decay themselves.

Two pretty squares surrounded by some fine buildings are the neighborhood's focal points, **Coliseum Square,** Coliseum at Melpomene, with the 1855 Gothic Revival **Coliseum Square Baptist Church** its major decoration, and **Annunciation Square,** Annunciation at Race. In the Irish Channel, churches are the prominent landmarks, testaments of the immigrant's faith expressed in brick and stone with a lavishncss often beyond the parishioners' means. Some are outstanding buildings: **St. John the Baptist** (1869) at 1139 Dryades, **St. Alphonsus** (1855) at 2029 Constance Street at St. Andrea and **St. Mary's Assumption,** next door at 2030 Constance. Both of the latter are establishments of the Redemptionist order, founded by the Catholic Church to aid immigrants; they found it convenient to have separate houses for the Irish (St. Alphonsus) and the Germans. The third of their churches, for the French, once stood nearby.

Garden District. Local historians seem to disagree on the dates and details, but there is a consensus that what created the Garden District was something called the Disastrous Macarty Crevasse. The crevasse appeared, whatever Macarty had to do with it, in the Mississippi banks—remember that the river here is higher than the land around it—and resulted in the usual Louisiana dilemma of Old Muddy turning up somewhere he wasn't welcome. Somewhere was the plantation of the Family Livaudais, and it had the effect of making them give up the whole business and sell their property for building lots to those busy Americans, the first generation of whom had made their fortunes and were ready to put on the dog.

Again, competition with the devilishly cultured Creoles across Canal

Street was the force that made the Garden District what it is today. Not only had the Americans to build imposingly, but status required that they build well, and to do so they borrowed some of the basic features of the Louisiana plantation house, the balconies and decorative balustrades, added their own Greek Revival touches, and so created their answer to the palaces of Royal Street. The great difference was that following the American sense of what a home should be, they gave each one its own large lot, beautifully landscaped into a garden for every man—hence the name. The Americans had made their point, and even the Creoles did not begrudge them admiration. Some of them even moved in.

Few American cities can boast a neighborhood as perfectly formed; only in San Francisco, perhaps, is there a collection of houses that provides such a delight for the senses as these, with their lacy ironwork galleries half hidden under venerable oaks. The oldest of them are from the 1830's, when a steam railway along the path of today's St. Charles trolley made the Livaudais subdivision, then the independent city of Lafayette, easily accessible to the city. Most of the homes went up before the Civil War, and the Garden District has kept its cachet as New Orleans' most desirable residential area right up to the present day. Unlike the French Quarter, where most old homes have become restaurants or museums, these are still lived in, and if you want to tour one, you'll have to stop at the **Seebold House,** 2504 Prytania Street, currently owned by the Women's Opera Guild (Mon-Fri 1-4, adm.). Although the Garden District's boundaries are somewhat hazy—in the real estate ads, it can mean anything for miles around—the choicest parts are south of St. Charles between Jackson and Louisiana Avenues and any walking tour should include these highlights: on **St. Charles Avenue,** no. 2265, one of the many homes designed by James Gallier Jr., and no. 2901, **Christ Church Cathedral,** the 1880's Gothic successor to the oldest Protestant church in the city; on **Prytania Street,** whose name comes from a *prytanée,* or high school further downtown, no. 2340, the District's oldest house (1838), and across the street no. 2343, one of the last great mansions, the 1870 Beaux-Arts pile that is now the **McGehee School,** no. 2423, the Adam-Jones Home (1860), no.2507, the Brennan House (1852), and no. 2605, the only Gothic style cottage in the District (1849); **Magazine Street,** the neighborhood's commercial strip, full of antique shops, classy restaurants, and boutiques; on **Jackson Avenue,** the 1851 **Trinity Church;** on **First Street**—the street numbering survives from the city of Lafayette—no. 1134, the **Fenner House,** where Jefferson Davis spent much of his time in his enforced retirement; on **Third Street,** no. 1331, the **Musson-Bell House,** has some of the grandest ironwork to be seen in all New Orleans, and no. 1415, the Robinson-Jordan House, with its curved portico, one of the biggest District mansions.

Further Uptown, you can see through the streetcar window how much of the Garden District has carried over into younger neighborhoods. The homes are only slightly less impressive, and the trees even thicker along this lovely stretch of the tracks. If you have wondered how New Orleans got its nickname "Crescent City," look at the map; from Jackson Square upriver to the city line, the Mississippi describes a neat arc, and the street plan follows it. Lunar influences may indeed be especially strong here, but that is only coincidental. Whatever, the name has been around almost as long as the city, and New Orleans cops have been wearing their crescent moon-and-star badges since the 1830's. The crescent of streets, really a grid twisted in several places to stay even with the river, can be traced to the days when everything uptown was still in plantations. The long cross streets, Jackson, Louisiana, Napoleon, Jefferson, Audubon, that measure the arc like pairs of calipers, were all once plantation boundaries, giving each planter on his slice of land a river frontage from which to ship his crops.

After thirty or so more blocks of the city's prettiest neighborhoods, the streetcar will take you past **Audubon Park,** the city's second largest—a beautiful spot entirely at home in these surroundings. Laid out for a long-forgotten fair, the 1884 World's Industrial and Cotton Centennial Exhibition, the park has as its major attraction the small but excellent **Audubon Zoological Garden,** with an aquarium, "grasslands of the world," "world of primates" and a children's zoo in one of the lush green settings that come so easy to Southern Louisiana (Mon-Fri 9:30-4:30, weekends 9:30-5:30 in the summer, otherwise 9:30-4:30, adm. $2.50; the zoo is at the southern end of the park, off Magazine Street). Across St. Charles from the park entrance, two of the city's leading educational institutions stand side by side: **Loyola College,** a Jesuit school founded in 1911, and **Tulane University,** which began in 1847 as the University of Louisiana, but changed its name in 1883 when a benefactor named Paul Tulane made them an offer they couldn't refuse. Tulane is best known these days for its medical school, the Newcomb School of Art, its Law School (one of the few places where Louisiana's future barristers can learn the intricacies of the Napoleonic Code that is still the basis of state law) and for the **Sugar Bowl,** at Willow Street, site of the annual New Years Day football extravaganza and the playground of Tulane's Green Wave during the regular season. Next to Tulane, New Orleans' poshest residential street shows off to the world with a stone and iron gateway and a sentinel at his post; **Audubon Place** is like the private streets traditional in St. Louis, only fancier. Where St. Charles Avenue ends at the river, Carrolton Avenue begins, heading back towards Canal Street through the old suburban town of **Carrollton,** swallowed up by New Orleans a century ago.

Downriver New Orleans. The city will always have a place in her memory for Monsieur Bernard de Marigny, a charmingly dissolute young man who left his mark on New Orleans more by what he didn't do than by what he did; had it not been for Marigny, "downtown," in the sense of the Business District, could really be downtown, and we would all be spared considerable confusion. Marigny, whose father's estate made him one of the richest men in America, was renowned in New Orleans as the most fervent, and worst, craps shooter ever. To cover his losses, in the early 1800's he subdivided the family plantation, which happened to be choice land adjacent to the Vieux Carré across Esplanade Street, and gave his new avenues names like Rue D'Amour (now a continuation of N. Rampart), Rue Des Bons Enfants (St. Claude Avenue), Champs Elysees (now Elysian Fields, it runs all the way to Lake Pontchartrain) and of course, Rue Craps, which had to be changed to Dauphine—it had three churches on it. In the 1820's, the movers and shakers from the American side of town were trying to buy all this land for a major development, nothing less than a new center of town. Marigny, impoverished though nonetheless disdainful, stalled for years, and when he was finally cornered into signing, his wife, who had a share of the ownership, wouldn't. The disgruntled Americans took themselves back across Canal Street and built their Garden District and downtown—uptown; today the **Faubourg Marigny** has changed little since then, still a quiet residential appendage to the Vieux Carré.

Further downriver, modest neighborhoods are clustered around the busiest part of the Port of New Orleans, the **Navigation Canal** and the **Industrial Canal,** connecting the Mississippi with Lake Pontchartrain and the Intracoastal Waterway. A neighborhood landmark, at Egania and Douglas, is the Doullut Houses, the "steamboat houses" built by a riverboat captain and his son in 1905. With their fanciful galleries and rooftop pilothouses they do look like steamboats—but also a little like the Japanese pagoda the Doulluts saw at the St. Louis World's Fair the year before. Nearby, at 6400 St. Claude, President Jackson's administration built the stately **Jackson Barracks** not far from the spot where General Jackson first made a name for himself. Now administered by the Louisiana National Guard, they are a military museum (Tues-Sun 9-4, adm.). **Chalmette National Historic Park,** about a mile over the city line in St. Bernard Parish, is a green island of tranquillity between sugar refineries and oil refineries. Back in 1814 all this land was swamp through which the British, who hadn't yet really learned the lessons in comtemporary warfare offered by American and Indian irregulars over the last fifty years, came marching in slow even ranks towards the American lines. Andrew Jackson's motley band, composed of Tennessee and Kentucky sharpshooters, New Orleaneans—both American and Creole—pirates and Indians, fired once, then twice and the Battle of New Orleans was decided. The British lost 2,000 men, the Americans 13, but all died unnecessarily—the peace had been signed in Paris a few days before. The battlefield, monument and national cemetery are maintained by the National Park Service, and their Visitor's Center in an old plantation house on the site can start you on a tour of the battlegrounds (daily 8-5, until 6 in the summer, free).

Lakeside. You wouldn't guess that New Orleans is as big as it really is, but because the city limits are coterminous with Orleans Parish, the city can claim as its own miles of swamps and bayous, almost as far as the Mississippi state line, through places like Unknown Pass and Blind Bayou. Out here, just beyond the eastward march of new subdivisions, you can trade city life for an afternoon of nature trails, exploring the unique Louisiana environment as well as a small nature museum, at the **Louisiana Nature Center,** 11000 Lake Forest Boulevard (Tues-Fri 9-5, Sat & Sun 12-5, adm.).

Working back towards the city, you'll discover one of New Orleans' best-kept secrets hidden away on the city's back door: **Lakeshore Drive,** which starts at the Navigation Canal and follows the Pontchartrain shore westwards, passing beaches and beautifully landscaped parks on the edge of some of the city's newer neighborhoods. At Elysian Fields Avenue, where the **Mardi Gras Fountain** sends up plumes of water illuminated in the Mardi Gras colors of purple, gold, and green, the drive passes the campus of **Louisiana State University at New Orleans,** keeping strange company with the **Pontchartrain Beach Amusement Park** (open April to Labor Day, weekdays 5 pm-midnight, weekends noon-midnight). Further west, **Bayou St. John,** an important shipping route in the early days of the city connecting the Lake with the system of canals, now serves only to decorate the surrounding neighborhoods and provide an eastern border for New Orleans' largest park: **City Park.** Here, among 1,500 acres of lagoons and groves dotted with statuary, you'll find the **New Orleans Museum of Art,** formerly the Isaac Delgado Museum of Art after its founder and benefactor, who financed this fine Beaux-Arts Ionic building to house his collections in 1912. The museum, one of the few important ones in the South, has grown fast since then, and it can offer a large and comprehensive selection of the world's art, particularly strong in pre-Columbian, Pacific island, and African works, French painting, glass, and American, particularly Louisianan, artists. Edgar Degas, who visited New Orleans in 1873 to see his dozens of relatives here, is a special favorite and has a gallery all to himself (Tues, Wed and Fri-Sun 10-5, Thurs 1-9, closed Mondays, adm.). The stand of ancient oak trees near the museum entrance is older than the museum and the park itself; back when such settlements were still legal, this was the traditional spot for holding duels. To tour the rest of the park, you can rent a horse or a bicycle, or ride the miniature train around it.

Leaving City Park by the Esplanade Avenue entrance near the museum takes you into one of the oldest parts of the city, a settlement on Bayou St. John along **Moss Street** that has watched the city grow up around it since the 1790's; among the plantation-style houses, at that date still looking more West Indies than Louisiana, there's one you can visit, the **Pitot House,** 1440 Moss, restored by the Louisiana Landmarks Society with period furnishings (open Thursdays only, 11-4, adm.). Nearby, on Esplanade, there's the **St. Louis Cemetery No. 3,** and the city's old racetrack, the **Fairgrounds,** a place that, for New Orleanean touts, is steeped in history and sentiment in the way of Pimlico or Churchill Downs. Some of the most fondly remembered old thoroughbreds are buried in the infield.

If you should take that Canal Street bus ominously marked "Cemeteries" up to this part of town, you'll end up at the corner of City Park Avenue, where there are, indeed, cemeteries—seven of them, including one just for firemen. **Metairie Cemetery,** the biggest and most interesting, has the remains of many of the city's notables: a platoon of Confederate generals including the luckless J. B. Hood, and Josie Arlington, a madam of the good old days who was the Mayor of Storyville's special friend. Her tomb has a bronze figure of a girl knocking at the door, apparently in vain, and the New Orleaneans will tell you either that this represents Josie being turned away from her father's house after staying out too late, which event started her on her career, or a virgin, being refused employment at Josie's. Until recently, her tomb was bathed in the red glow of a traffic light nearby, which provided New Orleans with one of its best inside jokes. North of the cemeteries, the **West End** squeezes itself between City Park and the city limits up to the lake, where it meets the curious shorefront community of **Bucktown,** rows of tiny raised cabins packed tightly together that serve as a kind of summer home for New Orleaneans and a place to keep their boats. Fishing is the major activity here, and there are lots of seafood restaurants.

Jefferson Parish. New Orleans' suburbs, sad to say, are as shabby and oppressively monotonous as any other city's. The biggest, with over 136,000 people, is **Metairie,** just over the city line; the name comes from a French-Louisianian word for sharecropping. Metairie has its own entertainment district, a kind of simulated Bourbon Street for the polyester set called **Fat City,** tucked among the shopping malls and parking lots along the Veterans Memorial Highway. The next suburb west, **Kenner,** is home to the **New Orleans International Airport,** and another racetrack, **Jefferson Downs,** 44th Street at Lake Ponchartrain. And also, Jefferson Parish is the southern destination of the world's undisputedly longest and least necessary bridge: the **Lake Pontchartrain Causeway.** It was built in 1956, twenty-four miles of concrete pylons over the shallow lake that leads to very little on the other side. The Expressway Commission would point out that they have already broken even on the tolls, so it isn't that much of a white elephant, and it may be worth it for the eerie experience of driving your car for miles with no land in sight in either direction.

West Bank. They haven't yet built a bridge over to **Algiers;** there's still only the Canal Street ferry, and this has allowed the trans-Mississippi part of New Orleans, within sight of the Business District towers, to remain the sleepy small town it has been since the 1840's, with streets of prettily decorated shotgun houses and a bizarre 1890's courthouse on Morgan Street. Nobody knows just how the neighborhood got its exotic name; they speculate about the old Frenchman who owned the land remembering years of service against the Barbary pirates, or that the Spanish named it this because so many blacks lived there. The two incorporated suburbs of the West Bank have interesting names of their own: **Gretna** has nothing to do with Gretna Green in Scotland, but so many people in the last century thought it did that the mayor soon found himself doing a booming business in marriages. **Westwego** was an early suburb along the first railroad to be built on the West Bank. Its developers, who also happened to be the railroad men, said "West we go!" They did, and prospered.

Restaurants. Food is a subject that New Orleans takes quite seriously—as do its visitors. They flock to Louisiana to experience the nation's outstanding regional cuisine, and the city's restaurants seldom disappoint them. New Orleans Creole cooking—part French, part Cajun, and the rest improvised over the last two centuries—leans heavily on abundent local seafood. Shrimps, crabs and oysters appear in a number of dishes (Oysters Rockefeller was invented here), and also crawfish in a gumbo or étoufée—both thick stews served with rice. Pompano, a speciality here as elsewhere around the Gulf Coast, is one of the best tasting kinds of fish anywhere. Just as important as the main dish, however, are such treats as French bread, pralines (pecan candy), turtle soup, Cajun sausages like boudin and andouille, and coffee. This comes in any number of ways in

New Orleans; the usual strong brew favored here, sometimes flavored with chicory, or café au lait as in the French Market, or even flamed with liqueur and spices as café brulôt. Some staples of the average New Orleanean shouldn't be too hard to find, like the "po-boy" sandwich (which might have anything in it, even oysters) and red beans and rice.

Some of the famous Vieux Carré spots: Galatoire's***, 209 Bourbon St. (seafood specialties); Armand's***, 813 Bienville St.; Antoine's***, 713 St. Louis St. (open since 1840); Broussard's***, 819 Conti St.; Acme Oyster House*, 724 Iberville St.; Felix's*, 739 Iberville (seafood); Buster Holme's*, 721 Burgundy (a neighborhood bar; they keep it funky to discourage tourists, but it's famous anyhow for red beans and rice).

Also in the Vieux Carré and Business District: Andrew Jackson Restaurant***, 221 Royal St.; Court of Two Sisters***, 613 Royal; La Louisiane***, 725 Iberville; Bon Ton**, 401 Magazine; Asia Garden**, 530 Bourbon; Cafe S'bisa**, 1011 Decatur; Castillo's Mexican**, 620 Conti; Kolb's**, 125 St. Charles (German and Creole); Marti's**, 1041 Dumaine; Messina's Oyster House**, 200 Chartres; Ralph & Kacoo's Seafood**, 215 Bourbon; Gumbo Shop*, 630 St. Peter; K-Paul's Louisiana Kitchen*, 416 Chartres; Johnny's Po-Boy*, 511 St. Louis.

Elsewhere around town: Christian's***, 3835 Iberville (in a restored church); Commander's Palace***, Coliseum at Washington; Corinne Dunbar's***, 1617 St. Charles; Le Ruth's***, 636 Franklin in Gretna; Versailles***, 2100 St. Charles; Bruning's**, 1870 Orpheum; Pascal's Manale**, 1838 Napoleon; Petrossi's Seafood**, 901 Louisiana; Scalafani**, 1301 N. Causeway in Metairie; T. Pittari's**, 4200 S. Claiborne; Turci's**, 1017 Pleasant; College Inn*, 3016 S. Carrolton; Parasol's*, 2535 Constance St.

Southern Louisiana—The Acadian Triangle

Louisiana claims to have more marshland than the other forty-nine states combined—five million acres of it—and once you have traversed the state's southern regions it's hard to disagree. This half of the state is also the homeland of one of America's oldest and most distinctive cultural minorities, the Cajuns (a contraction of "Acadians") who began arriving in the 1760's. Today they endure and prosper in their Triangle, bounded by New Orleans, Alexandria, and Lake Charles, doing their best to keep the French language and customs that contribute so much to making Louisiana the special place it is.

The Cajuns. The story of the Acadians is familiar to most Americans from Longfellow's narrative poem *Evangeline*. Britain's forced exile of the French population from Acadia, now the Canadian provinces of New Brunswick and Nova Scotia, in 1755, and the disgraceful act of genocide in which families were seperated and hundreds died, was not a conscious act of policy planned in London, but rather the work of one scheming imperial bureaucrat, Governor Charles Lawrence, a man with a single-minded zeal for the expansion of Empire, and a deep hatred of the French. Of the 12,000 Acadians to be shipped off, those who survived the arduous winter voyage to the American colonies were either sold out as indentured servants or enslaved (in Georgia and the Carolinas) and the few who reached the French West Indies fared little better—their own government pressed them into service building fortifications, where most of them died. Slowly but steadily, those who managed to escape trickled into Louisiana, whose Spanish government needed settlers, and granted them land along the Mississippi and the bayous.

Here, in the unpromising surroundings of the coastal swamps, the Cajuns rebuilt their village societies and even, on a few happy occasions, saw their familes reunited. Until this century, most of them lived simple lives as farmers, trappers, or fishermen, maintaining their island of French culture in the American South against intermittent oppression from a government dominated by Protestant Anglos from Northern Louisiana. For a time, it was even illegal for anyone to speak French in the public schools. Today, however, many Cajuns are not only determined that their language survive, they fight over what kind of French they're talking about. On the one hand, an agency called CODOFIL in the Acadian capital of Lafayette, assisted by France and Canada, tries to teach everyone the standard tongue, while on the other, Cajun insurgents publish books, journals and even grammars in the flat non-nasal patois their people have carried on for centuries (since they left their ancestral homes in Celtic Brittany in fact).

Many Cajuns still live on the bayou—that's from an Indian word, *bayuk,* for the small, sluggish streams in the marshlands that Louisiana has thousands of—and make their living in the old way. Many others live on the "Cajun prairie," raising cattle or growing rice, and today there are Cajun city folk, Cajun oilfield roughnecks, nationally known Cajun musicians, a Congressman and Louisiana governor, even a Cajun who pitches for the New York Yankees. The Cajuns' way of life, their style, has made them quite popular. The music is a big part of it, old French airs moderately Dixiefied, and played on the accordion and violin with a triangle for the rhythm—lately electric guitars and even steel guitars have been sneaking in. There's also a black Cajun counterpart to it called Zydeco, a little jazzier, whose leading exponent, Clifton Chenier, plays as many concerts in Europe as he does in the U.S. Cajun music is for dancing, as in the traditional Saturday party, the fais-do-do (means "go to sleep," which is the exact opposite of what happens).

Cajun cuisine is very popular, try gumbo and jambalaya, there are a thousand creative things to do with the ubiquitous crawfish (at their festivals they even have crawfish races), and you may encounter sausages like the hot homemade boudin for sale in grocery stores or gas stations. The tourist who comes to New Orleans for Mardi Gras usually don't know that even jollier parties are going on at the same time out in Acadiana: the big Mardi Gras in Lafayette, and smaller ones in the villages preceded by a band of maskers on horseback, doing the rounds of country homes to make monkey shines and demand "a fat little chicken to make a big gumbo".

Mississippi Delta. New Orleans has the most unlikely hinterlands a city could ask for. Just a few miles southeast or southwest of the river the streets end, surrendering to the wetlands kingdom of bayous, shallow lakes and bays, swamps and canals where the Mississippi and its countless distributaries make their confusing denouements into an uncertain shoreline. This sparsely populated territory—Terrebonne, Lafourche, Jefferson, Plaquemines and St. Bernard parishes—is inhabited largely by Cajuns, with a mixture of Spanish, Indians, even Filipinos and Croatians mixed in, living on the little settlements along the bayous. Those who do not work on the sulphur mines or oil wells, or own orange groves, still get by on the wetlands' abundant wildlife, catching oysters, crawfish or shrimp, hunting ducks, geese and rabbits, or trapping such local specialties as the muskrat and nutria, a fat, droll rodent whose presence in large numbers is helping the Louisiana alligator to stage a comeback. Even the Cajuns are not above dropping one into their gumbo now and then.

East of the city, in St. Bernard Parish, there aren't many Cajuns at all; most folks are Isleños—Canary Islanders, whose ancestors have been around for two hundred years. They live on oysters, in tiny villages like St. Bernard and Yscloskey.

To the south, few visitors ever make it down to the mouths of the Mississippi; it's an eighty mile trip along dead-end Route 23. **Port Sulphur** is the center of the mining region and further south the orange groves begin, also farms that grow most the nation's Easter lilies, which down here are called Creole lilies. **Fort Jackson,** between Buras and Truimph, was the bastion that proved so ineffectual in keeping Admiral Farragut out in 1862. Built in 1822, the fort is now open to the public (daily 10 am-sunset, free) with a view over the river to its companion Fort St. Philip, an important rendezvous for rum runners during Prohibition, now abandoned and in ruins.

In Lafourche and Terrebonne Parishes, sugar and oil have made the Cajuns quite prosperous, along with the tourist industry created by some of the state's best fishing. Shrimp are still important to the city of **Houma,** seat of Terrebonne, and the bayou villages to the south. In Houma, the 1859 Southdown Plantation, now entirely out of character with Victorian additions of the 1890's, houses the **Terrebonne Museum** which is full of porcelain birds and memorabilia of Allen Ellender, a Long crony who graced the U.S. Senate for years and years. (Take Route 311 just west of town, daily 10-4, adm.) Along the bayous, shrimping centers like Lockport, Golden Meadow and Chauvin, isolated and content, live simply and well in the kind of unmodernized existence that most people associate with all the Cajuns. **Chauvin** is famous for its annual fall festival, "Lagniappe on the Bayou," and another popular event occurs each July in **Galliano,** the Louisiana Oyster Festival. From here, Route 1 meets its Land's End at **Grand Isle,** a fishing resort on the shores of **Barataria Bay,** once the haunt of Lafitte and his pirates.

Thibodaux, the seat of Lafourche Parish, is one of Louisiana's most beautiful towns, with narrow streets, a fanciful domed **Parish Courthouse** built in 1856, some fine old churches and a park along Bayou Lafourche. From here, there is only one road to the west, Route 20, traversing Louisiana's Empty Quarter, a natural wonder whose future has become an exasperatingly insoluble ecological controversy, the **Atchafalaya Basin.** The largest of the Mississippi's distributaries, the Atchafalaya River drains (however slowly) over 2,000 square miles of central Louisiana with its own network of bayous, lakes and cypress swamps, and an abundance and diversity of wildlife surpassing even Florida's Everglades. Conservationists struggle over its destiny with farmers (much land is now planted in soybeans, even in places where no homes may be legally built); loggers, who want to turn the last magnificent cypresses into everlasting coffins; the Army Corps of Engineers; and oilmen who scar the landscape with canals and pipelines; but the Atchafalaya itself often seems determined to frustrate everyone's best intentions. The entire basin is silting up with topsoil from the upper reaches of the Mississippi and it could all be dry land some day if it gets its way. Another possible fate, incredible as it seems, is that the Atchafalaya will someday be the Mississippi, leaving the great ports of Baton Rouge and New Orleans high and dry. The Corps of Engineers maintains elaborate "control structures" and floodways up near Simmesport, to protect the big cities by diverting one third of Mississippi's floodwaters into the Atchafalaya, but the great flood of 1973 almost washed them away; some future flood could finish the job in spite of the Corps' efforts and change the course of the river permanently. For now, however, the Atchafalaya remains a world unto itself, where only long-time residents—mostly fishermen and trappers—can navigate the lace-like pattern of twisting bayous and canals. It is the Cajuns' pantry, the greatest generator of crawfish in the world.

Only two roads cross the lower Atchafalaya towards Lafayette. The newer and more interesting one, **Interstate 10** from Baton Rouge, must be the most bizarre stretch of the Interstate system, thirty miles of swamp traversed on high concrete pylons without a house in sight. Like the Everglades, the Atchafalaya has its seasonal flood cycle; if you drive through in the fall, when it's driest, you'll see what looks to be only a forest of willows and cypress, cut through by shallow meandering streams. Crawfish and alligators burrow into the wet spots to survive until spring comes, when almost everything will be underwater. The southern route, US 90 from Houma, crosses the Atchafalaya at **Morgan City,** not only the "Shrimp Capital of the World," but a booming oil center. The world's first offshore oil well was constructed here in 1947, and the citizens have commemorated it with a singular monument, an oil derrick surmounted by the "Eternal Flame of Morgan City". From the US 90 bridge through town, you will see hundreds of acres of stacked steel pipe ready for the offshore wells, and perhaps even the memorable sight of a newly built platform, like the steel skeleton of a skyscraper and just as big, floating down the Atchafalaya on its way to the sea. Morgan City also offers an introduction to the Atchafalaya Basin at **Swamp Gardens,** with a tour of the typical habitat along raised walkways, a small zoo of swamp creatures and explanatory exhibits (Tues-Sat 10:30-3:30, Sun 1:30-3:30, adm.).

Beyond the Atchafalaya, one of its tributaries, **Bayou Teche,** was a wealthy agricultural area before the Civil War, and retains a string of restored plantation homes like those along the Mississippi, from the pretty town of **Franklin,** founded by Pennsylvanians, through **Jeanerette** all the way to New Iberia and beyond. East of Franklin, on Route 182, the beautifully furnished **Franklin Plantation,** built of brick and cypress, is one of the oldest on Bayou Teche, built in 1820 (Tues-Sat 9-5, adm.). In Franklin itself, the 1851 Grevenberg House is now the historically-oriented **St. Mary's Parish Museum** on Sterling Road in Franklin City

Park (Tues, Thurs 3-5, Sat & Sun 1-5, adm.); and **Arlington Plantation** can be visited at 56 E. Main Street (Tues-Sat 10-4, adm. $3). To the west, also on Route 182, there's **Oaklawn Manor,** a fine example of Greek Revival, Louisiana style (daily 9:30-4:30, adm.) and the 1837 **Albania Mansion,** with a large collection of antiques (Tues-Sat 10-4:30, Sun 2-4, adm.); also, near Charenton, the small **Chitimacha Indian Reservation** offers a museum (Mon-Fri 8-4:30, free) and a crafts shop.

New Iberia and Iberia Parish got their names from the Spaniard named Francisco Bouligny who helped the Cajuns found it, on land already occupied by Canary Islanders. This growing town, the "Queen City of the Teche," is a busy port for oil and sugar, but it also cans seafood, digs peat moss, makes bricks, molasses and mattresses, and bottles hot sauce. Only in Cajun country would you find something like New Iberia's new **Civic Center,** between Main Street and Bayou Teche, decorated by a "Grotto of Our Lady of Lourdes," and an even more curious attraction can be found behind the big bay window of a bank on Weeks Street: a **Statue of Hadrian,** the Roman emperor, sculpted in about 130 A.D. and larger than life. Next to the Civic Center, one of the very best plantation homes, restored by a descendant of the original family, has come into the hands of the National Trust for Historic Preservation. They operate **Shadows on the Teche** as one of their seven major nationwide museum-home projects and also as a center to encourage local preservation efforts (daily, 9-4, adm.).

More plantations line the Teche on both sides of the city: to the west, **Dulcito,** used as a hospital in the Civil War, and to the east, **Justine Plantation,** on Route 86, including "Justine's bottle museum" (daily 10:30-5, by appointment, adm.). Travelling just a few miles south of the city, Route 329 takes you straight into the steamiest tropics. There's something in the air on **Avery Island,** something hot and conducive to languor even by Louisiana standards; it probably comes from the peppers, for Avery Island is the home of Tabasco Sauce, the most concentrated substance known to man and a staple of Cajun cuisine. The McIlhenny Company has been here for over a century, and they'll be glad to give you a tour of the neat brick buildings where they make their diabolical potion, after letting it ferment for three years; they'll also give you a little sample bottle (weekdays 9-5, Sat 9-noon, free). Edward Avery McIlhenny, in the 1890's, used his profits to create a 200-acre paradise, now open to the public as **Jungle Gardens.** February is probably the best time to see it, when all the camellias, azaleas and irises are in bloom, but throughout the year their spectacular gardens are well worth the trip, with their bird sanctuary, home to thousands of herons and egrets, lagoons and groves, bamboo forests and a huge 800-year-old Chinese Buddha in a temple (daily Spring and Summer 9-5:30, otherwise 9-5, adm.). Avery Island really isn't an island, but one of the hundreds of salt domes that push up the level of the land over the surrounding swamps. Louisiana has enough salt to supply humanity until the Judgement Day at least; they mine it here and use quite a lot to help the vats of Tabasco fester, other mining activities are pursued by the oil wells which peacefully co-exist.

St. Martinville, town of the Evangeline legend, started life in 1769 as a Spanish fort called Poste des Attakapas. The Attakapas were the local Indians and in the language of their neighbors, the Houmas, the word meant "cannibals". Nobody liked them and they met a bad end. In the 1790's the village took shape with a blaze of style Acadiana hasn't seen since, when a colony of French aristocrats, exiled during the Revolution, made it "Le Petit Paris," unpacking their fancy gowns to do the minuet at gala balls, and for the debut of Grand Opera on the bayou. When Louisiana became French again in 1803, they carried on a little civil war with sympathizers of the Republic—it began when one man started calling them "citizens"—that continued on under American rule. Many of their descendants still live in the area.

In the graveyard of **St. Martin's Church,** on Main Street, lies a girl named Emmeline Labiche. Up north in Philadelphia they'll show you another "Evangeline's grave" in an old cemetery near Washington Square, and according to Longfellow, that's where she should be, in the city where she was reunited with her lover on his deathbed. To that, the Cajuns responded with a resounding "Non!" Poets do embroider, and this Evangeline, really Emmeline, is the genuine item. Her lover was indeed torn from her during the Acadian expulsion, but when Emmeline found Louis here in St. Martinville, he was married to another woman, a highly unsatisfactory ending for any poet. The statue over her grave, however, isn't Evangeline at all; it's Dolores Del Rio, who played the role in a movie shot here in the 1920's. The cast chipped in to present this memorial to the town. There's also an **Evangeline Oak** in a park on Bayou Teche, where the girl supposedly finally caught up with her Louis, and the **Longfellow-Evangeline State Commemorative Area,** north of town off Route 31 (Main St.), with an **Acadian Craft Shop,** and the **Acadian House Museum,** a surviving building from Poste des Attakapas (Mon-Sat 9-5, Sun 1-5, adm.). Another museum, back in town across the street from St. Martin's, is the **Le Petit Paris Museum,** recounting the grand days of the settlement (daily 9-5:30, adm.).

All this territory west of Bayou Teche, incidentally, is the "Cajun Prairie," where, before new grazing lands opened up in Texas and beyond, the nation's first open-range cattle ranches were begun. St. Martinville was their market town. The first brand recorded in the Louisiana "brand book" dates from 1739, but hardly anyone knows that America's first legitimate cowboys were Cajuns, working on spreads that weren't called ranches, but *vacheries*. Even though most of the good land is now devoted to growing rice, there is still a cattle industry here, with Cajun cowboys in pickup trucks instead of horses, and more rhinestones when they're dressed up for festivals than any Texan ever dreamed possible.

Lafayette. The "Capital of French Louisiana" gives away its Gallic heritage not only in the serene, well-dressed old men you see on the streets, identical in every respect to their confrères in Paris or Lyons, but in the streets themselves. They're pleasant streets on the whole, and do their best to run somewhere, but if you try to follow them they will calmly digress you all over town, and when you pass the gargantuan revolving loaf of "Evangeline Maid" bread for the fifth time, swinging out dangerously in front of traffic to advertise a local bakery, you'll probably overcome your shyness and ask a Cajun for directions. Lafayette's first family are the Moutons, the first of whom arrived in the 1770's, and the second of whom laid out the town, originally called Vermilionville, in 1824. One later Mouton became a Confederate general—there's a monument in his honor at Lee and Jefferson Streets—and another, Alexandre Mouton, is well remembered as the first Democratic governor of Louisiana. His house, at 1122 Lafayette Street, has become the **Lafayette Museum** (Tues-Sat 9-noon and 2-5, free). Besides its restored period rooms and historical memorabilia, the museum has a collection of costumes from Lafayette's own Mardi Gras, a celebration second in size only to New Orleans', ruled over by King Gabriel and Queen Evangeline. Unlike New Orleans, the balls and pageants here are open to the general public.

Today, the population of Lafayette approaches 120,000, three times what it was in 1960. Just as Morgan City has become the center for offshore drilling, Lafayette is the oil industry's headquarters on land. To handle the boom, Big Oil has built what amounts to a new town on the southern edge of Lafayette, the **Heymann Oil Center.** Oil may be the basis of all Acadiana's current prosperity, but the inroads of Texas imperialism it brings with it are often controversial; Cajuns either mildly resent it, or are employed in it. Still there's hardly a hint of disruption back on the placid center of Lafayette. On St. John Street, near the business district, stands **St. John's Cathedral.** Every Cajun town has at least one lovely church, richly decorated and characteristically French, and this one, seat of the Acadian diocese, is one of the best, a brick and stucco structure completed in 1918. On its grounds are a cemetery of above-ground tombs like those in New Orleans and the 300-year-old "**St. John's Oak**".

The **University of Southern Louisiana,** a few blocks away on University Avenue, serves as the intellectual capital of Acadiana, conducting studies in Cajun history and folklore; its Dupre Library has an archive containing the colonial records from both French and Spanish rule in Louisiana. There's one unusual attraction on the USL campus, in front of the Student Union: **Cypress Lake.** a miniature man-made swamp complete with exotic birds and alligators, designed as an educational tool to reproduce various kinds of Louisiana swamp environment. After this you can continue your studies at the **Acadiana Park Nature Trail** on East Alexander Street north of town, or further explore the Cajun past at the **Acadian Village and Tropical Gardens,** a museum recreating a 19th century Acadian settlement with a church, store and Cajun-style homes moved here from various locations, and operated by the Lafayette Association for Retarded Persons (daily, 10-5; adm.; located on Route 93 south of town). Lafayette has two more museums, both on Girard Park Drive near the University: the **Natural History Museum** (Mon, Wed, Fri 9-5, Tues, Thurs 9-9, weekends 1-5; free) and the **Art Center for Southeast Louisiana,** with a collection specializing in 19th century French paintings and Louisiana artists (Mon-Fri 9:30-4:30; Sun 2-5; free).

To the west, the other cities and towns of the Acadian heartland form a crescent around Lafayette with its northern point at **Washington,** a quaint old town that was a busy port while its Bayou Courtableau was still navigable in the last century. Washington probably owes its well preserved state to the loss of commerce, and it has restored several of its pre-Civil War buildings and homes, including the old town hall, now the **Washington Museum** on Main Street (Mon-Fri 10-3, free) and the **Speyrer Home** from the 1830's (daily 10-5, adm.). The area around Washington contains several restored plantation houses, including **Arlington** (west of town on Route 103; daily 10-5, adm.) and **Magnolia Ridge,** which both sides in the Civil War used as field headquarters (also on Route 103; daily 9-5, by appointment, call 826-7795, adm.). **Opelousas,** a growing agricultural center, was the state capital for a short time during the war; one old house on Grolee Street is still called the "Governor's Mansion." Jim Bowie, hero of the Alamo, grew up here, and the **Jim Bowie House** is now the city's historical museum and tourist center (Mon-Fri 8-4 free). One of the most characteristic Acadian villages, **Grand Couteau,** is also one of the loveliest, with a center of pre-Civil War buildings and several Catholic religious establishments, under avenues of majestic oaks. Lake Chicot, a state park near the town of Ville Platte, is the home of the 300-acre **Louisiana State Arboretum,** a display of native Louisiana plant life in a beautiful setting (on Route 3042; daily, dawn until dusk, free).

Acadiana's towns each have a character that will likely pass unnoticed by the casual visitor; locally, however, almost all of them are known for some special thing, often it's an annual event. **Rayne,** for example, has more frogs than it can use, and its citizens have made a business of exporting them, but they also celebrate their presence in one of America's positively silliest jubilees; the annual, world famous Frog Festival in September. Nearby **Crowley** calls itself the Rice Capital of the World (but so does Stuttgart, Arkansas) and they uphold their claim with an International Rice Festival and a **Rice Museum** on US 90 (Mon-Fri 9-5, adm.). Another museum, a few miles away on Primeaux Road, has a collection of antiques in a century old Cajun cottage: the **Blue Rose Museum** (Mon-Fri 9:30-2, adm.). Opelousas, for its part, counters these festivals with its famous sweet potatoes, at the "Yambilee" in October; **Kaplan,** down near the coast, celebrates Bastille Day, and the little village of **Mamou,** near Ville Platte, is known all over Acadiana for the big Saturday morning fais-do-do at Fred's Lounge, broadcast on radio station KEUN.

Halfway between Lafayette and Lake Charles, **Jennings** got its Anglo name from the man who laid the Southern Pacific tracks through the Cajun Prairie and made the settlement worthwhile. The first successful oil well in the state was drilled here in 1901, and there's a replica of it and a museum at the **Louisiana Oil and Gas Park,** on Route 26 (daily 9-8:30, free). A local philanthropist, one of the town's first settlers, gave Jennings the **Zigler Museum,** with paintings by the likes of Whistler and Audubon, Reynolds and Constable, and other European and American, particularly Louisianan artists, as well as a room of dioramas depicting Louisiana wildlife (411 Clara Street; Tues-Fri 10-noon and 2-4:30, weekends 2-4:30 only, free).

Abbeville, at the southern limits of the Cajun prairie, lives on rice and the oil industry and it is one of the loveliest Acadian towns, with the live oaks, fountain and flowers of **Madeleine Square** at its center facing the tall steeple of the parish church, surrounded by narrow winding streets "patterned after the old towns of Provence". **Delcambre,** nearby, is a town that makes its living by catching shrimp. Here, we are back near New Iberia and Avery Island and in the vicinity of Delcambre there is another big salt dome, **Jefferson Island,** which like Avery Island has a salt mine and a jungle paradise: **Live Oak Gardens.** Besides the oaks there are formal English and Japanese gardens and a conservatory (on Route 615; daily 9-5, adm.).

Lake Charles. Charlie Sallier, the first settler, gave his name both to the little lake on the Calcasieu River and the town that grew up around it, but as the place grew its citizens eventually decided that Charlie's Lake wouldn't do and gave it a name that sounded a bit more dignified. The same Southern Pacific line that made a town of Jennings in the 1880's made Lake Charles a city, along with the mining activity that left its mark in the suburb called Sulphur (their Chamber of Commerce must have a difficult time with it). This mineral led the way to a petrochemical industry that is booming today, making this city in the southwestern corner of Louisiana one of the fastest growing in the South, as well as the sixteenth largest port in the U.S.

Downtown this prosperity is reflected in the new **Civic Center** on the lakeshore and the **Ryan Mall** created from the downtown shopping district along Ryan Street. Behind the Civic Center there's a public beach (a rarity in swampy Louisiana). South of downtown, on Sallier Street, the **Imperial Calcasieu Museum** recounts local history (Mon-Fri 10-noon and 2-5, Sat 10-noon, Sun 12-5, free), and out in Sulphur, that community's smelly past is remembered in the **Brimstone Museum** (Mon-Fri 9:30-2, free, in Frasch Park on Picard Road). Beyond Lake Charles this corner of the state is a rather empty place, but with an interesting diversity of natural settings and human activities. To explore it, stop at the Lake Charles Visitors Center on Lakeshore Drive for a brochure detailing the self-guided **Creole Nature Trail,** a short trip around Lake Calcasieu that will take you past wildlife preserves, marshes, salt domes, rice fields, Holly Beach, the shrimping village of Cameron, Indian sites, live oak-covered ridges called *cheniers*—and also tell you the best spot to see a porpoise, an alligator, or a field of beautiful Louisiana irises.

Tourist Information. Acadian Regional Information Center, Route 14 west of New Iberia (open Wed-Sun 9-5; 365-1540); **Lafayette Tourist Center,** US 90 at 16th Street (Mon-Fri 8:30-5, weekends 9-5; 232-2737); **Houma Tourist Center,** US 90 at S. St. Charles Street (Mon-Fri 9-5; 876-5600); **Morgan City Tourist Center,** Myrtle Street (daily 9-4; 384-3343); **Opelousas Tourist Center,** US 190 at US 167 (Mon-Fri 8-4:30; 948-6263); **Lake Charles Tourist Center,** Lake Shore Drive at Interstate 10 (Mon-Fri 8-4:30; 436-9588).

Restaurants. *In Thibodaux*: Jutz's*, 609 Jackson St. *In Jeanerette*: The Yellow Bowl**, US 90. *In New Iberia*: Patout's***, Abbeville Highway; French House**. *In Lafayette*: Jacob's Fine Foods***, 1600 Cameron St.; La Fonda***, 3809 Johnston St.; Chez Pastor**, 1211 Pinhook Rd.; Don's Seafood**, 301 E. Vermillion, Lagneaux's*, Ridge Road. *In Carencro* (north of Lafayette): Angelle's*, Route 167. *In Opelousas*: Soileau's**, 1620 N. Main St.; The Hut**, 130 N. Union; Palace Cafe**

167 W. Landry St. *In Breaux Bridge*: Thelma's**, 94 Lafayette Rd.; Schwet's Café**, 109 N. Main St. *In Lake Charles*: Chez Oca***, 815 Bayou Pinés Rd.; Plantation House***, 903 Broad.

Up the Mississippi from New Orleans to Baton Rouge

If, between the southern bayous and the northern plains, between the French and the Anglos, there is a heartland of Louisiana, it must be here, along the river between New Orleans and Baton Rouge, the first part of the state to be settled. In the "Golden Age" before the Civil War, Louisiana's richest planters, both French and English, built the finest of all the South's plantation houses, and presumed themselves into the same kind of riparian aristocracy the age observed along the Hudson—only with sugar cane and slaves. They were not the first to build in this country, however; in the 18th century this area saw the first colony of French refugees from Canada, the "Acadian Coast" it was called. Under American rule, the advent of sugar cultivation, fantastically profitable for large holdings, resulted in outside speculators buying up and consolidating the Cajun farms into plantations. Slave labor was already common; curiously enough it was introduced for sugar in the 1760's by Jesuit priests, and even some of the Cajuns were slaveowners. The Civil War, here as elsewhere, put an end to the fantasies of the plantation aristocrats, but did not change the area's agricultural role. That remained for the modern age; in the last thirty years the river between the two cities has witnessed the intrusion of oil refineries, docks and chemical plants in becoming one of the most industrialized corners of the South.

Tourists still come by the thousands to see the old plantations. They are different from the mansions you see elsewhere in the South; Louisiana's climate and history made them that way. There is much less of the formal Greek Revival spirit (though what there is of it is done better than anywhere else). The source of the architecture here is the West Indies, by way of the exiled Cajuns who spent time there before coming to Louisiana, and adopted that tropical style for their own early houses. Enormous verandas, pitched roofs with gables and delicate and fanciful wood carving and ironwork are the characteristics. Most are built of the almost indestructible cypress wood, with walls insulated by the old Cajun invention of *bousillage*—mud mixed with Spanish moss.

Leaving New Orleans towards the west along Route 48, you'll run into the first and one of the most famous houses, **Destrehan Plantation,** between St. Rose and Norco, built in 1787 and recently restored (daily 10-4, adm. $3.00). After Norco you'll pass over one of the engineering artifices that New Orleans is forced to resort to to keep itself dry, the **Bonnet Carré Spillway,** which in emergencies pumps Mississippi floodwaters into Lake Pontchartrain. The authorities keep the water's path clear by employing thousands of goats, who eat the grass in the spillway that would otherwise clog the gates. Across the river in this particularly industrial part of the Mississippi (there's a free ferry at St. Rose), is the "German Coast," where the Rhenish settlers attracted to Arkansas by John Law's Mississippi scheme were granted refuge by Bienville; the Germans have long ago melted into the rest of the population, but are remembered in the towns they left behind: Hahnville,

Luling, Kraemer and Des Allemands.

Although none of the plantations are still in the hands of their original families, most are privately owned, and determined plantation fans will have to be content with a peek from the two roads that parallel the river, Routes 44-48 (north bank) and 18 (south). One that is open, courtesy of Marathon Oil, sits on Route 44 just west of Reserve. **San Francisco,** built in 1849, was the first and by any measure the most spectacular piece of "Steamboat Gothic" anywhere—New Orleans novelist Frances Parkinson Keyes even wrote a novel with that title using San Francisco as a setting. Valsin Marmillion, who must have been the Louisiana equivalent of Bavaria's Mad King Ludwig, had his artists and woodcarvers busy for years decorating the place, tacking up ornate galleries and belvederes on the outside and filling the interior with cherubs, flowers and mirrors. Before the house was finished, however, Valsin Marmillion both went broke and died. If you're not fond of fancy homes, but duty compels you to see at least one Southern plantation, this should be it (daily 10-4, adm. $3.50).

Further west, through lands that now produce not sugar, but Louisiana perique tobacco and shallots, there's **Oak Alley Plantation,** whose name gives away its greatest attraction, some of the finest venerable live oaks any plantation can claim (daily, 9-5, adm. $3.50; Route 18 west of Vacherie); **Madewood Plantation,** for a side trip along Bayou Lafourche (daily, 10-5, adm. $3.00; Route 308 in Napoleonville); **Houmas House,** with unusual octagonal "garçonnieres"—decorative guest houses (daily, 10-5, adm. $3.50; this one is popular with Hollywood directors, the setting for "Hush, Hush, Sweet Charlotte," and other forgettable movies; on Route 942, a continuation of 44 near Burnside); and **Nottoway,** the largest house of them all, built in 1859 (daily 10-5, adm. $4.00; Route 1, an extension of 18, west of Donaldsonville; there's a restaurant—"Enjoy Mint Juleps on the Veranda" for the last word on antebellum fantasy). **Donaldsonville** is quite an interesting town in itself, founded by one of the first Americans to settle in this region, William Donaldson, who employed a New Orleans French engineer to lay it out in a formal axial plan, unusual for an American town. On the north bank you'll pass the town of **Convent,** named for the Jesuit base that now includes the beautiful Greek Revival building of long-deceased Jefferson College, now **Manresa House.** The town's parish church, **St. Michael's,** has an exact replica of the Grotto of Lourdes, built by a parishioner named Christophe Colomb. The final plantation, **Ashland-Belle Hélène,** is almost as imposing as Nottoway, cross the river from which it stands on Route 75; it too has had its share of movies (daily 9-4, adm. $3.00).

Baton Rouge. The *baton* in question, recorded by d'Iberville on his trip up the Mississippi in 1719, was a red pole planted to mark the boundary between the Houmas and the Bayagoulas. The French immediately set up a fort to subdue both, but somehow the name stuck. Even after the small town became the state capital in 1849, it never occurred to the Louisianians to rechristen it for some general, explorer or scoundrel of the past; perhaps the French and the Americans couldn't agree. These days "Red Stick" has become almost applicable, for the columns of flame that greet the traveler at night, leaping up from the miles of refineries and chemical plants that crowd the city's downtown, an industrial concentration of staggering size, the likes of which is to be seen nowhere else in the South except maybe in Birmingham. Baton Rouge has become a legitimate Sunbelt boomtown, the city that Standard Oil and Huey Long built, now the nation's seventh largest port and one of its leading petrochemical centers. It is pure Louisiana, with equally disorienting touches of tropical somnolence and northern boosterism.

You won't have any trouble finding Baton Rouge's landmark; the **State Capitol** is America's tallest, at 460 feet and 34 storeys. In 1930, the idea came to Huey Long that both he and Louisiana needed a proper monument. He got it in typical Long style, railroading the appropriation through the legislature as a rider to a highway bill after he had already cornered the architects and contractor with the command "Build it tall and build it fast!" With artists and craftsmen marooned by the Depression, Huey was able to hire them by the hundreds, to cover his monument with sculpture, reliefs, friezes and sententious inscriptions. Much of it, like the statuary groups of "Adventure" and "Patriotism" flanking the entrance, is first-class work—in a memorable, bayou-scented Ruritanian Imperial Art Deco that must have suited Huey fine.

They buried him in front of it. His statue, striking a democratic pose with his hand on a model of his capitol, stands over the grave, in the formal garden before the main entrance; at night, a beacon from the top of the tower illuminates it. The copious inscriptions on the pedestal explain Huey as he would like to be remembered. On one side there is a relief of the winged horse Pegasus, bearing a ribbon inscribed "Share Our Wealth". As in most state captols, they'll make you climb lots of stairs (here they are inscribed with the names of the fifty states, in ascending order of their admission) and haul open a door as heavy as the one on a bank vault, as if four hundred feet of Alabama limestone wasn't enough to make an impression. Huey obtained his stone from Alabama, Minnesota, Arkansas, Vermont and 26 foreign countries, everywhere but soggy Louisiana, which hasn't any. In the Memorial Hall, the black marble comes from Mount Vesuvius; the visitor's information counter is here and the hall is decorated with the ten flags that have flown over Louisiana, Sèvres vases of prodigious size sent by France and some fine murals by Jules Guerin. Around the back, behind the elevators, a small plaque marks the spot where the young Dr. Weiss shot Huey Long, just outside the Governor's Office. Flanking the Memorial Hall are the House and Senate Chambers, plain and elegant in marble, bronze and glass. Most visitors take the elevator up to the 27th floor **Observation Deck,** for a view of the Mississippi and everything in town.

Around the capitol gardens, among the newer state office buildings, Baton Rouge's oldest buildings remain from the 1830's, when this part of town was an Army installation including the **Pentagon Barracks.** There is nothing especially military about this sort of polygon; these five buildings were arranged over the site of an old Spanish fort. Only four remain, between Front Street and the garden; they have been restored as state offices, and are presently fought over by preservationists, who want to make them a museum, and the state legislators, who want to grab them to make apartments for themselves. To the right of the state capitol, the **Old Arsenal** has become a museum of Louisiana history (daily except

Tues, 10-4:30, free). The Revolutionary War cannons on the grounds are left from 1779, when the Spanish, with American help, seized Baton Rouge from the British in the only major battle of that war fought outside the thirteen colonies. There's a lake behind the Arsenal and State Capitol; singing governor Jimmie Davis built the new **Governor's Mansion** on its shore in 1963—a fake plantation like the other singers' homes up in Nashville.

For all its prosperity, Baton Rouge's downtown is one of the most distressed in the south, an orphan in a city hell-bent on suburbanization. Most of the city's past has been turned into parking lots, but some beautifully restored pre-Civil War homes can still be seen on North Street between Seventh and Ninth, a remnant of **Spanish Town,** the city's oldest neighborhood; west of downtown, across Interstate 110, the more modern end of Spanish Town survives as one of the poorer parts of town, with brightly painted houses on exceptionally narrow streets. The 1762 **Lafayette Buildings,** where the revolutionary hero stayed during his return to the U.S. in 1825, are other survivors, also the ancient commercial building at Main and River Road that has become **Le Petit Musée de Baton Rouge,** a combination museum, craft shop, bookstore and art gallery, and one of the best places to begin an excursion into Louisiana (Mon-Sat 10-4, Sun 1-5, free). A different way would be to tour the city on Louisiana's first main highway—the Mississippi River. An old riverboat, the *Samuel Clemens,* offers 1½ hour river trips every day except Monday at 10 and 1 pm, cost $5.00.

After the State Capitol, Baton Rouge's greatest civic embellishment is **North Boulevard,** divided by a strip of exotic flora and memorials (one of the statues is dedicated to Temperance, erected by the Women's Christian Temperance Union, and incredibly representing Hebe, the Wine Bearer to the Gods). Here, the **Old State Capitol** frowns over the Mississippi with the face of a Dickensian penitentiary. America's only Gothic statehouse was completed in 1852; its architect, James Harrison Dakin, was better known up North for his toils with the picturesque along the Hudson. Twenty years later, the sight of this building incited Mark Twain, in his *Life On the Mississippi,* to spend a few paragraphs explaining how everything that is wrong with the South could be traced to the novels of Sir Walter Scott. Twain, speaking for his "wholesome and practical nineteenth century" called the Louisiana capitol the ugliest building in the world and recommended dynamite.

That overly opinionated century is always good for a laugh, and you may even find yourself liking this ponderous affectation, with its cathedral windows, turrets and crenellated battlements. The people of Baton Rouge certainly do—it is a classic of the genre. The interior, probably the best sight the city has to offer, is the nineteenth century at its best, a breathtaking glass and cast-iron flight of fancy added in 1881, where a fan vault becomes a huge stained-glass skylight over a delicately cantilevered spiral staircase. It presently houses the **Visitor's Information Center** for the city (Mon-Sat 10-5, Sun 1-5) and occasional exhibits. On the grounds there's a non-sequitur in the form of a World War I French boxcar under a little pavilion. It carried American troops to the front in 1918, and in 1949 the French filled 48 of them with presents and gave one to each state. Behind the old capitol the city has constructed its attractive new

Riverside Centroplex—that's a kind of Sunbeltese word for convention hall.

A block away on the riverfront, the **Arts and Science Center,** once the city's train station and now converted to a museum with modern additions, contains scientific exhibits, old railroad engines, art shows, a collection of sculpture by Ivan Mestrovic (who deserves to be better known outside Baton Rouge and Split, Yugoslavia) and reconstructions of early Louisiana buildings. The Center also maintains the **Old Governor's Mansion** nearby on North Boulevard. Huey Long built this in 1930, a scaled-down version of the White House he always aspired to. They have it "restored to the period of the 1930's," and have added on a new structure that contains one of the largest and best planetariums in the U.S. (both parts of the Center open Tues-Sat 10-5, Sun 1-5, free, with plantetarium shows throughout the year, for schedule call 344-9463).

The business end of Baton Rouge commences just across the capitol lake from downtown, in the shadow of Huey's tower and stretches for miles along the Mississippi—an astounding landscape of tightly packed refineries and chemical plants, with forests of stacks and pipelines bristling in every direction. Standard Oil built the first refinery in 1910, and this industrial area has grown steadily ever since. The main road to the north, Route 61, passes it all; its name in Baton Rouge is the Scenic Highway and that may be the funniest thing in all Louisiana. Beyond the refineries, on Harding Boulevard, there's the modern campus of **Southern University,** an all-black school that is one of the largest in the state, and north of the city on Thomas Road east of US 19, the **Baton Rouge Zoo** (Mon-Fri 10-5, Sat & Sun 9-5, adm.).

South of downtown Nicholson Drive leads to the main campus of **Louisiana State University,** open since 1870 and one of the few land grant colleges in the South with a reputation and size equal to its counterparts in the rest of the nation, it's particularly renowned in the field of medical research. None other than General William Tecumseh Sherman, ironically, was LSU's first president. The campus spreads for 3,000 acres around **Memorial Tower,** and includes two Indian mounds from the Marksville culture, small museums in natural history, geology and art and a law school building modeled after the U.S. Supreme Court. They do take athletics seriously in this part of the country; Southern U. may have its cougar, La Cumba, prominently displayed on campus, but LSU answers with its mascot tiger, Mike the Third, in a cage near the 75,000 seat Tiger Stadium.

There's another plantation nearby, **Magnolia Mound** at 2161 Nicholson Drive, built in the 1790's (Tues-Sat 10-4, Sun 1-4, adm.) but you can also see how the antebellum other half lived at the **LSU Rural Life Museum,** on Essen Lane near Interstate 10. Here a small village of original and reconstructed buildings from all over Louisiana has been assembled to recreate a working plantation without the "big house"—only the slave quarters, overseer's house, mill, church, store and smithy, just as they would have looked in the 1850's (Mon-Fri 8:30-12 and 1-4, by appointment only, 766-8241, free).

Continuing north along the river from Baton Rouge, you can expect more plantations. On the west bank **Live Oaks Plantation,** on Route 76 between Rosedale and Maringouin still has some of its farm buildings and the slaves' church (open by appointment, 848-2346, adm.). By any measure one of the most interesting of all Louisiana's plantations, **Parlange** has stood by the Mississippi since 1750—or would have, had not the fickle river meandered itself a few miles away, leaving Parlange on a pretty oxbow lake called False River. Before the Civil War, this plantation grew indigo, another tropical contribution to early Lousiana's economy. It's still a working plantation (for sugar) and it is still owned by the family that started it—perhaps the oldest continuously run economic enterprise in the United States. The grand house, which is open to visitors, has a style taken directly from the French Caribbean, and it set the pattern for all the others in Louisiana (daily 9-5, adm.; Parlange can be found on Route 1, between Oscar and Mix).

St. Francisville, a perfectly charming town, lies just across the real Mississippi, best known for its association with John James Audubon, who made it his headquarters while studying Louisiana's exotic birds. The town's landmark is the Gothic **Grace Church,** built in 1858 and damaged in a Civil War bombardment. Many Audubon prints and memorabilia can be seen at **Oakley Plantation,** where he lived, on Route 964 south of town (Mon-Sat 9-5, Sun 1-5, adm.). Some other plantations nearby: **Rosedown,** as fancy as they come, has formal gardens with statuary from Italy (daily 9-5, 10-4 in winter, adm. $4.00; on US 61 at Route 10); **Catalpa Plantation,** one of the few built after the Civil War (daily 9-5, closed December & January, adm.); **Afton Villa,** where the house is gone, but the beautiful gardens remain, including a maze (north of town on US 61; open 9-4:30 in March and April; Wed-Sun 9-4:30 from May to December, adm.). You can learn more about these and other homes in the area, at the **West Feliciana Historical Museum,** on Ferdinand St. in St. Francisville (Mon-Sat 9-4, Sun 1-4, free).

East of the Mississippi, beyond Baton Rouge, the French influence dissipates considerably; there are towns called Pride and Wilmer and another named Baptist, in a countryside thick with pines that might as well be part of the state of Mississippi. All of this area, after the Revolutionary War, was controlled by the British and consequently attracted English-speaking settlers.

Two more pleasant towns lie just east of St. Francisville: **Jackson** and **Clinton;** the latter has a fine Greek Revival courthouse and both take pride in the number of antebellum buildings, churches and homes they have restored. Jackson, at one time, was a city of some pretentions, reflected in such grand works as the 1848 **East Louisiana State Hospital,** now with a small museum and gift shop behind its classical facade (daily 9:30-4:30, free), the **Baptist Church** and **Methodist Church** on Bank Street, and the remains of **Centenary College,** where Jefferson Davis graduated. There are plans to make the surviving building (the college moved to Shreveport in 1908) into a museum. Further east, **Hammond** is the home of Southeastern Louisiana University and still the "Strawberry Capital of the World". Until recently, the area produced almost all the nation's berries, and school children had their summer vacations in April so they could help with the picking.

Tammany was a Delaware Indian chief in Pennsylvania who was such an upstanding character and a friend to the settlers that he became something of a legend. In New York, Democratic politicos started a kind of lodge called the "Sons of Tammany"—later their political machine, Tammany Hall—and in Louisiana the good chief got himself canonized. **St. Tammany Parish** covers the northern shore of Lake Pontchartrain, across from New Orleans. Some of its towns were once busy health resorts because of the "Ozone Belt," around Abita Springs. Ozone is a form of oxygen that occurs when atoms are frazzled by lightning, and for some reason the air and water here are full of it; there's still an old pavilion in the middle of Abita Springs where the ozone water flows and you can try out its curative properties. **Mandeville,** on the shore at the northern end of the Lake Pontchartrain Causeway, is still a resort, a popular spot for New Orleaneans to get away to, with a good beach nearby in the **Fountainebleau State Park.**

Near **Slidell,** the parish's largest town and an industrial suburb of New Orleans, the Pearl River provides both the border with Mississippi and a popular place for fishing and duck hunting. Up the river in Washington Parish, **Bogalusa** makes its living from logging the pine forests all around. Here in Cassidy Park is the **Museum of Ancient Indian Cultures,** with artifacts excavated from all Louisiana's tribes (Mon-Fri 9-4, free).

Tourist Information. Baton Rouge Tourist Center, in the old State Capitol on North Blvd. (Mon-Fri 9:30-5, Sat 10-5, Sun 1-5; 3383-1825); **Gonzales Tourist Center,** 728 N., Ascension St. (Tues-Sat 10-4; 644-6000); **Point Coupee Museum—Tourist Center,** Route 1 (Tues-Sat 10-4, Sun 1-4; 638-7171); **St. Tammany Tourist Center,** 2020 First St. in Slidell (Mon-Fri 8:30-5; 649-0730).

Restaurants. *In Burnside* (across the river from Donaldsonville): The Cabin**, Route 44 & 42. *In Baton Rouge*: The Chalet Brandt***, 7655 Old Hammond Highway; Giamanco's**, 4624 Governor St.; Ralph & Kacoo's**, 7110 Airline Highway; The Place*, 5255 Florida Blvd. *In Jackson*: Asphodel Plantation***, south on Route 68. *In Mandeville*: Bachac's**, on the beach; Trey Yuen**, 600 N. Causeway.

Northern Louisiana

Although you'll leave the tropical ambience behind when you travel to the northern half of the state and also exchange the exotic environs of the Cajun and Creole for the familiar, tepid, Anglo-Saxon Deep South, there are some things that do not change with the trip north. The land is still flat, with an occasional highland outburst of rolling hills—the highest point in the state is less than 450 feet above sea level. The land is divided between pine forests and open field; agriculture, lumbering and oil and gas drilling are all important.

Shreveport contests pride of place with Baton Rouge for the title of Louisiana's second city; both are growing rapidly from oil and new industry. Far as it is from the civilizing French influence, Shreveport looks the arch-typical Sunbelt metropolis: wide straight streets, an abundance of skyscrapers and parking lots and dozens of Baptist churches in ghetto and sprawl alike. It isn't as bad as it sounds, though, for this city has lately been doing its best to put its prosperity to some good use. It has a number of attractions and a cultural life unusual for a city its size. Captain Henry

Shreve, the Pennsylvanian who founded the settlement in 1833, arrived with the job of clearing the Great Raft, a 150-mile log jam on the Red River that had accumulated for centuries. It took him five years, but if he hadn't opened the river to navigation it would be a much smaller Shrevetown today. The city is the seat of Caddo Parish; the Caddo Indians, who controlled much of this "Ark-La-Tex" region, were about the fiercest warriors the white man had yet encountered, but Shreve and Uncle Sam were able to buy them out in 1835, and their descendants still survive in Oklahoma. During the Civil War Shreveport was not only the rebel state capital, after the capture of New Orleans, but the headquarters of General Edward Kirby-Smith, the redoubtable leader of the Confederacy's trans-Mississippi military department, called the "Kirby Smithdom" from the somewhat regal pretensions of the general, whose big Texas army remained intact and largely untried, at the time of Appomattox. Until the 1930's, when the first oil and gas wells came in, cotton was the mainstay of the local economy, and in the last twenty years dozens of new factories have made the city an industrial center.

Downtown they've taken what's left of the old Shreveport and restored two blocks of 19th century commercial buildings into **Shreve Square,** painted in bright colors and housing restaurants and nightclubs (on Texas Street). Nearby, at 525 Spring St., the **Spring Street Museum** is a restored bank building with relics from the city's past (weekends only 1:30-4:30, adm.). At the riverfront, on River Parkway, the city has constructed a new **Civic Center,** with a statue of Captain Shreve and a botanical conservatory, the **Barnwell Garden and Art Center** with a tropical garden under its glass dome and a gallery for art exhibits (Mon-Fri 9-4:30, Sat-Sun 1-5, free). Whatever Kirby-Smith was doing in 1864, he wasn't contributing much to the defense of Shreveport; when Federal troops marched into northern Louisiana, the local garrison was forced to build **Fort Humbug,** a mile east of downtown along the riverfront—now on the grounds of the Veteran's Hospital. There were no cannon, so the defenders painted logs gray and set them up along the fortifications—hence the name, bestowed by the occupation force after the war. Nobody knows if the ruse would have worked; the Union General Banks suffered a defeat at Mansfield and never attacked the city. Little of the makeshift fortress remains, but there's a children's park where you can learn to play "frisbee golf".

Shreveport is bursting with museums. Near the State Fairgrounds, at 3015 Greenwood Road, there's the **Louisiana State Exhibit Museum,** a huge circular marble building that in itself is a kind of permanent state fair; everything about Louisiana, its history, natural wonders, agriculture and industry, is portrayed in enormous dioramas and endless exhibit cases (Mon-Fri 9-5, Sat-Sun 1-5, free). Smaller museums with a similar theme are the **Pioneer Heritage Folk Center,** a part of the Shreveport branch of LSU, Kings Highway south of E. 70th St. (Sunday only 1:30-5, adm.) and the **Bossier Regional Folk Life Museum,** 601 Barksdale across the river in Bossier City (Mon-Thurs 9-3, Fri 9-6, free). Both recreate frontier life in the area with demonstrations of crafts and everyday activities. Thanks to the donation of a local philanthropist in 1946, Shreveport also has a first-class art museum, the **R. W. Norton Art Gallery,** on a forty-acre park at 4747 Creswell; although European artists are also represented, this museum is best known for its large collection of American paintings, including works by Frederic Remington, the artist of the West, and other famous 19th century landscapists such as Bierstadt and Church (Tues-Sun 1-5, free). If you're fond of roses, you can see more varieties of them here than probably anywhere else at the 118-acre **American Rose Society Gardens,** west of the city near Greenwood off US 80. The society, which has its national headquarters here, registers every new variety and maintains this garden under the pines, with a "carillon" that is really a huge set of wind chimes (Mon-Fri 9-4, Sat-Sun 10-6; April to mid-November only; adm.).

In this metropolitan area, most of the action isn't in Shreveport but in its neighbor across the Red; **Bossier City** is a toadstool suburb, growing up from nothing in 1950 to become a town of about 40,000 today, and its prosperity has much to do with the growth of Barksdale Air Force Base next door. Bossier City has its "strip" of nightclubs along US 80, a popular, modern racetrack at **Louisiana Downs** (season May to October) also on US 80, and a country music show that has meant almost as much to the development of the twangy guitar and pedal steel genre as the Grand Ole Opry in Nashville. The **Louisiana Hayride,** on Route 3 (Benton Road) has been broadcast on KRMD since 1948, and claims to have launched stars like Elvis Presley and Hank Williams, as well as dozens of others. Shows begin every Saturday night at 7:45.

Around Shreveport, among the pines and oil wells, are at least a dozen lakes and reservoirs; some are state parks and stocked for fishing—the most popular activity around here, as in nearby Arkansas. **Mansfield,** to the south, was the site of a minor Civil War engagement, commemorated at the **Mansfield Battlepark and Museum** on Route 175; one of the last Confederate victories, this is the fight that kept the Northerners out of Shreveport. Nearby **Coushatta,** on the Red River half way between Shreveport and Natchitoches, has converted its old train station, the **Coushatta Depot,** into a crafts center that specializes in traditional quilts, which are for sale. **Saline** has another botanical park, the **Briarwood Gardens** (open April, May and August, Saturday 9-5, Sun 12-5, adm.), and **Winnfield,** an agricultural center in one of the most out-of-the-way corners of the state, and one of the last to be settled, deserves mention for no other reason than being the home town of the Longs. Earl gets a statue, at the **Earl K. Long State Commemorative Area,** but for Huey there's only an empty space in someone's backyard on Maple Street; the log cabin he was born in is long gone.

You will please the citizens of **Natchitoches** by pronouncing their home, correctly and inexplicably, Nack-a-tosh. This is the oldest city in Louisiana and shows it, with streets of charming 18th and 19th century buildings that make it seem a miniature New Orleans. The Spanish were here in the 1690's, and supposedly the earliest settlers in the area were Canary Islanders, but the actual town was not founded until 1714—four years before New Orleans—by Louis Juchereau de St. Denis, who created it as a post along the trail he was blazing toward Spanish Mexico to facilitate trade—later the great westward migration route called El Camino Real. The French colonial leaders up in Canada wanted this post primarily as a check against Spanish claims in the region; St. Denis would have planted it even further away, but Natchitoches at the time was the southernmost extent of the Great Raft, hence the furthest navigable point of the Red River. Natchitoches grew for a hundred years as a trading center second only to New Orleans, but no sooner was the Great Raft removed than the river shifted its course, leaving the docks below Front Street with only the little Cane River Lake, and insuring the town's survival as the preserved museum-city it is today.

Front Street, lined with homes and commercial buildings betraying a touch of New Orleans-style ironwork, has the city's **Tourist Information Office** at Lafayette. At Christmas the citizens put on quite a show here, covering the entire street with fairy lights for the Christmas Festival. **St. Denis' Grave** is on Front at Church Street, surmounted not by a tombstone, but a drugstore; the cemetery was closed a century ago. Below on the old riverfront on River Bank Drive, the **Roque House,** an 1803 cabin "en bousillage," has become a museum of local memorabilia (Mon-Fri 8-5, free). Two fine churches of the antebellum era are on Second Street; one, the Trinity Episcopal Church, was built by the famous Bishop Leonidas Polk, who put down his staff to become a Confederate general in the war. **Northwestern State University** is today the town's biggest employer, and its large shady campus, begun in the 1880's as the state teacher's school, commands the southern half of town.

Literary antiquarians may remember the turn-of-the-century novelist Kate Chopin (the critics, apparently, liked her better than the public). People in her hometown of **Cloutierville** certainly remember her; they have restored her house as part of the **Bayou Folk Museum,** just off Route 1 (closed in winter, open daily in the summer, otherwise Sat, Sun 1:30-5, adm.). West of Natchitoches, fifty miles of the Louisiana-Texas border have been turned into the fifth largest artificial lake in the U.S., the long, narrow **Toledo Bend Reservoir,** with 1,200 miles of shoreline given over largely to recreational use. The area was originally settled by the Spanish and though little of their influence remains today there's still an annual Tamale Festival in the village of Zwolle. **Hodges Gardens,** south of the town of Many on US 171, is the work of one man, conservationist A. J. Hodges, whose thirty years of work on once-barren land has resulted in one of the South's loveliest botanical gardens, covering almost 5,000 acres (daily 8-sunset, adm.).

Alexandria sits squarely in the geographical center of the state, a growing transportation center that offers little to the visitor but the **City Zoo,** on Masonic Drive (daily 10-6, free). Fifteen miles to the west, on Route 121, Louisiana has its answer to Arkansas' Hot Springs, the spa at **Hot Wells,** where the springs were discovered only fifty years ago.

East of Shreveport, towards the cotton country of the Mississippi, Interstate 20 and US 80 pass **Minden,** where a group of German religious dissenters led by a certain Count Leon established a communal experiment in 1830 that lasted forty years. The **Old Germantown Colony** has been reconstructed, with a museum (Wed-Sat 10-5, Sun 1-6, adm.). **Homer,** a tiny parish seat, has an 1848 Greek Revival courthouse, and **Mount Lebanon,** the **Stagecoach Trail Museum** (Fri-Sun 2-5, free). Further east, **Grambling State University,** at Grambling, is an all-black college, a relic of the days of segregated education; it has made a name for itself with its nationally known football teams and their flamboyant marching band. **Monroe,** like Shreveport, lives on oil and gas, as well as timber and cotton; it is the largest town in northeastern Louisiana. The **Lousiana Purchase Gardens,** off US 165 south, are Monroe's attraction, with a zoo, a botanical garden and an amusement park all tied together by a little train called the Lewis and Clark Railroad (daily 10-5, adm.).

In the northeastern corner of Louisiana on Bayou Macon near the village of Epps, stands one of the most fascinating of America's prehistoric monuments: **Poverty Point.** It is also one of the oldest, archaeologists place it back at least as far as 1,000 B.C., far older than any of the Temple Mound cultures of the South, and apparently a cultural predecessor to the mound builders of the Ohio Valley. The monument takes the form of a series of concentric octagons, the outermost three-fourths of a mile across. Apparently, half the figure was washed away by a long-ago change in the bed of the Mississippi, but according to one scholar, the volume of the whole must have exceeded that of the great Pyramid by thirty-five times (though it's only earth, not stone). Artifacts excavated from the site show that the area must have supported a large agricultural population, with trade connections that covered the continent. Who built it, and how they got such a jump on their mound-building colleagues elsewhere remain, for the moment, unanswerable questions. The culture seems to have sprung fully formed out of nowhere, suggesting influences that had come up the Mississippi from Central America or beyond (State Commemorative Area, open Mon-Sat 9-5, Sun 1-5, adm.). In Epps, the **Poverty Point Museum** displays artifacts found in the mounds (Tues-Sat 9-5, Sun 1-5, adm.).

Memorabilia of a more recent culture—the 19th century—can be seen at the **Louisiana Cotton Museum** north of Lake Providence, an oxbow lake of the Mississippi. An old cotton shipping station, marooned by the changing course of the river, has been restored with exhibits of the industry in the days when cotton really was King (daily 9-5, Sun 1-5, free).

From here southwards, the land is as empty as any part of the fertile Mississippi Delta—farms and pine bluffs, but no towns save Vidalia, across the river from Natchez. Back toward Alexandria, another prehistoric site is the **Marksville Indian Mounds and Museum,** on Route 5 in Marksville. This site, a thousand years after Poverty Point, gave its name to a culture that spread over the lower Mississippi, perhaps a colony of the Hopewell in the Ohio Valley. There is nothing of the peculiar symbolism of Poverty here, but a number of large mounds used for burials surrounded by earthworks; the state manages the site, and a museum of finds from the excavations (Mon-Sat 9-5, Sun 1-5, adm.). Also in Marksville, the **Hipolite Borden House,** a 1740 French cabin, has been restored as the local tourist information center, with a small museum. Another, similar house is in Mansura, the **Desfasse House** on Main Street.

Tourist Information. Shreveport-Bossier City Tourist Center, 629 Spring St. in Shreveport (Mon-Fri 8-5; 222-9391); **Monroe Tourist Center,** 141 De Siard St. (Mon-Fri 8-5; 387-5691); **Natchitoches Tourist Center,** 781 Front Street (Mon-Fri 8-5; 352-4411); **Many Tourist Center,** on US 171 south of Route 6 (Mon-Fri 8-4; 256-5880).

Restaurants. *In Shreveport*: Sansone's**, 701 E. Kings Highway; Smith's Cross Lake Inn**, 5301 S. Lakeshore Dr.; Brocato's**, 189 E. Kings Highway. *In Bossier City*: Studio Steak House**, 2565 E. Texas. *In Monroe*: Clyde's Seafood*, W. Thomas Rd. *In Natchitoches*: Lasyone's Meat Pie Kitchen*, Second Street. *In Alexandria*: Plantation Manor**, 1919 MacArthur Dr. South.

Annual Events in Louisiana

In January: Sugar Bowl, a week of sporting events including the New Year's Day football game, in *New Orleans*.
In February: Mardi Gras (see section under *New Orleans*) also in *Lafayette*, and most other Acadian towns, including *Thibodaux, Mamou, Houma*; Boudin Festival in *Broussard*.
In March: Audubon Pilgrimage, tours of historic homes in *St. Francisville*; St. Patrick's Day and St. Joseph's Day, Irish and Italian neighborhood parades in *New Orleans*.
In April: Holiday-In-Dixie, pageants, sporting contests and a carnival in *Shreveport*; Crawfish Festival, in *Breaux Bridge* (even numbered years only; New Orleans Spring Fiesta, festival and house tours in *New Orleans*.
In May: Contraband Days, *Lake Charles*; Jazz and Heritage Festival, *New Orleans*; Summer Arts Festival, *Baton Rouge*.
In June: Jambalaya Festival, in *Gonzalez*.
In July: Louisiana Oyster Festival, in *Galliano*; Bastille Day, Cajun fair in *Kaplan*.
In August: Tarpon Rodeo, at the fishing resort of *Grand Isle*; Louisiana Shrimp and Petroleum Festival, in *Morgan City*, with the traditional blessing of the shrimp fleet.
In September: Festival Acadians, Cajun music, cuisine and crafts in *Lafayette*; Frog Festival, Frog Races and Frog Dinners, in *Rayne*; Louisiana Sugar Cane Festival, *New Iberia*.
In October: *Natchitoches* Tour of Homes; International Rice Festival, in *Crowley*; Louisiana Cotton Festival, in *Ville Platte*; Louisiana State Fair, in *Shreveport*; Red River Revel, festival of the arts in *Shreveport*; *Baton Rouge* Fall Crafts Festival; Gumbo Festival, in *Bridge City*; Yambilee, yam festival in *Opelousas*; Lagniappe on the Bayou, in *Chauvin*.
In November: All Saints' Day (November 1) where in the *Cajun Parishes* and *New Orleans* the cemeteries become gardens illuminated by candlelight in the survival of an ancient ritual.
In December: *Natchitoches* Christmas Festival, parades, fireworks and a famous display of Christmas lights in the old town.

Accommodation in Louisiana

In New Orleans: French Quarter and Business District (Area Code 504)
Fairmont Hotel, University Place, tel. 529-7111. Very large, deluxe.
de la Poste Motor Hotel, 316 Chartres St, tel. 581-1200. Luxury hotel in the French Quarter.
Marie Antoinette Hotel, 827 Toulouse St, tel. 525-2300. Deluxe.

Maison Dupuy Motor Hotel, 1001 Toulouse St, tel. 586-8000. Also deluxe.
Le Pavillon, Poydras & Baronne, tel. 581-3111. Expensive.
Monteleone Hotel, 214 Royal St, tel. 523-3341. One of New Orleans' oldest hotels; in the French Quarter, expensive.
Place D'Armes Hotel, 625 St. Ann St, tel. 524-4531. Expensive.
The Inn on Bourbon Street, 541 Bourbon St, tel. 524-7611. Expensive.
International Hotel, 300 Canal St, tel. 581-1300. Expensive.
The Bienville House Hotel, 320 Decatur St, tel. 529-2345. In French Quarter, expensive.
Vieux Carré Motor Lodge, 920 N. Rampart St, tel. 524-0461. Moderate.
Felton Guest House, 1133-35 Chartres St, tel. 522-0970. In French Quarter, moderate, with kitchenettes.
French Quarter Maisonnettes, 1130 Chartres St, tel. 524-9918. Small, moderate-expensive.
Lafitte Guest House, 1003 Bourbon St, tel. 581-2678. Deluxe guest house.
La Mothe House, 621 Esplanade Ave, tel. 947-1161. Moderate-expensive, in restored mansion.
The Royal Orleans Hotel, Royal & St. Louis Sts, tel. 529-5333. Very deluxe.
The Warwick Hotel, 1315 Gravier St, tel. 586-0100. Luxury hotel.
St. Peter Guest House, 1005 St. Peter St, tel. 524-9232. Moderately expensive, in French Quarter.
La Salle Hotel, 1113 Canal St, tel. 523-5831. Inexpensive.
L'Auberge Hostel, 717 Barracks St, tel. 523-1130. Inexpensive, in good location.
Chez Nous Guest House, 727 Barracks St, tel. 523-4080. Inexpensive.
A Creole House, 1013 St. Ann St, tel. 524-0141. Moderate-inexpensive.

Elsewhere in New Orleans (Area Code 504)
The Ponchartrain Hotel, 2031 St. Charles Ave, tel. 524-0581. Deluxe, near Garden District.
Parkview Guest House, 7004 St. Charles Ave, tel. 866-5580. Moderate.
Sherwood Motel, 1015 Airline Hwy, tel. 835-9494. Inexpensive.
Royal Palms Motel, 7800 Chef Menteur Hwy, tel. 241-1577. Inexpensive.
The De Ville Motor Hotel, 3800 Tulane Ave, tel. 488-2661. Moderate.
Del Mar Motel, 8542 Chef Menteur Hwy, tel. 242-2770. Inexpensive.
Crescent Motel, 3522 Tulane Ave, tel. 486-5736. Inexpensive.
Columns Hotel, 3811 St. Charles, tel. 899-9308. Fairly inexpensive.
Hotel London, 1748 Prytania St, tel. 524-3007. Inexpensive, near trolley.

Southern Louisiana (Acadian Triangle)
Palace Inn, Rt. 90 East, tel. (504) 868-9021, *Houma*. Moderate.
Dixie Motor Inn, 1924 Rt. 90 E., tel. (504) 384-5750, *Morgan City*. Moderate.
Plantation Inn, 505 Universe St, tel. (504) 395-2841, *Morgan City*. Moderate-expensive.
Morgan City Motel, 507 Brashear Ave, tel. (504) 384-6640, *Morgan City*. Moderate.

Acadiana Motor Lodge, Rt. 90 E., tel. (318) 365-6711, *New Iberia*. Moderate-inexpensive.
Beau Sejour Motel, Rt. 182, tel. (318) 364-4501, *New Iberia*. Inexpensive.
Acadian Motel, 120 N. University Dr, tel. (308) 234-3268, *Lafayette*. Inexpensive.
Chateau Motor Inn, 404 E. Landry, tel. (318) 942-4944, *Opelousas*. Moderate-inexpensive.
Mid Continent Inn, I-10 and Rt. 13, tel. (318) 788-0970), *Crowley*. Moderate.
Heritage Inn, 2115 Charity St, tel. (318) 893-6420, *Abbeville*. Moderate.
Delta Downs Motor Inn, L-10 Frontage Rd, tel. (318) 589-7492, *Vinton*. Near Lake Charles, moderate.

Mississippi River and East Bank

Alamo Plaza Hotel Courts, 4243 Florida Blvd, tel. (504) 924-7231, *Baton Rouge*. Inexpensive.
Capitol House Hotel, Lafayette & Convention Sts, tel. (504) 383-7721, *Baton Rouge*. Moderate-expensive.
Bellemont Motor Hotel, 7370 Airline Hwy, tel. (504) 357-8612, *Baton Rouge*. Moderate-expensive.
Shades Motel, 8282 Airline Hwy, tel. (504) 921-2401, *Baton Rouge*. Inexpensive.
Billmar Hotel, Rt. 90 W., tel. (318) 828-5130, *Franklin*. Moderate.
H & H Motel, tel. (504) 683-8857, *Clinton*. Inexpensive.
Magnolia Inn, 1111 W. Thomas St, tel. (504) 345-3196, *Hammond*. Moderate.
Ozone Motel, Rt. 190, tel. (504) 626-7393, *Mandeville*. Moderate.
Bob's Motel, Rt. 190, tel. (504) 641-2992, *Slidell*. Inexpensive.
Fountainebleau Motel, 1330 Front St, tel. (504) 641-2560, *Slidell*. Inexpensive.

Northern Louisiana (Area Code 318)

Chateau Motor Hotel, 201 Lake St, tel. 222-7620, *Shreveport*. Moderate-expensive.
Mid-City Motor Hotel, 725 Jordan St, tel. 425-7481, *Shreveport*. Moderate.
Le Bossier Hotel, 4000 Industrial Dr, tel. 747-3000, *Bossier City*. Expensive.
Western Hills Inn, 3515 E. Texas St, tel. 746-0330, *Bossier City*. Moderate.
Vagabond Inn, 2102 Louisville Ave, tel. 325-5851, *Monroe*. Fairly inexpensive.
Plantation Motor Inn, 1919 MacArthur Dr, tel. 448-3401, *Alexandria*. Moderate-expensive.
Southerner Motel, 3405 MacArthur Dr, tel. 448-3481, *Alexandria*. Moderate.
Alexandria Inn, 1212 MacArthur Dr, tel. 443-1826, *Alxandria*. Inexpensive.
Park Hotel, 801 N. Pine St, tel. 463-8605, *Deridder*. Moderate.
Terrace Inn Motel, tel. 253-6528, *Marksville*. Inexpensive.

For more information on Louisiana, write the Louisiana Office of Tourism, P.O. Box 44291, Baton Rouge, LA 70804, tel. (504) 925-3860.

For information on camping in state parks, write the State Parks and Recreation Commission, P.O. Drawer 1111, Baton Rouge, LA 70821; fishing and wildlife regulations are available from Louisiana Wildlife and Fisheries, 400 Royal St, New Orleans, LA 70130.